poison

USA TODAY BESTSELLING AUTHOR
JADE WEST

Cover design by Letitia Hasser of RBA Designs designs.romanticbookaffairs.com
Edited by John Hudspith www.johnhudspith.co.uk
Formatting by L.J. Stock LJDesigns www.ljdesignsia.com
All enquiries to jadewestauthor@gmail.com

First published 2020

POISON

Dedication

For Timmy
For the inspiration on every level.
For the support, and the love, and for being absolutely
amazing in a whole new start.
Oh, and the ass.
This is for the magnificent ass, too. <3

8   POISON

Prologue

ANNA

It was one of his work social nights. Sebastian's.

I was sitting at our regular table, making the same regular small talk with the same regular group of other halves, twirling the engagement ring on my finger, ignoring my orange juice as the other women sipped at their wine.

Bored.

I was so damn bored.

But it was more than that.

I scanned the club, our usual venue after the usual restaurant, the ongoing cycle, swirling month by month, like it had done for years. My eyes glossed over the man who was supposed to be the love of my life as he stood in his usual pose, one elbow on the bar top, laughing along with his pompous work friends like their lives were the epitome of worldly success.

I should have been happy. I'd been convincing myself I was for months on end – a mantra of smiles and telling everyone *we were great, we were great, we were great.* That Sebastian Maitland was the best future husband anyone could wish for. Attentive. Smart. Successful. Invested in our future.

But still, I was bored of it all. And bored of me.

My heart was a static flatline. I'd forgotten who I was, fading into myself for so long that I didn't recognise my own soul anymore.

I was trapped in my own little box, with a fake smile and fake hopes and dreams.

My mind was constantly churning, desperate for Sebastian to be the one, but I knew deep down that he wasn't. I was scared to all hell that nobody could ever find the spark in me that made me alive and love me for that, when I didn't even know me myself.

And that night, I was flatlining. Numb and lost and fading into the background.

Until I looked away from him and saw them there. A couple I'd never seen before.

She was leaning back against the wall between two seating booths and he was up against her, their mouths just inches apart, eyes hard on each other's. Magnetic. Transfixed.

They were simmering.

And I felt it.

I felt the thrum and the want and the intensity of the fire between them.

I felt the pull of true, animalistic need. The craving for flesh on flesh. The screaming of her body to have him inside her, and the screaming of his to deliver.

He leaned in close, his lips to her ear. Her back arched at his words, her hands coming up to reach for him. One swept up his chest, the other snaked around his neck, fingertips to his skin, desperate. She was desperate.

So was he.

And shit, so was I.

My heart was thumping as I watched, the other women's voices fading to nothing as I found myself hungry to know what he was saying.

And then he kissed her.

Oh God, how he kissed her.

His mouth claimed hers so hard, with so much need that I felt it in my stomach – that pang of need myself. I clenched my thighs, and I fluttered down deep, and I couldn't tear my eyes away. I was a voyeur just a few booths over, but I couldn't stop staring.

It didn't matter.

They were so consumed with each other they'd never have noticed my voyeurism. They'd never have noticed anything – the whole club could be on fire and they'd be oblivious.

His mouth was fierce. Hers was hungry. Their breaths were ragged, bodies grinding. Their tongues were conquering, submissive, battling and loving, all at once.

Oh, how I wanted to be her. Every single inch of me wanted to be her.

But it wasn't about the man next to her. I'd barely even noticed what he looked like. He was a hot guy in a suit, sure. But that wasn't it.

It was the flash of memory that flared up from the depths of me. The flash of the only time in my life I'd ever felt like that about someone else's flesh. Someone else's mouth. Someone else's hands, and words, and cock.

I'd only ever kissed one man like that. I'd only ever wanted one man like that. Needed one man like that. Craved one man like that.

And it wasn't the man whose engagement ring was on my finger… it was the man who had totally destroyed me all those years ago.

"What do you think, Anna?" Kelly asked from the other side of the table. "Do you fancy a girls' night next Saturday? The guys can hang out and play some poker, we'll hit the wine and gossip."

"Sure," I said, forcing my eyes across to her. "Sounds great."

Her voice became a blur again in a heartbeat, planning our usual chatty girls' night, and I was right back to staring at the couple whose lust was on fire. The kiss broke, and she smiled a knowing smile as he took her hand, both of them pressed hard to each other's side as they made their way to the exit.

I shivered as they walked on by, my heart thumping to a whole other rhythm as he held open the door for her and she stepped on out.

It was still thumping through the rest of the table's chitchat, my tummy still panging when Sebastian and his friends broke up from the bar and headed on over. I grabbed my coat and said my goodbyes, smiling an empty smile at my fiancé as we walked to the taxi rank outside.

He didn't even look at me.

I stared at him as the taxi drove us home, but he was scrolling through his phone, oblivious. I tried to summon the want for him I should be feeling, but there was nothing there.

He opened the front door, turned off the intruder alarm and hung his jacket up. He tossed the keys onto the kitchen counter and scrolled through his phone some more, and I watched him. I watched him and tried to feel something. Summon something. Anything.

"Did you take your meds?" he asked.

"Yes," I said. "I took them before we left."

"No seizures?"

"None," I said.

He poured me a glass of water and put it on the counter. I sipped it while he scrolled some more. Then he yawned, and finally he looked at me.

"Bed time," he said.

I hadn't even taken my coat off, but he didn't notice, just walked on by me and headed upstairs. My hands were shaking as I took off my heels and got ready to follow him. My legs felt bandy as I climbed the stairs, my heart still thumping as he finished brushing his teeth with the bathroom door open.

He was already in bed when I'd done mine and taken my makeup off. His face was lit up by the glow of his phone screen, and I knew he was attractive, but I didn't see it. He wasn't interested in the slightest as I slipped my dress off, unclipped my bra and slid my knickers down. He didn't even shoot me a glance as I pulled the covers back and got in bed beside him.

I wanted to sleep. I wanted to turn off the churn inside and forget about the lot of it, but I couldn't. My eyes were wide open and fixed on the ceiling when he finally put his phone down on the bedside table and flicked the lamp off. They stayed there when he closed the distance between us and climbed on top.

His kiss was wet, but not passionate.

His hands were dancing their regular groping tune, but they weren't really trying.

Mine were dancing their regular tune right back, my legs spreading to let him in, where he thrusted and humped and grunted.

I didn't even pretend to come this time. He didn't notice, just rolled away when he was done, patted my thigh as some kind of *thank you*, and then he was off to sleep. His back was to me, his breaths deepening, and I was lying there wide awake, still churning.

Still staring at the ceiling.

And then I said it. On a breath, I said it.

"I can't do this anymore."

There was fear, and sadness, and a whole part of me screaming inside that I was crazy, but I couldn't stop it. I was done. My heart did one final frantic leap and begged me to dig, to find myself again, and I knew I couldn't do it here. Not in this life with the man so determined that I was a sick little liability who needed to be a smiling nobody on his arm, nodding at his every word.

He didn't wake up until I grabbed his shoulder and shook him. He started before he rolled on over, and my voice sounded unsteady as I said it again.

"I can't do this anymore, Sebastian. I'm sorry, but I can't. I just can't do this anymore."

He laughed. He actually laughed as he flicked the lamp back on. He was still laughing until he saw my face, and then he tensed, propping himself up on one arm with his eyebrows pitted.

"What the fuck are you talking about?"

I was up and out of bed before I could answer him. The room was a blur as I pulled some clothes on and took the overnight case down from the top of the wardrobe. I piled in the first couple of items hanging up, and he was up and out of bed right after me, following me around as I got my things together.

"Jesus Christ, Anna. What the fuck are you doing?!"

"I mean it," I said. "I'm sorry, Seb, but I can't do this anymore. I can't do *us* anymore."

And then he got it.

He forced my case from my hands and threw it on the floor, and his cheeks were red, his mouth a scowl, eyes glaring as he backed me up against the wall and told me I was *fucking insane.*

"Have you forgotten the fucking obvious?" he asked me, and his voice was ice cold. "Have you forgotten just how much of a fucking mess you were before I picked you up from the floor and gave you a fucking life again?"

No, I hadn't forgotten.

I'd never once forgotten in all the years we'd been together. Not in the least because he reminded me regularly – as did everyone else in our world.

It panged hard. The guilt. The fear. The self-doubt that rose up inside and made my chest heave as I stared right up at him.

But tonight I couldn't stop myself. Through everything that begged me to gain some rational thought and climb back into bed for the night, I just couldn't choke it all back down. The need for release. The need for life. For soul. The need for flesh on flesh that truly meant something to me.

"Is this about you wanting to be a disgusting little slut again?" he seethed, and my cheeks scorched under his stare. "Don't think I didn't see you goggle-eyed over those freaks in the club who needed to get a fucking room. Is that what you want? Huh?"

I hated the way his mouth twitched as he scowled. His hands reached out to grab at me, and I hated that too. He pawed at me like I was a cheap whore. A whore worth nothing.

"Come on," he spat. "Tell me you want it like this. This is what he did to you, isn't it?" He squeezed my tit hard and I batted his hand away. "That pervert prick who left you in a pitiful heap with his bullshit. Want to be a slut, do you? Want to soak yourself in filth? Want to take it like a desperate bitch like you did with that vile piece of shit?"

I didn't want it like that. Not from him.

"Don't," I said.

"Oh, but it's what you really want, isn't it?" he hissed. "It's you wanting to chase that sick excuse for fucking I pulled you away from. That sick excuse for *you* I pulled you away from."

I shook my head, but there was that embarrassment blooming. The humiliation at knowing just who I was when *he* came into my life.

But at least then I *did* know just who I was.

He picked up on that embarrassment and rammed it home.

"You think there's anyone else out there that would pick you up from the dregs like I did?" He laughed a vile laugh. "How much of a kinky bitch do you think you're going to look when you're spasming in bed and waking up in a pool of your own piss, Anna?"

"Please stop," I said. But he didn't.

"You were in a shitty fucking state when I met you, and you'll be in a shitty fucking state all over again without me. See what your parents think if you tell them you're going it alone. See what the whole fucking world thinks of your selfish bullshit."

I hadn't seen him like this for years.

It was the drink. The drink and the dent in his pride.

It wasn't love.

It wasn't him seeing me as the person I truly was and loving me for me.

It wasn't freedom. Not to be myself. Not to be a woman who chased her own destiny.

I was wrapped in baby softness cemented hard by constant judgement; I just hadn't wanted to see it. I was plugged into scrutiny masked as caring

– answering a running commentary on everything I ate, and drank, and thought, and did. I was boxed in on all sides and smiling through it by telling myself it was my life now. That it was all I was capable of now.

He really had been there for me where other people had left me to scrape my way through my own shit. He wasn't wrong on that score.

If only I could believe we were real, him and me. That what we had really was all that mattered.

But how could it be?

How could he be in love with someone who didn't really exist anymore?

"Tell me you love me," I said. "Tell me like you mean it. I don't think you've said it in years."

"What?" he asked, eyes still glaring.

"Just say it, Seb. Tell me you love me and mean it."

But he didn't say it.

"I take care of you, Anna. I put up with your medical crap and make sure you're okay every fucking day. I keep you from being an utter state with yourself. If that isn't enough for you, I don't know what will be."

He stepped away and tutted, and looked at me like I'd gone mad.

Maybe I had.

I was questioning my own sanity, and wondering *myself* what the hell I was doing when he finalised my thoughts for me by laughing that cold laugh of his.

"Just get back to fucking bed and sleep it off, will you?" he said. "Have you been on the wine or something? You'd better not have been fucking drinking."

Maybe I should have been. Maybe a couple of glasses of wine would have seen me asleep in bed and immune to the feelings spinning deep.

My tears were brimming as I picked that case back up from the floor. I could barely take a breath as I summoned the last of my words to the man I'd pledged my heart into marrying.

"I can't do this anymore," I said again. "I mean it, Seb. I can't do this."

"Your brain really is a poor excuse for one tonight," he said, pacing the room. "This is madness. Total fucking madness. They need to up your fucking meds and get your stupid head back in gear."

It may have been insanity, but madness was better than living an illusion for the rest of my life. It had to be.

"Goodbye, Sebastian," I told him.

"You'll be back when you realise what a stupid cow you're being," he said, and got back in bed.

I left my engagement ring on the counter next to his keys, and then took my first shaking footstep into a whole new world.

Chapter One

ANNA

Three months later

I pulled my phone from my handbag at the ping, calling up the message with one fumbling hand as I carried on up the street back to the office. I shoved it back in my bag without answering. Sebastian and his regular text, the same routine as every other lunchtime these past few months.

Have you come to your fucking senses yet?

No, I hadn't come to my senses yet. So many nights I'd paced up and down my new apartment living room when my new housemate, Vicky, had bailed off to sleep, trying to make myself see reason and return to the man everyone was continually telling me I was insane for leaving. So many nights I'd failed.

This Friday lunchtime wasn't any different.

He didn't even put kisses at the end of his messages. No attempt to tell me he was missing me, or wanting me, or loving me. Just that same blunt question, as though it was inevitable I would one day realise I wanted to go wedding dress shopping and walk up the aisle to him, the god of an ideal existence – Sebastian Maitland and our world of *perfect*.

Life might've been so much easier if I did.

I answered the messages from Mum, desperate to know if I was still alive and free from seizures, then walked into work with a smile at Lucia on reception and dropped myself down at my desk to prepare for the afternoon project meeting. I had my sales strategy notes all mapped out, the coming quarter plotted for Pewter Security's campaign, and that's when another ping sounded from my handbag.

This was a different ping altogether. One that did actually have my heart racing.

Trojan from the online dating app. *Trojan,* the huge specimen of a man who'd been promising me all kinds of wonder in the bedroom if I agreed to a meet-up.

I'd been replying, flirting, asking about his preferences and his wants and his needs. It seemed they matched pretty well with mine. Fire and lust and flesh on flesh. The churn of animalistic excitement and desire coming to life.

Stacey from the marketing team headed on over with a file pressed to her chest, and I dropped my phone on the desk. She was one of the only people far enough removed from my life to avoid giving me scathing attacks at every opportunity.

"Is that him? The hot guy? Trojan?"

I nodded. "Yeah, it's him. He wants to meet up this weekend. His promises are quite attractive."

She nodded back. "So, are you going to do it? Bite the bullet and give him a shot?"

I leaned back in my seat and tapped my pen against the desk top. "I don't know."

"You've got to do it sometime," she said. "It's not like the local populous is offering you much fulfilment." She put her hand over her mouth as Steve from accounts walked on by.

Cringe.

I screwed my eyes shut.

He'd been the last member of the local populous I'd spread my legs for in the hope of getting a genuine orgasm. I'd been disappointed. Same as usual. I'd fucked up in my stupid thrill-seeking. Same as usual.

"Sorry," she said. "Hopefully he didn't hear me."

But he had. He fired me a seething glance from Peter's desk at the other end of the room, and I cringed afresh. His seething glance could join the club along with everyone else's, but still, it slammed me hard.

I should never have fucked anyone at work. It was a mistake. Hooking up with a couple of random hot-looking guys after nights out with some of my work friends had been one thing, but responding to Steve's flirty work emails had been a whole other league.

"At least the online app should be good for anonymity," I told her.

"Maybe he'll actually be a good fuck," she replied. "You'll have to fill me in with the gossip on Monday. I can always give you an *emergency bail out* call if you need one. We can pencil one in."

I thanked her – the one person in my life who wasn't constantly shaking their head and demanding that I should run back to Seb. My parents were devastated, our entire network of mutual friends was still reeling, *my* friends too. Even Nicola, my *bestest bestest bestie* in the whole bloody world.

"I'll let you know when to put in the call," I said. "Honestly, I appreciate it."

She tipped her head. "Sounds like you are planning on hooking up with this one, then."

I guessed I was.

Maybe he'd be the one who finally got me off and gave me just a scrap of what I needed.

I sent him a reply.

Saturday? Eight pm? Oscars on Bath Street?

He'd replied before I'd even put my phone down.

I'll see you there, you gorgeous kinky bitch.

Finally, my heart got a flutter. Hopefully my clit would follow soon enough.

The afternoon project meeting went fine, and I finished up another successful work week, at odds with the carnage of my personal life. I finished another day by taking my lamotrigine meds before bed and ticking the chart. Five days with no seizures – a slight improvement on the few weeks prior. I thought about *Trojan* as I laid there, picturing us as that same burning couple in the club that night. The pair who had ignited each other as well as a shitstorm of chaos for me.

Even one night with that kind of passion would make it worth it, though. Enough to remind me for even just a heartbeat that I was still Anna Blackwell, a woman still herself somewhere underneath the fear and the numbness and the crud of having a brain that couldn't be relied on to function anymore.

Or so I prayed.

I got ready on Saturday evening with a sprinkle of nerves dancing all over me. Thirty-five years old, and in that moment I felt it – a world away from the early twenties-something girl who could hit the clubs and dance all night without even tossing a thought to the life looming ahead. Hell, what I'd give for a taste of that girl again.

I'd at least have a try at it.

I picked out my finest little black dress and tousled my freshly-dyed jet-black hair, and made my makeup even sultrier than any of my last dates – an ever increasing style since moving away from Sebastian. I was ready, teetering in my highest heels as the taxi dropped me off in the city centre. I grabbed an orange juice from the bar at Oscars, cursing again that my meds made alcohol forbidden to me. And there he was, leaning against the bar at the other end, a beer in his hand as he stared on over with a smirk.

Trojan.

I flashed him a smile back and he headed on over, and there they were again, those nerves dancing hard.

He was huge. Huge and hot. His shirt stretched tight over his chest and his shadow of stubble just right on a firm, hard jaw. Dark hair, dark eyes. Dimples perfectly at odds with the strength of the rest of him.

Yeah, he could well be the one to give me an orgasm. Several if I was lucky. A whole night of them if the universe cut me a break.

"You look even better than your profile picture," he told me, and I felt my cheeks burn up.

"The feeling is mutual," I replied. "You're quite something in the flesh."

His smirk grew brighter. "I hope you'll be saying that when the night is done."

So did I.

Small talk was small talk, but I kept looking at his mouth, wondering what it would feel like pressed against mine. How hot his tongue would be as it sought mine out and ate me up. How solid his hands would be as he took my dress off and reached down between my thighs.

I should've told him about my epilepsy to prepare him for any potential seizures but opted to avoid the topic. I kept up on the orange juice as he necked back the beers, and small talk turned to dirty talk, him telling me how much he wanted to slam me deep, and hard and plough my ass with the kind of intrusion I hadn't felt in years.

Yes, my clit was fluttering.

Finally, it was fluttering.

Stacey called with our pre-arranged potential bail out call, and I told her I was *great thanks*, and then we were off. Trojan – who was actually called Sean – finishing up his beer and knocking back a double whisky before we headed on out of there.

He didn't take my hand.

Maybe that was the first sign.

We got into a taxi and he put his hand across to squeeze at my knee, but he didn't snake it up my thigh like I hoped he would. I gripped his knuckles to encourage him, but it didn't make any difference. He smelt of beer over the top of his cologne, and his words were more bolshy and less dirty as the journey took us back to mine. More about slamming me hard than how adventurous he could make our encounter.

I encouraged him to find the heat. Holy shit, how I encouraged him to dig down deep for more.

He stumbled a little as we piled out of the taxi and I got my front door key out. He tried to grab me in the hallway but his hands were clumsy. His mouth was clumsier. Hot and wet and swishy.

My clit flutter was fading fast.

I led us through to my bedroom, past Vicky's lightless doorframe, and got down on my knees as he dropped his pants, and then I sucked him. I sucked him like I wanted him to claim me whole. Like I wanted to love his dick. Like I wanted to taste every inch of him and have him taste every inch of me.

"Fuck," he grunted. "Fuck, you're fucking good at that. Too fucking good at that."

And then he came.

He shot his load in my mouth after one lousy minute, and reeled back clutching his dripping cock.

"Shit," he said. "I'll get it up again, don't worry. You were just too fucking good."

Bullshit.

He barely even tried while we were waiting for round two. We got cosy on the bed and he rubbed my pussy but ignored every attempt from me to get the rhythm right. I ignored every urge to pretend I was coming just to get him the hell away from me and stop wasting my time.

I stared at him and knew he was hot, but yet again that was flatlining, fading to nothing and leaving my heart in the gutter, abandoning every scrap of optimism for the evening.

"Fuck, yes," he said with a grunt, and showed me his stiffening dick. "Let's get this show back on the road."

Like it needed his dick to be hard to get the show rolling again. Selfish prick.

Still, I gave him another chance like the idiot I was sometimes, glass half full and all that crap. I let him take his fill, squirming away underneath to try to angle him at my g-spot, and letting my tongue find a rhythm with his. But it was shit. No matter how hard I tried, and encouraged, and pulled him closer and lifted my legs up his back, it was shit.

He'd done with round two in no time and ditched the condom, and I wiped his spit from my mouth, my clit hating my guts for believing in this fumbling loser and his promises.

Even Seb had given more of a shit for my pleasure.

"I'll be more up to it in the morning," he said, and buried himself down under my covers. "I had a bit too much beer. So damn excited it made me nervous. Your fault for being so hot."

Sure it was. Yeah.

Even my glass half full mentality didn't give me faith in this guy's morning potential. I rolled over on my own side and stared at the wall, just like I had done so many nights of my life with Sebastian, and my thoughts were still going there. Heart, pussy and tummy still screaming out for the passion I'd felt from that couple in that club.

The passion I'd felt in *anything*.

I wanted that so badly.

I needed that so badly.

I was seriously fucking desperate for that. Just one night. Just one taste of who I was.

The light was streaming through the front window next morning, and I was still awake when he stretched out his arms and headed back over for another go. I shied away, and told him I had stuff on I needed to get to, and he shrugged before slipping out of bed and pulling his jeans on.

"Some other time then," he said. "That was really damn hot last night."

I didn't have any words, just a weak little smile as he smoothed down his hair and said he'd ping me later. *Sure thing, can't wait.*

Super-hot *Trojan* was a big buzzing fly in my optimism ointment. A let down that had me collapsing like a starfish flat under my bedcovers as soon as the front door slammed shut after him.

Fuck you, Trojan. Fuck you.

I was tired and scuttling towards a day of potential seizures. Tired and zany and still reeling. Tired and zany and desperate when I scrolled through my phone to the very depths and found his number. The man who'd burned me up harder than diving straight into Hell.

I had no idea if it was even still his number as I wrote out the text message at eight a.m. on a Sunday morning and fired it off.

Hey, it's Anna. Long time no speak. Was just wondering how you're doing.

Damn fucking fuck, I regretted it as soon as the sent tick flashed up.

I consoled myself with the hope that maybe he had indeed got a different number this past decade. I mean that would make sense. A decade was a long time.

I consoled myself with the hope that he was probably busy with a whole new world, with no time or thought to even read my message, let alone fire back a response, as cringeworthy as that may be.

But I'd heard… just the faintest scrap of a whisper at the very edges of our extended social circle… I'd heard he might be single…

I consoled myself with the chatter of my brain telling me I really had been insane and really would come to my senses and return to boredomville and Seb with a smile on my face, resigned to my fate forever.

But then it came.

The ping.

The ping from him. The poison in my veins, even after all these years.

The ping that changed my whole fucking world.

Chapter Two

LUCAS

The buzz of my phone was enough to drag me out of my slumber.

I blinked at the sun streaming through my gaping window like a piece of shit to burn my retinas. My mouth was parched, bedsheets crumpled underneath my sprawled nakedness. Anything but a lovely way to greet the morning. Still, a regular one.

I coughed and stretched, and my arm landed on two empty wine bottles, cast away like fallen soldiers. The usual deal. The usual shit.

I scrabbled around for my phone, expecting it to be the alarm bleeping at me, but it wasn't. My gut did a thump as I saw the text icon, no doubt a spiteful whinge from Maya and a cancellation of me having Millie. Another usual deal.

Only it wasn't Maya's flashing name that greeted me, it was number unknown. One that had my attention on full alert as I propped myself up and opened the message.

Hey, it's Anna. Long time no speak. Was just wondering how you're doing.

My eyes scanned that message over and over before my brain would accept I was really conscious. I considered it must be a joke. Or a balls up. Some kind of crazy cockup in the communication ether.

It had to be. There was no way that Anna Blackwell would ever be asking how I was doing on a random Sunday morning, or any morning for that matter – I'd swear she'd rather eat her own shit. But still, that message was staring back at me in cold hard text.

My fingers took on a life of their own, typing out a response before my brain had even caught up with the flow.

Very long time no speak. Doing so so. Can't complain. How about you?

I wondered what the hell she would say, or if she'd say anything at all. I wondered what the fuck could have led her to message me out of the blue, like we were just old friends needing a catch up. I wondered if she'd been on some crazy binge and had her phone stolen by some idiot friends playing some prank.

But no.

I was out of bed and brushing the stale alcohol from my teeth when the next ping sounded.

Life has been quite a whirlwind these past few months. How is yours?

Our old social circle was still attached on the outskirts, but I rarely heard anything about her in passing from distant connections. I rarely heard anything whatsoever these days about Anna, and she certainly hadn't been keen to forge a friendship from our explosion of a break up. Not at any point this past decade, and I can't say I blamed her.

I wondered if she'd heard about my split from Maya. About how much of a train wreck people were judging my life to be these days. About how much of a train wreck people were judging *me* to be these days.

They had a point.

Maybe this was a gloat fest on her part, but it didn't feel like one.

I swilled out the toothpaste and let my fingers fire off a reply.

Good thanks. You still in Cheltenham?

I hadn't heard of her leaving the city, and a weird little twinge in me hoped she was still local. I'd vacated well and truly to the outskirts with Maya and Millie in tow, and had no intention of venturing back onto city turf, but it was still my locale.

I hoped she was still my locale too.

Yeah, I'm still here. In the city centre. You?

I pinged right back.

Close enough.

And then she said it. She actually said it and sent the string of texts to a whole new level.

Fancy a game of tennis?

I caught my smile in the bathroom mirror. One I hadn't seen on my face in an age. Just a shame it was there under hollow eyes.

Tennis.

Our stupid sport with stupid competition. I remembered her face as she raced to slam that ball back across the net at me. I remembered how she blew her loose straggle of hair back from her forehead and swayed on her feet for the next serve.

I couldn't stop myself.

I'd love a game of whatever you fancy.

I cursed myself for dashing the fuck ahead, contemplated following up with something less provocative, but it didn't matter. She texted back before I could manage it.

Let's start with tennis.

I'd start with whatever she wanted, but today wasn't the day for it. I had Play Planet and dog walking with Millie and teatime with my mother to follow. Hardly the freedom to schedule in an impromptu session of tennis with an ex-girlfriend.

I pinged back.

When did you have in mind? Today is a bit rammed...

Her reply was instant.

Next weekend? Work is a bit crazy this coming week. Want to have a clear head for it. Maybe I'll fit in some practice to get me back in the zone.

My smirk was still there in the bathroom mirror, imagining hers as she planned on kicking my ass.

She'd never managed it yet, but she'd had a few decent tries. Maybe that's what this was really all about – her making a spectacle of me on the tennis court. I'd take it gladly if it meant a conversation. I'd even fall down flat and play dead on the tarmac.

Next weekend is good. I don't have Millie. Book in wherever you want and I'll be there.

Now was the moment. Conversation starter or sign off.

She opted for conversation starter.

Ah yes. I heard you'd had a little one. How old now?

She'd sure heard more about me than I had about her.

Five. Shooting up daily. Quite the little princess.

I'd made it downstairs and let the dogs into the paddock by the time she replied to that one. This time the message cut off the stream short and sharp.

I'm sure she is. Next weekend then. We'll work it out.

I sure hoped so. A game of tennis would be a sliver of relief in the disgrace of an existence I'd created these past few months. My thumbs-up was a positive sign off, and we were done.

I tried to file my Anna Blackwell thoughts into the *for later* box, but they wouldn't go there. My mind was churning them up and over as I got myself showered and ready for the Maya crossover. I knew I shouldn't dwell on any of it. There was no doubt she might come to her senses and bin off a random tennis game well before next weekend. Either that or her social group would manage to bark some common sense into her before she had chance to give me a single minute of her time in person.

They hated me.

I didn't blame them.

Maya hated me too. Standard.

Even my own mother fucking hated me these days, even if she tried to smile through the scowls.

Luckily, Millicent Isabel Pierce didn't hate me. Her arms flung wide as she raced down her mum's garden path on my arrival, her *Daddy* scream at full volume.

She, out of everything – career and sport and general lifestyle bullshit all considered, even when relationships were a write-off – was by far my biggest success story. I did a pretty damn good job where my little princess was concerned.

Unfortunately, nobody else seemed to think so. Maya's face was the usual condescending grimace as she stomped down the path to join us at the gate.

"Don't let her trash her shoes again. Not like last time. These are new."

I looked down at Millie's feet. Glitter and bows. Typical.

"I'll put her in wellies."

"And keep her away from the dogs. Her dress was caked with muddy paw prints when she came home last."

I'd heard this crap already, but nodded regardless.

"Yeah, yeah," I met her eyes, and felt the ice there jab hard. "Anything else?"

Her folded arms formed a barrier between us on every level. I'd have formed one too quite happily. I absolutely despised the woman my wife had turned into these past few years.

"Just don't cock up," she hissed under her breath, then pasted on a goodbye smile for Millie. "See you later, sweetheart. Wrap up warm."

My little girl was already sighing as she dropped herself into the passenger seat of my truck.

"I don't want to keep away from the dogs, Daddy."

I ruffled her hair and reached over for a kiss. "No chance of that, Mills. They love you too much."

As usual Play Planet was a win of an afternoon and the wellies did well enough to guard Millie's feet as she stomped through the mud puddles on the hillside. My mother gushed and story read, and I stared across with another churn of frustration, wondering again how the hell I was going to fix the bullshit shitstorm I was caught up in.

She was a zing of a presence right through it all though, Anna Blackwell. Rife in my thoughts as we ate our cottage pie at the dining table and I prepared to drop Millie back home for the night.

Memories of us. Of her laughter. Of her dirty grin as she coaxed the filth out of me. How she lapped it up and begged for more. Always more.

Of the way she would bite her lip as she came, and I'd bite it right back after her. Harder.

How I took every fucking thing her body had to give me, and she took it all right back from me.

Dirty. Little. Slut.

I'd almost forgotten what that felt like. Almost.

I'd almost forgotten the very depths of the beautiful filth we'd summoned from each other, but not quite.

I'd never quite forget that.

"I don't want to go back to Mummy's yet," Millie said once my mother had done her hugs.

"Hopefully it won't be for too much longer, sweetheart. Hopefully you'll all be living back at Daddy's soon," Mother whispered, and I almost spat out a curse.

Her eyes spoke volumes as they met with mine. Disappointment. Disgust.

She could be disgusted all she liked without bringing Millie into it. Our stare off was heated as hell, just like everything else lately. She shrugged like she was stating the obvious, and I was grateful we didn't have any alone time left for her to grill me on *what the hell I was doing to fix things with Maya.*

Maya the angel. Maya the perfect mother and perfect wife and perfect everything as far as the rest of the world were staring in at, jangling her crystals around in the air for her angelic *self-development* bullshit.

Me? I was just the selfish prick with the mountain of failings.

"School tomorrow," I said to Millie once we were back on the road. "Got to get you a good night's sleep and ready to roll."

I was lying. We didn't need to get her anything that required me dropping her back to that self-righteous cow for the night, but as usual it would do me no good to protest.

Predictably, Maya pulled Millie around when we were back at hers, checking out her shoes, and dress, and hair before giving me a scathing nod. Part of me wished I'd spent the day laughing and joking and dancing with my little girl in the puddles just to be an asshole, but it would've cost me dearly for weeks.

She shooed Millie into the house before joining me back at the gate. "Have you been drinking?"

"No, I haven't been fucking drinking," I said, and made to walk away, but she pulled me back.

"We still have a whole load of things to finalise. You need to give me some assurances. I need to know what you're doing to get yourself back on track."

I shook my head. "I'm not doing this now. It never gets us anywhere."

"Nothing ever gets us anywhere with you," she spat. "We have so much ground to cover, Lucas. But that doesn't matter, does it? Do we matter a shit to you anymore? What did your mother say today? She's just as keen for you to sort yourself out as I am."

Fuck the never-ending rat run of criticism. I was nothing but a wages workhorse there for the milking and had been for years. A failure at everything other than stuffing the cash into the bank account every month.

Pervert.

Alcoholic.

Filthy smoker.

Arrogant piece of shit.

"Maybe you should just move in with my mother. You can spend all your time bitching about what a useless cunt I am."

I walked away with nothing more than a wave up at the window. Millie waved in return.

"Fine," Maya snapped at my back. "Fuck off again. It's always you, wrecking every attempt at working things out. I'm sick of it."

But she was wrong.

It wasn't the fucking off again that caused the issues, it was the clashing and cursing and screaming that ensued when we tried to build any damn fucking bridges.

She hated me and had done for years. She'd looked at me like I was a piece of shit for years. Judged every fucking thing I ever did as worth nothing for years.

On top of that, she'd spat at me for being some kind of deviant every time I'd tried to fuck her for years.

Maybe I really was too much of a deviant to make a life with. To want to be with.

Anna had never seemed to think so.

Anna whose life I'd fucked up and mine along with it a whole decade ago.

Maybe this was karma. The universe sucking me in and retching me up the way I'd done to her. I should ask Maya for her fantastic bloody *psychic perspective* on it.

It came again out of the blue, before I was back at home and through my own door that night – the next text message that set my blood pumping like it hadn't done for months. Years maybe.

That thrill of knowing something was coming. Something that set your very soul alight with the need. The want. The craving.

The fire and the burn and the crazy pull of flesh on flesh.

Fuck tennis, Anna's message read, *that's not the game I want to play and you know it.*

Oh hell yes, I knew it.

I knew it, and I was damn well on the same page.

Just let me know when and where, I replied. *I'll fucking be there.*

Chapter Three

ANNA

I was insane. Absolutely insane.

I'd been insane the moment I fired off a message, and even more insane for still considering a meet up.

I daren't tell any of my friends, and definitely none of the family still ramming Sebastian down my throat at every opportunity. They'd only tell me I was insane in an even more brutal manner than I was telling myself. I could barely even imagine the fallout.

Especially Nicola. Nicola would nail my wrists to a post before she'd see me hook up for a game of *tennis* with the man she'd cursed about through the past decade.

I'd heard about him getting married to Maya Brooks. Even though it was a good three years after our breakup, it had still slammed me in the gut like a hurricane. I'd heard about them having a kid and doing the whole family game, and I guess that was one of the reasons I'd grabbed hold of Seb so hard when he offered me the engagement ring and said we were all in for keeps.

I'd wanted him to be the love of my life. I'd wanted that more than anything.

I guess what I'd really wanted was the security of an alternate life to the one I'd been dreaming of with Lucas Pierce.

The very last thing I should be wanting was a fuck fest with him, the man who tore me to shreds, but I couldn't stop myself. I couldn't stop myself imagining his mouth slamming into mine and eating me up. I couldn't stop the shudder as I pictured him grabbing my hair and holding my head back tight, forcing his fingers in my mouth and stretching my lips open as I gurgled and drooled and spluttered. Couldn't stop the heat boiling through me as I remembered how hard he would suck on my clit. Hard enough that I'd buck against his face like a woman possessed.

I couldn't stop myself remembering how much I'd wanted that man. How every cell in my body and mind had screamed for more of him every single day and night we were together.

How I'd cursed myself for playing in bed at night with him starring in every fantasy through every year since.

Oh, the fantasies.

Oh, the insanity of the games we used to play. The filth we used to dance with.

I'd sworn there was no way I'd ever speak to him again. Not in this lifetime, no matter what.

Not for the sake of my health, and my mind, and my self-respect. Not out of gratitude for everything people had pulled me out of when I was falling apart in his aftermath.

Still, I'd sworn I'd be happily married with a couple of mini Sebastians running around me by now, so my own self professions didn't seem all that watertight. Neither did my sanity. Epilepsy wasn't even playing a factor in these brain fuckups, these were standing strong all on their own.

I was in the office meeting room, having a regular team performance meeting when I heard my phone buzz on the tabletop. Something told me it was him before I'd slyly clicked on the screen, and that something was right.

I hated the flutter in my belly. It was the same tingle it had always been when that prick of a man messaged me. Fuck you, Lucas, but only after you've fucked me first. Because that was all this was. Just one splurge. One solitary fuck fest to set my senses free and wild. One tiny scrap of fun to relieve me from the years of need and boredom, and hopefully give me a hint of myself again.

Any news on the tennis date? I have some ideas...

And with that the work meeting was done for me. The voices of our management team blurred out, and my heart was racing and my thighs were clenched tight. I had plenty of ideas of my own and every one of them involved his naked flesh and how well he knew how to use it. The guy was a monster in the bedroom, a monster of pure perverted brilliance.

Just a shame he'd been so much of a monster outside of it.

Tell me, I texted back.

Those two simple words were asking for it. I knew his reply would seal my fate, whatever it may be.

The tease was always a tease.

I'll show you. When and where?

I was supposed to be scanning through the group stats for the month when I fired off the response.

Next Saturday. Hotel?

The ping was right back.

My place? I'll send you the address... safe in the middle of nowhere...

But I couldn't get to a place in the middle of nowhere. My heart dropped at yet another example of the damn condition screwing me over and taking my transport with it.

I can't drive anymore. Train station?

Another ping. *No driving? How come?*

A flash of memory of him teaching me to drive around country roads rose up behind my eyes, and I banished it. Like I'd always banished every memory of us when it rose up to bite me.

I pulled the phone under the table as I typed the reply.

I have epilepsy. Can't drive. Not until I'm twelve months clear of seizures which hasn't happened yet.

I really didn't want to tell him this. Didn't want to show him even the barest hint of personality or weakness or anything even vaguely related to anything other than getting me off.

Shit. I'm sorry. When did you last have one?

I hated typing out my response.

Five days ago. It's been an intense few months. They are upping my meds at the moment.

If he even dared back out of the fuck fest now, I'd storm around to him myself and tell him all over again what I thought of him. I'd pile through the epic security at GCHQ – Government Communications Headquarters, where I'd heard he'd been rising up in the ranks, so people said – and give him the middle finger right up in his face. But he didn't back out.

I could pick you up from yours, or you could get the train to Lydney? I'll get you from the station?

There was no way I wanted to risk being seen with him anywhere near my place. The train was the safer option by a clear mile.

Train works. I'll look up the times.

I was back at the apartment that evening, listening to Vicky gossip about one of her annoying workmates when I called up the Lydney train times for Saturday afternoon. I'd scrolled back through to the morning timetable once I weighed up just how likely we were to take the whole day up with our filth fest.

11:32, I told him.

I'll get the prosecco in, he replied.

It was a bitch that he couldn't get the prosecco in. Not on my account.

No drink for me, I said. *Not allowed on my meds.*

Bummer, he said back. *I'll make sure you don't miss it, don't worry.*

And there we had it. The date and time set and confirmed. I felt guilty as I focused back on Vicky's chatter – guilty at myself and the loads of people who would hate me doing this crap. Guilty at how I was betraying my own self-worth. Guilty at how I'd sacked off Seb just to end up in a splurge with the man who'd ripped my heart into pieces and left me a wreck for months.

He really had left me a wreck for months. I'd been besotted with him. In love with him. Dedicated to a future with him and his delicious mind and delicious lifestyle and delicious cock to match.

Jesus Christ, I'd been in love with that man.

Jesus Christ, I'd paid for it.

My fingers really did hover over a half-formed message to him. *Scrap it, this is crazy* – it began, but I couldn't send it. I couldn't force myself to fire those words in his direction.

So I aimed the sense-making words in another direction. I spat them out and hoped to hell Vicky could talk some sense into me. She'd known me long enough to know this was a shitstorm waiting to happen.

My words came quick and fast.

"I'm meeting Lucas at his next Saturday. We're going to have an afternoon of fucking, and it's going to be a one off. Just a one off. Definitely."

She stopped talking mid-flow, her face an absolute picture of horror as she digested my outburst.

"Lucas Pierce? You're going to fuck Lucas Pierce? Are you fucking serious?"

My shrug didn't match up with just how serious I really was.

She shook her head as she gathered her words. "Hell, Anna. What the fuck? Does Nicola know?! Please tell me you've told her..."

The shake of mine was a whole load more frantic. "No! She doesn't. Not yet. Please don't tell her."

I felt easily as dumbstruck by my own dumbness as she did.

"You broke up with Seb, and are going to fuck Lucas? Have you lost your mind? Lucas Pierce was an absolute prick to you, and he's allegedly been an absolute prick to his wife, too. Just ask anyone who knows shit about him. He's still a complete bloody asshole. He's probably screwed her brain up nearly as bad as he screwed yours."

I had no doubt about any of that. Another shrug, and I confirmed I had lost my mind. I'd most definitely lost my mind.

I wasn't expecting the way she reached out along the kitchen counter and grabbed my hand. I had no idea that the look in her eyes would be so genuinely concerned as she moved closer.

"Please don't," she said. "Please, Anna, don't do it. It won't do you any good. Not with your seizures. There's no way you'll come out good from this. No way at all."

The stab in my ribs was hard as I caught the truth in what she was saying.

"Please," she repeated. "I won't tell Nicola, but you have to come to your senses. Please don't do this. He fucked you up last time, and you didn't even have them then... don't do this... it won't be fair on anyone. We'll all be worried sick."

Yeah, they would be. Yeah, I was an idiot even considering it.

I was nodding, even though my heart was a racing mess. I knew I would be risking a step back into more seizures if I pushed my own stresses with games and emotions and crazy sex.

I knew full well he could fuck up the progress I'd been striving to make for years, and screw up the months of setback and upped meds on lamotrigine even further.

I knew all of this, but still I couldn't stop myself craving Lucas Pierce.

"I know it's crazy," I told her. "Don't worry. I'll come to my senses. I will."

And I truly intended to. I really did.

I went for a walk past the Neptune fountain in the city centre every lunchtime that week, and threw a coin in the water, like I always had. I urged myself to stay sane and back away from this stupid splurge and put my health and brain and respect for my past ahead of whatever my clit was begging for.

I threw a coin into the water every day that week and wished that I could forget about Lucas and his depraved filth and gorgeous body.

But I couldn't.

The messages kept coming and I kept firing them back, and the weekend came closer without me daring to talk it through with Vicky again. I pulled out my best underwear from my top drawer and made sure I was shaved to perfection. I dug my toys from under my bed and packed them up in a little black case.

I thought through all the things I wanted him to do to me, and what difference the past ten years might have made to him. To his body. To his tastes. To his smirk.

No matter how many times I wrote out a message to back out of the hook up, I never sent it off.

No matter how many times I wrote out a message to Nicola, forcing myself into the hailstorm of her talking sense into my stupid skull, I never sent that off either.

It was the sex. The passion. The thrill and the need and the craving of my body for his.

Fuck that couple in that club that night and the glimmer of lust they'd reminded me existed.

Somehow, no matter what I did, or thought, or tried to reason with myself, I was a fluttering mess on that Lydney bound train on Saturday morning, with a case packed up with smut and filth and an overnight supply of my epilepsy meds, even though I swore I wouldn't ever sleep in a bed with him and would be back home that evening.

No matter what I did, my heart was pounding hard as the train pulled out of Cheltenham station and I sent off the final ping that sealed my doom.

On my way, I told him.

I'll see you soon, he said.

Any time this lifetime would be too soon, but it was too late for that.

The train pulled up at the little town station and I stepped out onto the platform, then climbed over the bridge to the other side. I headed out to the front and scanned the car park for a sign of him, but he wasn't there.

I cursed my stupidity again as I dropped myself down onto a battered bench with my cases at my feet, cursing the rain on top as it started to spit down from high.

And then he came for me.

A truck pulled into the station and my heart did a stutter, before I even knew for sure it was him. Call it instinct.

He turned around in one of the spaces and drew up in front of me, and down came the passenger window.

And there he was.

The man who'd broken my heart into a thousand pieces and left me clutching at the shards.

I hadn't seen him in glasses before, but they suited him. He was wearing a suit on a Saturday, and I knew full well it was because he knew I liked them. His smirk was the same smirk that set my clit pulsing. He looked older, but not all that much older.

His hair was cropped shorter and his beard was longer, but he was still him.

Holy shit, he was still him. Still him, and still hot as hell, and I was still crazy for him.

Crazy nervous to match, too. But I wasn't going to show him that.

"Hey," he said, as I climbed in beside him and dumped my stuff in the footwell.

"Hey," I said back, and it was there. The same thrum between us.

The same crazy spark. The same crazy need that set me on fire.

"Back to yours then?" I asked, hating how my thighs tensed when I met his eyes.

He shook his head. "Not just yet."

And then he started driving.

POISON   41

Chapter Four

LUCAS

She didn't say a word as I drove us to the Hawthorn Inn. I kept casting looks in her direction, but she was staring out of the window, or at her feet. At just about anything but me.

Yet still, it was there. That undeniable zing that had always been tight between us. It was bubbling deep, from my cock to the thump in my ribs, to spin off filthy thoughts of just what I wanted to do to her.

They were totally fucking obscene.

No matter how many times I shot a look her way, I still couldn't believe she was sitting there beside me. But she was.

She was undeniably her. Every dirty little bit of her the same dirty little bit of her I'd claimed a thousand times over, and still craved more of.

She was wearing black, with high heels tapping in the footwell. Her legs were crossed, and I knew her thighs were clenched tight together. It took every scrap of restraint I had not to reach over and slide my hand up between them.

Her hair was longer, but just as dark. Her lips were painted red and her eyeliner was every bit as dramatic as she'd ever worn it.

It would be smeared all over her face by the time we were through, and I'd love it. I'd fucking love the way I'd destroy her makeup, and make her pant and scream and beg. I'd leave her a sweating, soaking mess and love the wreck of her. Fuck, all those memories came flooding back and my cock was twitching for it.

For her.

She'd love the sweating, soaking wreck I'd make of her too. I'd make sure of that.

I pulled up in the inn car park, and she finally shot me a look.

"What's this place?" she asked, and I gave her a grin.

"Thought we'd grab some lunch before I plough my cock into you all afternoon. Let me treat you before I claim you."

She tried to hold back a smile, but failed.

Her heels sounded delicious as she paced her way across the gravel. She gave me a thanks as I held the door open for her, then paused as she surveyed the host of empty tables. We were the first ones in for lunch. I gestured to a pew at the far end of the place, opting for distance between us and the range of diners who'd be sure to arrive after us.

She slipped off her coat and dropped into a seat with self-conscious grace. My eyes were fully on her as I dropped into the one opposite, but hers were focused on the menu.

The zing was even stronger between us in that place. You could feel it. Alive. Screaming. My body hungry for hers and hers hungry right back, without giving two shits for whatever treats the menu was offering up for us. Still, I played interested in the food as I scanned the listings.

"I'll have the chicken salad, please," she said, and I nodded.

"Sure thing. Drink?"

She pouted and sighed. "Orange juice, as per. My choices are crap these days."

"Epilepsy, right?"

She nodded, but cleared her throat, clearly not wanting to engage in the topic.

I didn't push her, just gave her a nod right back and headed to the bar. I could feel her eyes on me every second of the way now I wasn't looking back at her. I pondered what the hell I should say as a conversation starter, while I waited for our drinks. Whether I should burst out a straight up apology and risk an explosion, or skirt every issue and make small talk.

Maybe I should avoid both and just urge the dirty out of her with a whispered list of filthy promises.

I opted to scrap all of it, keep mute and see what the fuck she wanted to say to me.

She answered my question when I dropped her juice on the table.

"So, life's been a whirlwind?" she asked. "All good, though?"

I tipped my head. "A whirlwind about sums it up. You?"

She sipped her juice. "Things have been pretty crazy."

The awkwardness was zinging almost as hard as the lust. She was tight in her posture, guarded in her words, and I felt it. I felt it all.

She was a fragile magpie behind a thorny barricade. The same feisty little firecracker behind the same pretty lace smile as she'd always been.

She was still the Anna Blackwell I'd fallen in love with and broken apart as a result of my idiocy.

I'd be breaking her to pieces again today, but this would be an entirely different performance.

"Things have changed a lot for me this past decade," I told her. "I guess that's universal when you've suddenly got a little person that means more to you than you do."

It was the wrong conversation starter. She met my eyes in a flash, and there was a coldness to them I wasn't nearly so used to.

"Let's clear this up now," she said, and leaned in closer. "This is a one off. Sex. An afternoon of crazy filthy fucking and nothing else."

"Agreed," I replied. "Your call. However you want it."

Her words were hard. "We need to keep this quiet, because everyone will go mad about it. I don't want anyone to know I was here, or anyone to know I took your dick all afternoon. I could do without the drama or the backlash, and there would be plenty of it."

I laughed a little. "Also agreed. I too could do without the drama or backlash. I get enough of it already."

"So, we eat up then go," she said. "No silly chat, or pretending we give a shit about each other."

Those words cut me more than they had any right to.

"Sure thing. I just thought we could at least do with a hello lunch. It's been ten years."

"Not nearly long enough if I had any sense," she said, and there was a snap in it. She caught herself and shook her head, waving her hand in some kind of half-assed apology.

Yet again, I didn't blame her for any of it. I was still in utter shock she was sitting opposite.

She looked around the room. "Is this your local? Seems nice."

I shrugged and smiled and played at ease.

"Kind of. I don't have all that much that's my local. You'll see what I mean when we get there."

The food turned up, and she picked at it with her fork. I knew her belly would be fluttering, craving the contact like mine was. I knew she'd be nervous, because I was bristling with a strange nervous anticipation myself, even under the pulse of the pure primal urge to fuck her senseless.

I'd looked up epilepsy, but the condition seemed to cover a whole spectrum of different symptoms and effects. I was certain Anna would be telling me what she needed to, and the rest of it was her business and nothing to do with me.

Still, I was curious.

Curious and concerned. Yet still, I had no right to be.

I ate my steak and swigged back my red wine, then patted my mouth down with a napkin as she did the same, and we were done. Dessert was out of the question for both of us, and it didn't need saying. But something else did. Something that wouldn't keep quiet in me if I tried.

"I'm sorry," I said, and I meant it. "Seriously, Anna. I'm sorry. For everything that happened. Sorry doesn't cut it, I know, and I wanted to say it sooner, but –"

She held a hand up, her lips pitted hard. "Don't," she said. "I don't want to hear it. I don't want to hear anything. I don't want to talk, or chat, or laugh, or pretend this is anything more than wanting a crazy afternoon where I actually get off for once."

I couldn't argue with that. I daren't.

"You'll be getting off a hell of a lot more than once, don't worry about that," I told her, and went to pay the bill.

She was standing with her coat over her arm when I headed back to join her. She gave me a polite thanks, and stepped on ahead of me, and it was all I could do to stop myself from grabbing her and tugging that dress down hard from those pretty pale tits of hers.

My dick strained in my pants, my mouth watering at the thought of her juicy cunt, but it kept on simmering under the surface. We were silent all over again as I drove us out to my place. The roads turned to lanes, and twisted and climbed, and the tracks were muddy and potholed. She took an audible breath as I pulled off to the right and parked up outside the house. She leaned forward and stared up at the sprawl of it, eyes wide.

"Wow, this is really something."

"Yes, it is," I agreed and bailed out.

The place was a converted barn, with ivy growing all over the front of it. The gardens were lawned, but wild, with vegetable plots all up the one side, and the door was heavy wood, and made a loud creak as I pushed it open. I took her cases from the car and dropped them inside while she was still standing on the doorstep.

"It really is in the middle of nowhere," she said, and looked around the grounds one final time before stepping over the threshold. There were no neighbours in sight. One of the reasons I'd chosen it in the first place. No neighbours. No noise. No intrusion.

I called the dogs back as they charged at her, and they listened, but only after they'd managed to bundle her into the kitchen wall and wagged their tails like rudders on speed.

I'd have let them do it all over again just to hear the slightest hint of the laugh that sounded out of her.

"Good dogs!" she giggled. "Wow, what cuties!"

It was her.

Finally, it was really her in the room along with me.

"They are amazing!" she laughed when they'd taken my instructions and zipped outside for their toilet break. "Collies?"

"Bill and Ted," I said. "They are indeed collies."

She stepped on through to the windows at the far end of the room while I held the back door open for the boys. My eyes were on her as she leaned into the sill and scoped out the horizon.

"This really is quite something," she told me. "It's beautiful."

"Yes," I said. "It's really beautiful. There are plenty of things that are beautiful right here and now though."

The dogs dashed back inside and made their way to their beds without accosting her a second time. I closed the door, and held back a minute, staring at the woman who'd set me alight again as she stared out at the sunshine. I saw her shoulders tighten as I stepped in her direction. I heard her breath catch as she felt me approach.

"Really, Lucas," she whispered, and my heart thumped along with my cock, just to hear her say my name. "You've got a great place. So different from the city. It's really amazing out here."

"We'd better get started on that really amazing one off afternoon of yours, then," I said, and my voice was low. So fucking low. So fucking alive.

She was shuddering before I'd even reached her. Her breaths were shallow before I'd even made contact, my body tight to hers.

"I've really needed this," she said. "It's crazy, but I need this."

"That makes two of us. Maybe we're both fucking crazy, or maybe the rest of the world is."

"Just a one off," she whispered.

"Just a one off."

But I didn't believe that.

We were already in too fucking deep for that, and we hadn't even started yet. It was a shitstorm of lightning threatening to zap us both alive. It was a barrage of pain, and regret, and stupid decisions flaring back up to bite.

It was everything I cursed, and everything I craved, and just about everything that could add salt to the wounds I was trying to heal up around me.

Trying and failing.

Trying and failing at so fucking much these past few months.

"I mean it," she said. "It has to be a one off. This doesn't mean anything. It's just stupid fun. A stupid way to spend a stupid afternoon, and nothing else. It can't ever be anything else."

She was waffling. Nervous.

She was edgy as hell as I slipped my hands onto her waist and pressed my mouth up close to her ear.

"This will never be a stupid way to spend an afternoon," I told her, and she whimpered as she tipped her head back.

"Just fuck me, Lucas," she hissed. "Make this one off worth the absolute insanity and just fucking fuck me."

Chapter Five

ANNA

My whole body was screaming out YES, even as my mind was screaming out NO.

He was toxic. Poisonous. The fatality of every scrap of my heart when he'd trashed it all to pieces without even looking back. The man who consumed me, promised me the stars, then destroyed me and left me a betrayed mush on the floor, sobbing my guts up and retching myself to sleep at night.

I hated him.

I'd sworn I'd always hate him.

But I couldn't stop myself. I couldn't stop my clit begging and my heart pounding and my breath quickening. I couldn't stop myself giving my needy, filthy shards over to the man who knew how to consume them.

This was me. The real me. The crazy me.

The me everyone I knew would curse at and tell me I was a stupid bitch for letting loose.

The me I'd thrown to the side and ignored through ten years of trying to live a cookie cutter life for my own wellbeing.

And failed.

I'd failed.

I was doomed the second I felt his heat at my back. His hands on my waist. His warm breath alive on my neck. His words a whispered hiss at my ear.

"I'll do more than fuck you, Anna. I'll take you so fucking hard, you'll be a mess for weeks, and you know it. You know full well the things I'll fucking do to you, that's why you're here."

Yes. I knew it.

Yes. That's why I was there.

I let out my first desperate little moan as I turned to face him. His mouth was waiting. Open and fierce and wet.

My lips pressed to his, but his tongue was already set to take mine. It pushed in deep and danced a beautiful dance as his fingers gripped my face and held me tight.

And there it was. That simmer deep inside that you can't fake or substitute. That heavenly desire that buzzes right through you and lifts you to your toes.

He did that to me.

He always had.

And I needed it right now.

I grabbed onto his hair and kissed him like my whole world depended on it. Like he was my salvation. My saviour and destroyer both at once. Enough to drive me out of my mind and lap it up in an orgy of the purest sin.

He was panting now, and there was that smirk of his I knew so well and loved so much, his mouth barely breaking contact.

"You'd better be ready to show me what a filthy little slut you still are."

"Make me one," I hissed right back. "Fucking take me."

He bit my lip hard enough that I whimpered, then he snarled and shunted me backwards. I didn't know where I was going, and didn't have a care. There was only his kiss, his hands, and the strength of him. His chest was every bit as firm as he'd ever been. The swell of his cock was high against my belly.

My eyes were wide and I'm sure I shrieked when he lifted me up onto his dining table and slammed my ass down. He tossed the chairs away with a clatter and was right up and at me, his mouth right back on its attack.

His hands were masters as they tore my dress down and yanked my horny little tits from my bra. My nipples were every bit as hungry as the rest of me, tight and straining for his mouth before he'd even broken it from mine.

"Good little slut," he growled, and spat on his fingers. He pinched my nipples slick, and his eyes were on mine – that mottled hazel green I knew so well – that fatally filthy stare that had always sent me wild.

He knew what I was going to say before I said it. My voice sounded pathetic as the words came out of me.

"Do it, Lucas. Make it hurt."

"My fucking pleasure," he said.

I rocked back on my arms, tits offered up and legs spread wide as he lowered his face. His hands gripped tight enough that I sucked in a breath, well aware that he'd drive my tits to such sore tenderness they'd sing their thrills for days. His lips were a vice, his teeth nipping and pulling, and I was lost as I bucked up against him.

"More!" I begged, and he gave it.

His fingers twisted, and his mouth clamped tight, and I was squirming as he sucked my tit so hard. My grab was fierce on his scalp, my legs wrapped around him tight. He dribbled and drooled and spat all over me. He rubbed his dirty wet spit all over my skin and teased my nipples with the very tip of his tongue when he wasn't hurting me. Tender and brutal, tender and brutal. A seesaw that had me dazed and giddy.

His palms skirted up my thighs and my clit was already going crazy. My knickers were soaked, pussy tingling underneath as he lowered his mouth and licked his way down there.

He hitched me forward on the table, and I shuddered.

He let me feel the heat of his breath through the lace, and I tipped my head back on a moan.

"I've been looking forward to tasting this slick little cunt of yours," he said, and my cheeks burned up.

"Please…"

I squirmed forward but he didn't give me his mouth. I knew he was smirking in denial without even looking at him. I could feel it. Feel him.

"Please…" I said again. "I need this…"

"So do I," he said, and reached up to slam me flat on the table.

My back arched the moment he buried his face into my sopping knickers. He knew every groove, every spot, every slick thrill there to drag from me. It came flooding back, the passion and the thrum and the zinging pulse of my pussy, and he had me. He had me so fast that I was already murmuring by the time he pulled the fabric aside and spread my lips so wide my clit was bare for the taking.

So many years of faking a half genuine orgasm. So many years of feigning the moans, but with him they were all real. His instincts were sharp and always on point. He lapped and sucked in perfect rhythm, taking hold of my clit and coaxing the waves. Pure. Fucking. Mastery.

Nobody else could have slammed his fingers into me the way he did. Three in hard, all the way in deep, and I was ready. Ready and begging. He curled them up, and ground hard until the spot was crying out, and I rode them, I rode and bucked and writhed like the filthy little slut I'd always been with him.

I held his face pressed tight, my fingers digging into his scalp without giving a shit for how hard my nails were grabbing at him, but he didn't give a shit right back. He was grunting and panting and eating me up like I was his sacred fountain, and I loved it. I fucking loved it.

He sucked. Hard.

I bucked. Hard.

He fucked me rough and fast, his fingers spreading to stretch me, and I craved more, cried out for more, pleaded for it harder and harder.

He delivered.

One final wet lap and he swirled his tongue in just the right spot, flicking at my clit like a damn snake and the explosion was everything I'd been seeking and denied. It was everything that had always set me on fire, enough to have me a pool at his feet in every way possible.

My ears were ringing, and my screwed-closed eyes flashed with white, and my moans sounded distant but raw enough to have me shuddering.

Loud.

Needy.

Wild.

Lost to everything but the pure brilliance of my pussy losing control.

And I was done.

I was a shivering wreck. Heart thumping loud. My knickers were still on, and he ran his thumb right over the crotch once they'd settled back into position. Fuck, I was wet. Soaking wet.

So was he.

His face was as drenched as I was, my wetness glistening in his beard as he climbed back up and onto me, bearing his weight right down.

I reached up to brush his cheek, and he was smiling. Smiling dirty in just the same way I'd fallen in love with all those years ago.

He licked my open mouth all the way around my lips before he kissed me deep. I tasted myself on his tongue, but that wasn't enough for him. He hooked his fingers in my cheeks and stretched them wide, and I knew what was coming. I was whimpering ready before he even did it.

He spat into my mouth, my own pussy juice undeniable, then plunged his fingers in so deep I retched.

"Suck," he said, and I did. I sucked his fingers while he licked my face, and I was already straining up at him, my clit already desperate for more. "I love making a filthy mess of you," he whispered, and pulled his fingers free to smear the pitiful remnants of my lipstick right across my cheeks, and with that I was lost all over again, his to do whatever the hell he wanted with.

Just like always.

His grin was toxic beauty as he pressed his forehead to mine. His nose was its usual pressure, his lips their usual puffiness after eating me up so hard, and I loved it.

Damn my own stupidity, but I loved it.

"Nice to see you after all these years," he said, and he was laughing.

Part of me hated how I was laughing back, but I couldn't stop it. Didn't want it to stop. The euphoria was too instinctive. Too beautiful.

He collapsed on top of me, his laughter at my neck, his firm body pressed into mine.

"Such a filthy little slut," he said with his mouth touching mine.

He bit my lip before pulling away and getting to his feet.

He was still fully suited and looking damn fine for it. His tie was still in position, his damp shirt still perfectly buttoned underneath, and I was a wreck with my tits bare and heaving, my dress still hitched up my waist while my thighs still trembled.

I despised myself and him along with it, but it was a distant whirlwind amongst the rest of my tattered senses, lost under that ridiculous high.

I watched him walk across the kitchen and reach a pack of cigarettes from a shelf. I watched the suck of his mouth as he lit up and took his first drag, his cheeks still glistening with my wetness, and I wanted one.

He knew me well enough to tell.

He was holding the pack out as I propped myself up on my elbows, and for the first time in years I accepted with a nod.

Seb's face would be a picture of horror as I dropped myself to my feet and headed over to take a cigarette from my filthy destroyer. He'd curse and bluster and moan about my fitness, and insist I lapped up the mineral water and banish such travesties of mankind to the gutter.

I tugged my dress back up in some shitty attempt at modesty before I lit up, then coughed like an idiot before I'd even managed a decent breath.

His face was pure amusement, one eyebrow raised as he stared down at me.

"Given the shit sticks up, I take it?"

I nodded. "A long time ago."

I expected a lecture, just the same as I'd been getting from everyone in every capacity for years, but it didn't come. Instead, he headed over to the fridge and pulled out a bottle of wine, then grabbed a glass from the cupboard.

"I have prosecco?" he said, and it was another counter offer to everything I'd been living for as long as I could remember.

"I'm on meds," I reminded him. "I'm not allowed."

"Of course," he said. "But you've always done plenty of things you're not allowed. Just wanted you to know it's an option."

My lungs adjusted to the smoke, and I managed a decent drag of nicotine.

"You shouldn't let me," I told him, but he looked at me like I was speaking a foreign language.

"Shouldn't let you what? Have a drink? You're perfectly capable of knowing whether you want a drink or not."

I had a weird zing in my belly as he reached another glass down.

"Juice, then?"

I nodded. "Yes, please."

His smirk was as filthy as ever as he grabbed the carton from the fridge and poured one out. It was the strangest contradiction in my ribs – the urge to grab him and tear his shirt off pulsing down deep, while another part of me wanted to scream abuse and storm right out of there like the asshole deserved. Or like I deserved.

I did neither, just took that glass from him and took a swig.

"That was quite a pleasure," he said, then stubbed his cigarette out in a jar lid on the side. "I'd forgotten just quite how deliciously explosive you are when you come like that."

I hadn't.

That's why I was there in the first fucking place.

I held back from making that statement, just stubbed my cigarette out in the jar lid to match and leaned back against the kitchen counter.

Our eyes met and held, the tension already building right back up again.

He was a gorgeous specimen. Fit and filthy and toned just right. His face was angular in just the right places, eyes heavy and focused as he pulled at his beard in the same habitual way he'd done for ever.

It suited him.

Everything always suited him.

"Let's get on with making the most of this one day fuckathon," he said, and downed the rest of his wine.

Chapter Six

LUCAS

Spit and smeared lipstick made a glossy mess of her face and she looked so damn delicious.

"What next?" she asked with a grin on her wet face, and there it was again. The horny slut in her that set my pulse racing all the fucking faster and my dick eager for more.

Oh, so many answers to her question. Oh, so many choices. My brain was a slideshow of crazy ideas, desperate to take advantage of every single one of them.

"Spit it out, then," she prompted, licking her lips as she stepped closer. "What's next in the filthy fuckathon? It's a one off, remember, so we'd better make the most of it."

Her tits were still slick, cleavage shimmering over the top of her dress as she pasted on the cool act. The cool act didn't matter. She could puff away on cigarettes like we were just two casual unknown hook-ups all she wanted, but it would make no difference. There was nothing unknown about this hook-up.

I knew everything about the woman whose taste was still a pleasure on my tongue. Every nook, every curve. Every want and fantasy and muffled little squeal.

I knew her. All of her. Every fucking thing there was to know.

I was damn fucking well going to exploit it.

"We'll be making the most of it alright," I told her. "Get your dirty little ass upstairs!"

She didn't need telling twice. I gestured the way and she dashed on ahead, lifting her heels nice and high over a ride-on toy unicorn at the bottom of the stairs before she started up. Her eyes were flashing back at me every step, fully ready and waiting for me to grab her at the top.

I didn't disappoint.

I wrapped my arms so tight around her waist that she could barely grab a breath, half carrying half dragging her across the landing past Millie's room and straight into mine. Her mouth was already open as I shoved her to her knees at the bottom of my bed, head tipping back nice and ready like the little slut she was.

She was so fucking beautiful like that.

I tugged my cock free from my suit trousers, clutching at her hair to keep her firm, and then I gave her what was coming. My balls were throbbing, dick fucking desperate, and I took her mouth like the perfect little fuck doll she was so fucking good at being.

It was rough and retching and beyond any kind of sanity. She loved it and I loved it as I slammed her throat until her eyes were streaming, smearing tears of mascara across her face as she drooled and spluttered.

I couldn't hold it back.

My gut was a hum of absolute craving, right the way up to my chest. I was fried by it, her swirling tongue and wet little mouth driving me fucking wild.

She knew it. Oh fuck, how she knew it. It may have been her taking the pounding with me destroying her makeup into tatters, but she was the true vixen in this exchange.

She knew just the way to flick her tongue along my shaft to make me grit my teeth and grunt like a savage.

She knew how to suck just hard enough to get that pressure just fucking right.

She knew how to twist her face to billow my length out of her cheek like a filthy little bitch, and how fucking wild that would make me as I stretched her pretty face.

And she played it. She played it all just like I was playing her.

"Rub that filthy slit," I grunted, and she did. She spread those knees further apart and dipped her fingers right the way down to those sopping wet panties. And she was rough, wet, noisy with it, moaning and whimpering and shuddering, and that drove me fucking wild all the more.

"Give me your cum," she muttered, nice and sloppy with my dick halfway in.

"No fucking way," I grunted back, and pushed her away.

My balls hated me, and my dick wasn't far behind, but it was just the beginning. I'd be banking up every scrap of my seed until she was a squirming mess on the floor, begging hard enough to scream the walls down. She moaned all over again as I dropped down and lapped at her dripping wet face, breaths hard and heavy as she fingered her sopping wet cunt.

No way was she taking that damn fucking pleasure herself.

"Down," I said, and twisted her onto all fours and shunted up to her rear, tugging those slick wet panties right down from her ass cheeks.

She wriggled them further without a word, shooting me another flash of her dirty glinting eyes as I pulled them from her ankles. I spread her ass cheeks so fucking wide and buried my face in so fucking hard that she cried out, and I had her. She was soaked through. Dripping so slick it was a fucking treasure.

She cursed out filth as I squirmed my tongue into that tight little asshole and dug in deep, rubbing back against me as her fingers strummed hard. I was a slavering beast, taking everything, and she was the slut I knew so well, begging me for more. She came so hard her thighs were shivering to a whole new tune, and I didn't let up. I twisted under her and pulled her puffy little slit right down onto my open mouth, so hungry for more of her wetness that I'd have stayed there a lifetime, sucking that perfect cunt into my mouth. She ground and circled, whimpering as she claimed it all, and fuck me, I gave it. I fucking gave it all, but we'd barely scratched the surface yet.

She swung her leg over and grabbed my tie, yanking me up onto my knees like a woman possessed. She tore at my shirt in a frenzy, and I helped her on her quest, freeing my skin bare enough that her mouth was on my naked chest, biting at my nipples like a desperate little bitch as her hands helped me wrestle off my suit pants, then she reached for my straining cock.

But it wasn't her hands I wanted.

She was on her back in a heartbeat, dress and bra torn off, knees up at her shoulders as I sank my cock right the way into that hungry pussy and thrust like a beast.

We were animals. Feral and desperate. Lost to everything but the slam of flesh on flesh. The heat of skin on skin, of breath on breath.

She gripped my face, fingers tight, eyes piercing mine as I fucked her deep.

And then I kissed her.

I kissed her and she kissed me right back and our doom was fucking sealed.

The whole world faded into nothing and there was just us, wet and thrusting and panting, mouth to mouth in a kiss that was beyond all human reason, and I needed it. I needed it so fucking bad that my body was on fire, my chest heaving and heart thumping, pressed tight to feel hers thumping right back. The decade was destroyed, lost into the background. Flesh never forgets, and ours sure remembered every fucking thing we'd ever done.

Jesus Christ, how I wanted more of it.

I don't know how many times I fucked her that night. I don't know how many times I squirmed my tongue against her clit until she screamed out my name like a banshee. I don't know how many times I was balls deep into that hungry little cunt, so hard that her nails were talons on my back.

I don't know how many times she kissed me with so much meaning that I swore she'd be bare naked in my arms forever, and I don't know how many times I rewarded her by filling up her begging mouth nice and slick with my cum.

I don't know how we managed a trip downstairs to the kitchen and put some semblance of a steak dinner on to cook. I don't know how I managed to drink nearly two bottles of wine and she managed to take her medication at the proper time.

I definitely don't know how I managed to find her snuggled tight in my arms under the bedcovers with a smile on her face as we soaked in the euphoria of a day to remember.

I was just so damn fucking pleased I did.

I eased off to sleep with no idea what time it was, only that the very first scrap of morning light was blooming outside. She was breathing deep and steady, lost in dreams with her head still tight into the crook of my shoulder as I closed my eyes and said goodbye to the ten year hello.

And then, finally and truly gratefully, I slept better than I had in a decade.

Chapter Seven

ANNA

I woke up in instinctive panic, my hand plunging straight down between my thighs and patting around the bedsheets.

Please, please, please.

Clammy, but not dripping. No wetness. Not that kind of wetness anyway.

Thank fuck I hadn't pissed myself in someone else's bed as an embarrassing farewell.

I took a breath and settled back down, letting the calm wash over me – what little there was of it, at least.

There really wasn't any calm left in a ten-mile radius once I looked over at the man who'd fucked me senseless, kicked free of covers with his shoulders rising and falling steady, still lost in slumber. His ass was the ass I knew so well, so perfectly shaped, he looked like he'd been pulled down from a podium in a Roman amphitheatre. He was worthy of tourist snapshots, sculpted from stone and hot enough to scorch a thousand souls.

Screw my life. One look at him and I was thrumming desperate for another go.

His back had the same glorious ladder of a spine, with dips at the base that made me want to dig my fingers in and lick a road all the way up. His butt cheeks were screaming out to be pulled apart, my eyes desperate to snatch and steal every sliver of his privacy.

Holy shit.

I was doomed.

My whole body was rattling, desperate for another taste of him eating me alive, but no. My brain was fighting it this morning, holding on to the frayed edges of reason. Finally. I had some. At least thirty seconds of frayed reason enough to swing my legs out of bed and shove myself to my feet.

I didn't have a clue where most of my stuff had been cast aside – not even my phone – but luckily my medication tray was on the top of his chest of drawers with a half full glass of water standing next to it. I ate up my morning dose, then resolved to drag myself to some kind of order and get the hell out of there, party over, see you later.

See you never fucking again, more like it.

I'd clipped my bra back on and tugged my dress down over my head by the time I realised he was looking at me. His leg was lazily kicked out, arms deliciously muscular as they grabbed a load of pillows and propped his head up.

His stare was anything but lazy as he lapped me up. I could feel him. Drinking me in and swigging me deep.

He patted the covers next to him with a smirk, but no. Just no.

"Fuckathon over," I said. "One off, remember. Nice to know you."

I sounded a whole load more sure than I felt.

"You're really fucking off before a morning repeat?"

My back was to him when I nodded. "Yep, I'm really fucking off."

I didn't hear him moving and I daren't have looked around to check, just kept on grabbing my stuff up from the carpet and piling it back into one of my cases. Still no sign of my phone.

"I can give you a lift back to your place," he said, but I shook my head.

"I need the train," I replied. "Can't have anyone seeing us together. If I'm a scrap of lucky, I'll get away with this bullshit without having to spend the next decade explaining my crazy."

"Maybe a decade explaining the crazy is better than a decade living without it," he said, and his words thumped me deep.

There was only one person on this planet responsible for the decade living without it, and he could go and get fucked. I spun to scorch his stare with mine, wishing my clit believed a sliver of the spite the rest of me was such good friends with.

"I'll be living without it for more than a damn decade this time around," I told him. "It was a splurge. A stupid splurge. That's all."

"I can still taste your pretty cunt," he said, and I hated him. I hated the way he licked his lips and kept that smirk at full volume. I hated the way he was bursting for more without even breaking a sweat. I hated the way he had me on fire, even though my heart was ice cold and seething.

I hated the way his cock was hard and my mouth was watering.

I hated the way I was fluttering like a weak little heartbreak with jelly legs.

"Get me to the train, please," I said, and he held my stare for a few long seconds before getting to his feet.

"Sure."

He kicked aside his strewn shirt and pants and grabbed some jeans from his drawer. I cursed myself for watching as he pulled them up, and cursed myself harder when his eyes met mine in the mirror, catching me in the act. I got the hell out of there and found his bathroom at the bottom of the landing.

My heart was panging weirdly as he burst right on in while I was taking my morning piss, that same smirk on his face as he checked out my pussy as I peed. He loaded up his toothbrush and got to work, and I couldn't stop that pain at the familiarity. His presence was so matter of factly at ease with mine. I knew his movements by heart, even after all this time. The way he tilted his head as he washed his hands up and smoothed down his beard. The way he cleared his throat and shoved his toothbrush back in the holder.

"Know when the trains are?" he asked, and I forced myself not look at him, just kept my eyes on the toilet roll and wiped myself dry.

"It doesn't matter," I said. "Just get me to the station, please."

"No breakfast?"

"No thanks."

I prayed he wouldn't play on my favourites. That he wouldn't offer me his speciality poached eggs and fried mushrooms, and his smile across the breakfast table.

He didn't.

"I'll get ready to roll, then," he said, and my heart dropped.

Disappointment.

I hated myself in that moment almost as much as I hated him.

I found my phone downstairs on the kitchen counter, blinking with low battery and a whole ton of missed calls and texts. *Mum. Nicola. Vicky.*

Shit.

No doubt they all thought I was spasming somewhere, with no idea of my own name.

Again, I hated myself for letting them worry like that, all for the sake of getting my clit sucked by an asshole.

I was ready to leave and petting his dogs when he joined me downstairs. He was so much more casual today; a regular t-shirt that he buried under a regular coat and grabbed his shoes from the rack. He let the dogs out, then grabbed up his keys and tossed a glance in my direction, heading down the hallway and holding the door open for me to step out.

I hated myself a whole load more for just how much my tummy churned at the knowledge that this was really it. Goodbye forever. So long for another long decade, and hopefully loads more of them to follow.

He took my cases and dumped them in the back of his truck, then climbed on in as I clipped my seatbelt up.

We didn't speak. No small talk. No laughter. No grinning memories of an epic night together. Nothing but the countryside rushing past outside the window and Lydney train station getting closer.

Until we were there.

I didn't know what to say, so I didn't say anything, just dropped on out of the passenger seat and grabbed my cases before he had a chance to.

Please God, don't try to hug me goodbye or wave me off.

Luckily, he did neither.

I wanted to thank him before I went, but the words burnt my throat too hard. I wanted to at least throw him a smirk and a *hell, that was a fuckathon*, but I couldn't. I just pushed my feet to walking a step at a time on stupid heels, feeling like an idiot as I made my way to the platform.

He didn't join me, and I was grateful.

I had enough battery in my phone to fire off some *don't worry, sorry, be back soon* messages to the blinking contacts, then shoved the handset back in my bag as the next train pulled up at the platform. I took a seat and a breath along with it, resolving afresh that this was really it. No more Lydney train station and no more Lucas Pierce.

I just wished it didn't feel so bloody hard.

I also wished I hadn't broken enough to leave my dirty knickers tucked under his bedcovers when I'd been zipping up my case and bailing on his bedroom. Because why? Why would I leave a parting gift like that, knowing full well it was one of his *drive you crazy* fetishes?

Because I wanted to drive him crazy.

Because I'd always wanted to drive him crazy.

Even half as crazy as he drove me.

I should have felt better as Cheltenham pulled closer and normality pulled closer with it, but I didn't. I was still a mess from his flesh on mine, and his tongue in my mouth, and his fingers digging tight on my scalp. I was still a pool of want with my pussy still dripping for another fill of his dick.

There were so many things we hadn't gotten to. Toys still to play with, and filth still to explore. An ocean of repeat performances stacked up and looming with no chance of expression.

Turns out that one night isn't enough to fulfil a decade of need. Who'd ever have thought it? Not this little moron with her stupid notion that this could have ever been a sane enough move to skip right away from. I scrolled through my messages, contemplating using the last of my battery on a confession text to Nicola, to seal my fate and push this crazy night aside for ever. My thumb was paused over her name and Cheltenham was just a stop away when a ping tried to seal my fate in an entirely different direction.

Thanks for the panties. Tennis this p.m.?

And there it was. A picture to follow. My knickers around his dick. His magnificent dick with the precum glistening.

Fuck you, Lucas Pierce and your perfect manhood.

Fuck you, clitoris, and your idiot needs.

No tennis, I fired back. *And no more dick pics, please.*

My brain tried another bullshit argument, shouting to my pounding heart that this would truly be a game of tennis. Just us on the court with me trying to kick his ass and failing miserably.

Maybe I'd manage to break his nose with a super strong serve and gritted teeth. That would be a game worth playing.

Scared of getting thrashed? he replied. *I've still got your racket, btw.*

There was a burn with that. A weird little burn I couldn't place.

My racket.

I remembered the pink flash on the handle. The way it felt when I would spin it in my hands between serves.

Surely, I could check out my racket one last time? Surely, it wouldn't have to mean the world to share a match on a Sunday?

But it was about more than the racket or the memories. There was something bursting in my chest. A stranger over the years, so long buried that it brought a stranger of a smile to my lips along with it.

Fun.

It was fun.

I was having fun.

Not scared of getting my ass kicked, I replied, and I meant it. *I might well kick yours, asshole.*

I clicked on a smiling emoji and sent that off to follow.

Show me then, he said.

And I could. I could remind him just how fierce I battled when he summoned the spark of fight. Just one game to revisit another great snippet of the great life I thought we'd been living together until he chewed my heart into nothing.

Tell me when and where, another ping followed up, and I cursed myself out loud as I used the final few battery percent to look up the sports clubs on the city outskirts and pull up an available court. I cursed myself again as I fired off the details, and trusted he'd got them when my phone blinked out.

And then I made my way home for a shower of shame and the terrible travesty of another looming Lucas Pierce experience.

Chapter Eight

LUCAS

I dug the rackets from the case above the weed killer in the garage and wiped them down. Still fit to serve. I hadn't played tennis in years, barely venturing near a court since Millie was born, but the rackets felt familiar in my grip.

Just like Anna. She'd felt plenty fucking familiar in my grip.

It didn't matter that I'd busted an ocean of seed from my balls the night before, and another round into the dirty lace of her panties just a few minutes previous. I was still craving. Still strung tight with filthy lust for the filthy little bitch who knew my cock even better than I did. The strung rackets bounced off my palm, mirroring my tension.

If I couldn't claim her tight little ass in my bed that afternoon, I'd damn well claim it on the tennis court.

I took the dogs out before heading into the city, taking the time to stretch my legs and pick up into a jog to get my limbs in gear. I was washed and dressed for the game, well stocked up on a brunch of poached eggs before jumping in the truck and setting off. I fired up the stereo and put on some usual radio chatter, but my mind was nowhere on the voices spouting on.

It was all on her.

No matter how hard my sanity of rationale was trying to cast this aside as a blip in hers, I couldn't shake off the undeniable. I was excited. Bristling with the spike of adrenaline. Nothing the fuck whatsoever to do with tennis and everything to do with Anna Blackwell.

I pulled up in the sports club parking area, checking again on her message to make sure that this was the right venue. It was a way out of town, right on the outskirts and no location I recognised from days gone by, but yeah, it was the right one.

I was still sitting in the truck, ready to jump out when a taxi drew up in a space in front of me. I watched her legs appear before she did, her sweet little backside poking up high as she leaned back in to pay the driver.

She looked absolutely fucking divine. Hair scooped up messily, in the style I loved so much on her. Cheeks flushed with the taste of life as she stared on up at the building, seemingly as unsure of it as I was. Her top was tight and stretched just right over her perky little tits. Perky little tits I'd pushed hard in the way that drove her crazy, and drove me insane to match.

I knew they'd be tender as sin under the fabric, begging for a flick of my tongue on her nipples. Bruised just right to set her churning, grabbing hold and squealing for more if I dared to squeeze just so.

Her shorts were high enough to show off the legs she'd wrapped so tight around my back the night before. Socks cute and white in sweet little tennis shoes.

I dropped out of the truck and was up close behind her before she registered my presence.

She sure fucking registered it when she did, though. Her eyes were wide when she spun to face me, mouth open in the perfect invite to slam my tongue in deep and claim her for another battle of skin on skin. But then she saw her racket in my hand. Those wide eyes lit up as she snatched it from me, spinning it in her grip like a long lost friend.

"Wow, you really kept it."

It seems she had considerably more affection for the strung plastic sports weapon than she had for me. Yet again, I couldn't blame her.

"Let's see if you really kept up with how to use it," I said and saw the flash in her eyes I knew so well. Competition. Spirit. Drive to push herself to the limit.

It turned me into a prick every bit as desperate to claim victory as she was to win the fight.

"I'll remember how to use it," she said, and spun it in her hand again as we reached the entrance. "Let's just see if you remember how to kick my ass as hard as you used to."

"I'll kick your tight little ass so hard you'll scream like a bitch all night long," I hissed at her ear as she grinned at the reception attendant on the main desk.

"Blackwell," she told them, but her voice was goofed up and unsteady. "Three p.m., for tennis."

"Court four," they replied, barely shooting us a glance.

Anna didn't speak a word until we got outside. She took up her side of the court and did some stretches, and my dick was a total loser, straining hard in my shorts as she bent and scooped and danced around the place. She flaunted her ass, and knew it, flashing me a dirty glance over her shoulder and smirking like a minx as she saw my stare.

Yep. If that was her game, she'd stand a chance of winning. Slamming the bastard tennis ball over the net was right down on my list of priorities. Slamming my tongue in her asshole was a whole fucking world more captivating.

She bounced the ball on the tarmac. I braced myself for the serve.

It was a disaster when it came. She judged the racket swing wrong, barely scooting the ball over the net where it bounced in a pitiful little stutter.

She cursed. I laughed. She cursed louder and shot me the middle finger, and I shrugged. Then she was laughing too.

"False start," she shouted, and I shrugged again.

"Start as many times as you want, I'll always be the one to finish."

"We'll see about that," she said.

Next time she caught it good. There was spirit in her slam, the racket connecting with the ball and striking hard. She delivered. I delivered right back. She leapt and dashed and swung like it was her life purpose to win the match, but I didn't let her. There was no way I was letting her take the crown. She was mine to be taken, both on the court and off it, she just didn't know it yet.

She was blushing pink in no time, breaths ragged as she fought the battle. My pulse was strumming, but steady, enjoying the rhythm of the game. Two people in the groove, predicting each other's movements and using it to spur their downfall.

She scored a point. I scored three back.

She did a jig when she scored her second, told me it was only a matter of time before she kicked my ass, she was still just finding her feet again.

Her feet were actually a fuck ton more steady than I remembered them. So was her swing.

"Have you been practicing?" I asked, but she shook her head.

"No. Maybe you've just been getting worse."

I tipped my head and gave her another smirk, cheeky little minx. She was right on that score. I'd been getting worse at life for a whole long drag of it, but I wasn't going to show her that. Not today.

So I did it. I kicked her ass. Pulled my mind from the filth and charged myself to the maximum.

She was sweating and panting, letting out those delicious little grunts as she tried to batter the ball back, but I couldn't help myself. I kept on stealing it, aiming the ball just outside her stretch to watch her straining.

I loved watching her straining.

"I will beat you one day," she told me through the grunts. "I swear, I'm going to beat you one day."

"Be my guest," I said, and slammed another point home.

There were another couple of players waiting at the sidelines by the time we clocked that our time was done. I met her at the net, but she had none of my outstretched commiseration handshake, putting her thumb to her nose and poking her tongue out.

Jesus Christ, I loved that silly little side of Anna. She had me poking my tongue out right back at her, laying a hand on her back as we walked away from the court.

We strolled our way back out through reception into the parking zone with a *thanks* to the attendant, and she pulled her phone straight from her bag, scrolling through the numbers.

"Where next?" I asked, and she shot me a glance that feigned disinterest.

"I'm calling a taxi," she said. "I'm going home."

But I was done with the stupid facade. She let out a squeak as I grabbed her tight and forced her across the gravel to my truck. She stole a gasp before I slammed her into the passenger door, my thigh pressed tight between hers and my breath in her face.

"You're not going anywhere near home until you've come around my cock, and we both fucking know it," I said and the glare she gave me was the headiest mix of want and hate I'd ever seen. "Now buckle the fuck up," I said. "We'll see who wins the next game… in my fucking bed."

"It was a one off," was all she could say.

I told the truth right back at her. "It'll never be a one off while your pussy is dripping for more and my dick is so keen to deliver."

The silence ringing back at me had me grinning like a twat.

"This is just sex," she said eventually and I nodded.

"It can be whatever you want it to be, Anna, just give me that pretty little mouth and that pretty little cunt to match."

"I mean it," she snapped, then turned to yank the door open. "It's just sex. You're a prick, and I know it this time around."

"I'm a prick with a prick you want a ride on," I said, and made my way to the driver's side. She was already belted in when I dropped into the seat.

I wasted no time in getting the hell out of there and back on the road.

We were back out of town when I opted to strike up conversation.

"Don't you wanna talk about it? Not any of it? Maybe we can churn things out a bit, cover some ground."

"I don't want to talk about one single snippet of the bullshit you put me through. Get fucked."

"You can get fucked," I said. "You can get fucked really fucking hard as soon as we get through that front door."

It was another thing I was telling the truth on.

She barely even bothered petting the dogs when they charged at her, and I wouldn't have let her if she'd wanted to. They were bounding around outside and she was up against the wall in a beat, my mouth on hers so hard she could barely take a breath, and she was right back at me, nails digging into my shoulders like she wanted to spear me, even as I ripped those shorts down her thighs.

And she'd known it. She'd known she'd fucking be here, even if she'd set out to deny it in a court of fucking law.

She was wearing my favourite kind of panties. Lace and white, pulled so tight between her pussy lips that they were slick little rose petals on a tightrope. Anything but suitable for a tennis court.

"Fuck," I said, and she bit my lip. She bit my lip and pulled tight, and I growled, pulling that tightrope a damn sight tighter.

"Fuck *me*," she said. "Fuck me *hard*, Lucas."

"My fucking pleasure," I said, and dragged that horny little bitch on upstairs where she belonged.

Chapter Nine

ANNA

I was done for. Scrambled by everything but the pure need for that asshole's perfect form. Senseless. Stupid. But, for the first time in years, not damn soulless.

My mouth wouldn't leave his as he bundled me upstairs. He'd torn me out of my t-shirt and shorts before we'd made it even halfway up, but I was just as unstoppable, ripping him from his clothes like a shredder. I was crazy for the sweat on his skin, and he shared the insanity, lapping it up from between my tits and ploughing his tongue back in my mouth with the salt fresh for the tasting.

We were a tornado of limbs and kisses, and this time he was even more primal as he wrenched me from my feet and threw me onto his bed. I landed with a bounce, and he was straight on top, his dick grinding so fiercely against the wetness between my thighs that I was panting just as hard as on the tennis court.

"Yes!" I hissed, and he knew it. He knew the fucking spot and worked it hard.

I tried to buck and grind, but he had me pinned. In control and loving it, eyes so raw on mine that I could feel the heat of him.

"Dirty little tease," he growled, and his voice gave me shivers. "Playing me like a horny bitch with those filthy wet panties."

I'd known it. I may not even have admitted it to myself, but I'd known it when I'd sought that tiny white thong out of my top drawer and slipped it on before my tennis shorts.

My legs were spread wide and his cock was ploughing hard against the criminal lace, bunching the fabric so tight against my clit that I was moaning like a slut beyond all reason. I barely even recognised my own voice.

Fuck me, Lucas. Please, fuck me. Please!

But he didn't. He kept grinding, dick straining hard, and he held me bound at his mercy. My wrists were clenched in his and my head tipped back as I squirmed underneath his weight and I was coming. It was loud. Desperate. Needy.

So fucking needy.

And holy shit, how those thrills kept on coming.

He shoved me further across the bed before I'd even come down from the first explosion, mouth hot and hungry, sucking my clit through wet lace with grunts from the back of his throat. My hands took his head and got my comeback for his bondage, holding him so tight that he could have suffocated and I wouldn't have fucking cared.

Good. I'd have suffocated him gladly.

But not today.

He didn't pull my thong to the side, just made me explode a second time with his mouth sucking hard through the fabric.

I knew he would.

Wants and needs don't change with time. Not even a decade.

His weakness was still dirty knickers, and my weakness was still… him.

My weakness was him.

Screw the universe, but my weakness was Lucas Pierce and his filthy prowess.

I had to tip my head to the side and pin my lip between my teeth as he shoved his fingers inside me. I could hear the squelching, and hear his breaths, and once again I knew what was coming. He thrust inside deeper and twisted his hand.

"Let's make these nice and wet," he barked, and I gasped out a *yes*, wanting it too.

It was his pinkie finger that pushed its way into my ass first. I gripped the bedsheets under me on the in and out, still feeling the tightness of my thong tugged to the side. The second finger was a nice stretch. I clenched and moaned, clit still fluttering, but he didn't let up, working them back and forth like the same fucking professional he'd always been.

"Spread those legs for me," he said, and I did. I raised them wider and used them to lift my butt from the bed, just like he wanted me to and before he said it. "Good girl," he grunted, and it made me burn up even brighter.

I whimpered at his depth as he pushed those fingers deep, but I could take it. That animal instinct took over and I was moving with him, seeking out more.

"I'm going to fuck your dirty ass," he told me. "If I wasn't so totally consumed by that sweet little cunt of yours yesterday, I'd have claimed it already."

"Fuck me then," I replied, but he didn't.

He kept on with those fingers and used his thumb on my clit, even though it was still crying out from earlier.

"Slick and swollen, just how I like it," he told me.

I could imagine the puffiness. Imagine the dribble of my pussy as he drove me crazy.

"I'm still shaky from coming," I said, and he laughed.

"You'll be a whole load more shaky when I'm done with you."

I had no doubt about that, just braced myself for more.

It felt impossible, just how well he played my body. He was a musician on some kind of complex flute thing, playing a masterpiece where nobody else could even get a note. He even got more than I got myself on my own damn instrument.

"Do it," I said. "Take my ass."

"Not yet," he said, and worked his thumb in harder circles.

No. Fucking. Way.

I arched my back, and the squelching got louder, and there I was again, bucking like the same needy bitch as he ploughed my ass with his fingers and worked my clit to a whole new song. I'd forgotten just how good he was, faded by a decade of mediocrity at other hands – one set of which belonged to the man I'd pledged my life to. Go figure.

"These panties are going to be absolutely filthy," he said, and I didn't even manage a nod.

He scissored the fingers in my ass and I cried out, panting afresh, losing everything but the sensations between my legs. I gulped and spluttered and gushed so hard I could've wet myself, but he was right there, grunting and lapping it up, urging me on.

"That's it," he hissed. "That's the filthy little slut that drives me crazy. Beg me to fuck your ass, Anna."

The world was a blur, my name on his lips, I had no problem begging for it.

"Please, Lucas, please fuck my ass."

"I said fucking beg!" he barked and my asshole stretched tight as more fingers went in.

I gasped out a breath. "Please, Lucas… I beg you, please."

"Louder, Anna."

So I did it. I lifted my head and took his hair in my grip and I shouted it. I fucking shouted it, but it was hardly a beg.

"FUCK MY ASS, LUCAS! JUST FUCK MY ASS!"

"My fucking pleasure," he grunted, and it would be. It would be his fucking pleasure.

And mine, too.

He flipped me in a heartbeat, and ploughed me into the bedcovers, hand on the back of my neck to pin me down. His cock made me squeal as he thrust in hard. It took a few shunts of his hips before my body opened up for him, and I was the same grunting bulk of flesh as he was, both of us ravenous as he claimed that dirty hole.

And yes. My thong was still on, bunched so tight that my tender pussy was a heady combination of love and hate.

There was a strange silence as we both held our breath, the slam of skin on skin the only beat in the room. He was the one to break it.

"Fuck," he said. One simple word that had me moaning right back.

I couldn't believe my own words until they were out of my mouth.

"Harder, Lucas! Fuck me harder!"

He pinned me tighter, his chest pressed to my back, and he gave me everything, pumped me so hard I thought I'd be unable to walk for a month. It was an animal burn, a searing heat of pleasure, and I didn't stop bucking up, couldn't stop bucking up.

I cursed and hissed with every frantic thrust.

"Fucking take it," he hissed right back, and I wanted it. I wanted it all.

I'm not sure what happened to my body as Lucas Pierce came in my ass for the first time in a decade. It was a blur of sensations sparking somewhere down low. A moaning, whimpering mess of me that wanted nothing more than that man shooting his load inside me.

I cried out again as he pulled his cock free, feeling the spurge of his cum bubble out along with him.

Again, I knew what would happen before he did it. I was already moaning out a *yes* as he smeared his cum across the crotch of my thong. I was already moaning even harder as he pulled that filthy scrap of fabric down my thighs and whipped it away from me.

I rolled onto my back before he asked me to, his dick still hard and glistening with his cum as he told me to open my mouth.

I did.

He shoved the filthy slick crotch of my thong in there.

I sucked on his fingers through the lace like a dirty bitch, moaning as he pushed them right the way in. They tasted creamy and filthy. A cocktail of thrusts and climaxes and need.

"Beautiful," he said as I sucked, and I felt that vile little bloom of pride in me. A betrayal of still being moved by what the fuck that prick ever thought of me.

But I did care what he thought of me.

I'd always cared what he thought of me.

Which is why I was so fucking broken when he left.

He got back up from me and took the thong with him. I closed my eyes and caught my breath and didn't bother to look where he took it, just knew it would be somewhere safe for later.

"Cigarette and shower," he told me, and I nodded, knowing full well there was no way I'd be turning down a cigarette after that performance.

I followed him downstairs with my ass on fire and glugged my water from my sports flask as he pulled the packet down from the shelf. He lit one up for me and handed it over.

And then he laughed. A laugh that had me laughing along with him, incapable of immunity to the thrill of the euphoric high.

I took deep drags on my cigarette, and looked at that man grinning at me, and I couldn't stop it. I was grinning right the way back, loving life with a crazy flash in me that I couldn't deny.

I should've come to my senses and got him to take me home, but I didn't. Couldn't.

I should've confessed my sins and reached out to some scowling associates of mine to talk some sanity back into me, but I didn't. Couldn't.

Instead, I sent off some stupid *be back soon, I'm fine* messages to the bleating contacts and showered alongside his perfect body and perfectly hard cock. I washed my hair with his expensive shampoo while he teased my clit all over again and washed us down with some foam.

I dried off with towels that smelt like him and loved them for it.

We ate some great tasting salmon pasta and then he fucked me over the kitchen counter.

And then he got the wine from the fridge, and asked me if I wanted a prosecco this time around.

Curse my life, I said yes.

I had one glass.

He had three and finished the bottle.

He put his stereo on and played his tunes high enough that the bass throbbed through the walls.

I hadn't heard music like that in years.

He danced.

I danced along with him.

He picked me up and spun me around and I was heady from one little glass of fizz and it had me laughing. Singing. Enjoying myself more than anyone should have enjoyed anything with this prick of a man.

And then the prick asked me for a song of my choice.

One song of all songs that he could play at full volume while we danced around together.

So I chose it.

The song I'd played for years and always thought of him and cursed his name while I played with myself.

The song with the words that had always given me a shiver and a pang for how much I still wanted that total asshole who destroyed my heart.

And a pang for how much I hated him.

"*Poison*," I said. "By Alice Cooper."

He put it on.

Chapter Ten

LUCAS

S he was addictive and I couldn't get enough. My burn for her was scorching the air between us, steaming against the ice of her stare, pure unbridled lust as that song struck up.

Her hair was wild, messy from my sweaty grip, and her makeup was a mess to match, what little there was of it. But it was her eyes – jewels of a glare that had me transfixed more than anything.

Fire.

Spark.

Passion.

Us.

I knew I was her poison. I knew I was the toxic need that drove her crazy, just as crazy as my need for her drove me. Only mine had no hate chained along with it.

She was bristling along with those lyrics as she glared across, lips still puffy from my kisses and the filthy panties I'd made her take from me.

Anna Blackwell could never have looked more beautiful than she did in that moment, fighting the need to be here with every scrap of her being and failing.

I closed the distance in a flash, grabbing her tight. Her arms closed around my shoulders, that same glare at full volume as her eyes crashed back into mine. She was living the lyrics. Breathing the lyrics. And I was breathing them right back at her, snaking my hands down her ass and hitching her against me all the harder.

And then I kissed her all over again.

Her fingers gripped so tight that it was undeniable she wanted to destroy me. Her whole body bristled with spite, and disgust, and regret for ever messaging me that Sunday morning.

But still, she kissed me right back.

Her mouth was an attack in its ferocity, her tongue battling with mine even as her body surrendered. She softened against me, heavy against my thigh as it ground fresh on her ragged clit. My teeth nipped at her lips, demanding her filthy little soul with the rest of her.

She gave it, but she had mine right back.

Jesus Christ, she had mine right back.

We were both fucking doomed, finding each other in one unholy mess of pure life carnage with no way on this earth we'd ever negotiate the fallout. Ghosts of a former life that consumed us both amongst a shitstorm of pain, and regret, and bullshit.

If only there was just a sliver of light left between us – a chance to fix that beautiful spark we'd had so strong, so long ago. But I didn't feel one. Not from Anna. Not as that song played loud.

I spun her away from me with a grunt and wrapped my arm snug around her neck. She rested her head back against my shoulder and breathed heavy against my grip, and I moved for the both of us, rocking to the pulse of the music and sliding my fingers right down to her sacred spot.

Again.

She'd come for me again.

She shuddered and tried to buck away but I wouldn't let her. I kissed her temple and held my mouth pressed tight.

She stumbled on trembling legs, and her hands reached back to steady herself, her weight holding itself up with mine. And as the song reached its climax, she did too.

It was pure fucking magic.

My filthy little minx lost every tiny scrap of restraint her body had left and cried out for me, her throat humming against my arm as her nails dug into my hips.

I loved her like that.

I'd always loved her like that.

I'd always loved every little scrap of her soul with every scrap of mine, I'd just been too much of a prick to ever deserve her.

She came down as the music changed, and she didn't start up again, just moved away from me with ragged breaths and took a cigarette straight from the pack.

The song was real to her. The pain was real to her. I could see it all over her face.

I opened another prosecco and took a swig from the bottle, then turned the volume down on the stereo and waited for her to speak.

"I shouldn't be here," she said, stating the obvious.

"I shouldn't be drinking wine from the bottle," I replied, stating the obvious. "But I want it."

She took a long drag and turned away from me.

"Shall we talk about it?" I asked. "Cover some damn fucking ground that's been churned up for a decade?"

She held a hand up. "Don't even think about it. I don't want to talk about shit with you."

I chanced it. I closed the distance and wrapped my arms around her waist from behind, but this time there was no quest for her clit in my motives, just the solid press of my skin to hers.

"I'm sorry," I said, and she tensed. "I'd have said it a thousand times already, but I couldn't."

"Stop," she hissed, and tried to tug away from me, but I held on tight. "Just let me say it."

"I don't want you to say it," she snapped. "I don't want you to say anything, I just want your fucking dick."

There was an unwarranted pang in my gut at the coldness in her voice. She wrenched herself free until her eyes were on mine, then carried on.

"Believe me, Lucas. I like your dick a hell of a lot more than I like you."

I took a cigarette out of the pack. "Fine. Have my dick all you like, just know that I'm sorry."

"A one off," she said. "This is a one off, remember?"

I laughed. "This is already a two off, remember?"

She didn't laugh along with me. "It's a very long one off. This weekend and then it's see you later. Farewell. Enjoy the next decade."

I don't think either of us truly believed that, but she wanted to. I didn't fight her resolve, just shrugged.

"Sure thing. We'd better make the most of it then, hadn't we?"

But she was done. Spent and bristling and fighting off whatever burst of hurt was blooming down deep. I'd no doubt there would be a lot of it.

"Take me home, please," she asked, but I shook my head.

"Sorry, but I can't take you home after a fuck ton of wine."

"Call me a taxi, then," she pushed, but I shrugged again.

"It's expensive and pointless. I'll take you home in the morning, I'm on my way in anyway, just rest up a few hours."

"Ah, yes," she said. "Some massive high flyer at GCHQ now, aren't you? You must be there for about four a.m."

"I'm a director of security and cryptography. Hardly some massive high flyer, and hardly four a.m."

She stubbed her cigarette out and filled her sports flask up with water. I watched her fingers fumble with her bag from the floor and pull out a tray of tablets.

My gut struck up with another pang, and my words kept on coming.

"What's going on with your epilepsy?" I asked her. "How long have you been having it?"

She smirked but shook her head. I didn't get the humour in it.

"Like you give a shit about my epilepsy."

But I did. I gave one hell of a shit about her epilepsy.

She was guarded to the max, that thick shell of her, and I hated it. I hated every scrap of protection around the most beautiful parts of Anna Blackwell and her stunning, addictive soul.

"Fine, don't call me a taxi," she cut off before I could carry on with my thread. "Let's just fuck off to bed and you can drop me home in the morning before the world is awake enough to see us together."

At least she'd be in my bed for the night.

She took her meds and I let the dogs out, then grabbed myself a water and got the lights on the way upstairs.

I noticed how she turned her head to stare for a few seconds at one of Millie's *Daddy* paintings stuck to the wall and cursed inside that she wouldn't let me open up to her about the whys and the wherefores, not even a little.

I washed up in the bathroom, hoping she would join me, but she didn't. She held back until I was finished then took her own turn. I was already sitting up in bed when she came through, armed ready with her bottle of water for the bedside table when she threw the covers back on the other side and climbed on in.

"Goodnight," I said, but she said nothing, just settled down with her back to me.

I flicked the lamp switch off, then couldn't sleep, churning over things to say and staring at the ceiling like a total moron, lost. I despised myself for my fucked up life choices, and despised the universe along with me for how one fucking mistake can cost you everything, snowballing like an acorn on Everest until your whole existence is smashed beyond reason.

Fuck me, how that snowball had kept on rolling.

Fuck me, how I wished I could really apologise for it and have her listen.

"I'm sorry," I said again, quietly, knowing full well she was still listening, bristling just as hard in the darkness as I was.

"Sorry means shit," she said back. "It will never mean anything from you. Not to anyone else anyway, even if it ever did to me."

She was right on that front. I couldn't imagine anyone in her entire circle ever doing anything but spitting in my face before trying to stab me.

I heard her sigh. "Not that it will ever mean shit to me, either. It won't."

She must have finally been half asleep when she inched her way closer and laid her head on my chest. I was anything but half asleep as I shuffled down and pulled her closer, pressing my lips to her hair and breathing her in.

"I'm sorry, Anna," I said, one last time, but this time it was a whisper.

And this time she was breathing so deep and so steady there was no way she'd ever hear it.

Chapter Eleven

ANNA

The room was barely lit – just a dull orange glow of light shining through from the landing. Still, it was enough to make out the obvious. There was no sign of Lucas.

The other half of the bed was empty, covers tossed back in my direction, just me alone in his silent bedroom before sunrise.

I didn't expect to be alone in his silent bedroom before sunrise.

Along came a flood of dread that him bailing from the bedcovers was due to a flood of piss between my legs, but no. I patted down the sheets underneath me and found them dry. No seizures in the night. At least I could hold on to what tattered scrap of dignity I had left around the man who'd destroyed it in the first place.

I found him downstairs making coffee at the kitchen counter with a cigarette in his mouth, already suited and groomed for the day ahead, and seemingly immune to the hangover from the decent volume of wine he'd guzzled the night before.

I felt anything but immune to anything as I stared over at the creature who'd torn my heart to shreds and yet still managed to get me off ten times in a row.

"Breakfast? Coffee?" he asked, but I shook my head, wrapping myself tighter in the robe I'd taken from behind his bathroom door.

"No, thanks."

"Suit yourself," he said, and took a sip of his drink.

Silence.

We both stood in stupid silence, his stare on me, while I cast my eyes around anything in the room that wasn't him.

He didn't try to make conversation to ease the tension. Small talk wasn't high on his agenda seemingly. Just as well since it had no place whatsoever on mine.

"We need to be out of here soon," he said, finally, and gestured to the wall clock. "Monday morning is calling me loud and clear."

"Ditto," I replied. "I've got plenty to be doing, too."

But I didn't move as he got on with kitchen duties, glued to the spot like a stupid mute fool, blindsided by the way that stunning creature went about his regular life.

I watched him pet his dogs and grin at them, then put some toast in the toaster. I watched him clean down the countertops and shove a few plates in the dishwasher, and there he was. The man I'd fallen in love with. Mannerisms, and breaths, and expressions. The bounce in his step as he crossed the kitchen to the back door and let the dogs out into the garden.

I knew this man.

I knew his usual bright-eyed morning brilliance.

I knew the way he clicked his tongue and whistled to call the dogs back inside again once they'd done their business.

I knew the way he wriggled his tie into position and smoothed down his jacket once he'd laced his feet into his brogues, ready for the outside world.

I knew everything about him, because I'd known everything about him. He was still him. The same Lucas Pierce who'd captivated me from the beginning.

With that realisation came a nagging little twist in my belly – a gust of something far deeper than words. Something way beyond my control. Way beyond anything I'd ever want to feel in a thousand years.

Please, universe, no.

Please, brain, get a goddamn grip.

But I couldn't deny it. I couldn't even hide it from the part of myself screaming for his blood and his tears and the battering retribution for all the tears he'd given me.

That twist in my belly was stating the very damn obvious.

I didn't want it to be time to go soon. Not from Lucas Pierce and his stunning dick and his stunning countryside bolthole. Monday morning could get stuffed, because I wasn't ready.

I wasn't ready for this one off to be over.

"Sure I can't tempt you with breakfast?" he asked again, when he noticed I was still standing there staring over like an idiot.

It was enough to snap me out of my immediate stupor.

"No, thanks," I repeated. "I'm not hungry."

I wasn't lying on that score. I wasn't hungry, and I didn't want any breakfast from that asshole. I should never have taken anything from him in this place, especially not his cock. It was my own fault for being led so easily by my bleating little clit.

I should have told him he was a prick all over again and come to my senses, but I didn't. In the cold light of morning, as it dared to peep its face through the kitchen window, I forced a smile at his hospitality. Manners cost nothing, after all.

He flashed me a smile right back, both of us hovering there with this awkward hint of a grin on our faces. Paper thin on both sides. A pathetic little veneer hiding a whole churn of bullshit highs and lows.

So much unspoken.

So much that would never be spoken in this lifetime.

It was time to end this shitstorm for good.

I told him I'd get my things together and bolted away upstairs. Collecting my crap was an easy mission. There was only a stupid scrappy tennis outfit minus the lace thong to dress myself in, and a bag crammed with makeup, and my meds, and a sports bottle I filled back up with water in the bathroom. I popped my lamotrigine pills from the packet and washed them down, then cursed myself as I realised my phone was dead to the world. Flat out of battery.

Clearly, I hadn't entirely planned on being here overnight again. If I had, I would have packed my damn charger. And my toothbrush.

I didn't bother with makeup, but I did smooth my hair down as well as I could before getting set to step back into my regular life. I cast myself one final sigh in the mirror, then trekked back down to my nemesis with a newfound determination that this was really it. Party over.

He'd finished up his coffee and dumped the mug into the dishwasher by the time he noticed me in the kitchen doorway wearing the same skimpy shorts as the day before.

"Nice," he said, and gave me a smirk. "Fancy a rematch?"

"Don't even go there," I replied, and he shrugged.

He sorted the dogs and grabbed his coat, just a regular morning for a regular guy heading into the office. But it was anything but a regular morning for me.

My heart was aching fresh for the life I'd been devastated to lose, but was now crying out to a whole new tune along with it.

The scribbled *daddy* pictures taped to the wall upstairs had slammed me deep and hard.

Knowing he'd put a ring on someone else's finger was still enough to make me feel queasy now that he was right beside me in person.

I hated it. I hated that I gave even the slightest shit about any of it.

"Ready to go, then?" he asked, and I nodded.

I didn't say anything as he said goodbye to his dogs and headed on out to the truck, just followed him and clipped myself in. I stared out of the window when he put the radio on, assuring myself that this was really still a nothing whatsoever. Just a stupid sex splurge. Just me seeking out a decent orgasm and not a scrap more. My mind was firmly churning on that when his voice cut over the radio.

"You do know I jerked one off in those dirty white panties this morning, I hope. Very nice."

I shot him a glance to find him smirking, That usual filthy stare of his eating me up like a whore.

"You're welcome to them," I said, and forced myself to look back out of the window.

"I'd prefer them considerably more if you were wearing them," he told me, but I didn't respond, just gave him a *turn left here* and pointed him towards the city centre.

I directed him to my street, gesturing he should park up far enough along from my apartment entrance that nobody would stand a chance of seeing us. He pulled up, then turned in his seat to face me, eyes burning hard with that same filthy stare.

All he found waiting was another fake smile on my face.

"Thanks for a great one off," I told him.

He tipped his head. "This is really a one off?"

I dropped down from the truck before I answered.

"Yes, Lucas. This is really a one off. Enjoy your next decade."

I daren't risk looking at him, just slammed that passenger door shut behind me and started walking. My heart was thumping, belly twisting, but I kept on moving, step by step, determined to get my head straight and leave that asshole behind where he belonged.

I thought I'd almost made it. I could see my apartment entrance when his voice called out across the street.

"Anna, just stop and bloody wait a minute, will you? At least let's fucking talk about it."

But I couldn't.

I daren't.

I wasn't sure where that minute would ever stop for me if it started.

It was a huge relief when I reached my apartment doorway. I let out a sigh and threw myself into our communal hallway, dashing upstairs like the place was some kind of safe haven from Lucas Pierce cravings.

It wasn't. I still felt them every bit as strongly as I ditched my bag onto the coffee table and opted to head straight through to the shower. If only I could scrub my brain down in the same foamy wash as the rest of me and get him away from my thoughts as well as my skin.

As it turns out, I didn't make it that far.

Vicky was already up and in the kitchen, dressed in her work uniform with her blonde curly hair swept up in a bun for her checkout duties. She was chomping down on a piece of toast with her phone in her hand as I walked on through.

Until she saw me.

Her eyes widened as she clocked my appearance, mouth dropping. Mine widened right back, a shitty pulse of guilt no doubt blooming on my cheeks.

Horror. All I felt was horror.

And so did she. I could read it all over her face – she was both mortified and relieved at once, gulping in a breath before shaking her head at me.

I'd been caught in the act. There was no way this wasn't caught in the *I've been fucking Lucas Pierce* act.

"I've been worried sick!" she screeched. "Your phone went to voicemail every time I tried to get hold of you last night. I wondered what the hell was happening to you! You could've been a total mess, convulsing in a ditch somewhere!" Her eyes searched mine. "Please don't you dare tell me you've been with that asshole all weekend, Anna. Please, don't."

Oh shit. I'd fucked up with the phone thing.

There was no getting out of it, so I tried to play it down.

"It was a game of tennis," I told her. "Just a stupid game that made the one off a bit longer. It was still a one off. It still *is* a one off."

"Fucking hell," she hissed, and her voice was genuinely strained.

"You've actually been fucking that prick for two days straight?!"

I didn't bother confirming with an answer, and she paced the kitchen as she carried on.

"What the hell is it about that jerk that has you out of your mind enough to hole up for a whole weekend with him?! Are you still losing your mind over that piece of shit?"

"No," I said. "I'm not losing my mind over him."

"Why, then?" she pushed. "Why the fuck did you spend another night with him? Tell me!"

I blustered through my reasoning, but couldn't find any answer other than the truth of it.

"Incredible sex."

She shook her head in disbelief. "Incredible sex from an incredible piece of shit."

I shrugged. "An incredible piece of shit I won't be seeing again."

She didn't look convinced, just kept on pacing and shaking her head at my stupidity.

"Honestly, Anna, you can't do that again. He's no good for you. Being anywhere near him is no good for you. He'll fuck you up again."

I nodded along with her wise words. "I'm not planning on being anywhere near him again, don't worry."

"I mean it," she said. "He'll leave you an even bigger state than he did last time, and this time he'll cost you a whole load more. People will never live with you doing that to yourself. We couldn't."

"It's nobody else's business who I fuck on a weekend," I snapped, but she glared right back.

"It's *everybody* else's business when you cast off Sebastian to chase after the absolute loser who fucked you over. That's friendship, Anna."

She had a point.

"You're not bullshitting me, are you?" she asked. "That really was a one off? You're not seeing him again?"

I swallowed down everything but my resolve.

I dug into my pain, and humiliation, and the burning bloom of shame.

I dug into the disrespect I'd shown myself for firing off that message to him in the first place.

I dug into the hurt, and those scrawled drawings lining his landing. I dug into the way I'd spent too many nights pining his loss.

And then I believed it.

I believed it when I said it, eyes burning hard with the honesty.

"I'm not seeing him again," I told her. "It *was* a one off. Just please don't tell anyone I was with him."

She squeezed my arm as she passed me, and this time her expression had a whole other flavour to it. "It's a bit late for that," she said.

Chapter Twelve

LUCAS

There was a strange thrill to my Monday morning. A simmer running through the office I hadn't felt in years. I could feel it in the air, see it in people's faces, sense it all around me as people went about their day.

The morning was almost done by the time I realised the simmer wasn't running through the office. It was running through me.

Hell, what a difference it made.

People were seeking me out, talking strategy with a zing to their tone, and I was a grinning optimist as I joined in the discussions. There was something burning down deep. Something I'd have taken for granted when I first took up the directorship position in the cryptography sector of GCHQ several years ago.

Excitement.

Passion.

Life.

Since Maya left and took Millie with her, leaving me at a loss as to what to do with the pitiful scrap of my former self wallowing in her wake, I'd thrown myself into my work. My position was intense, needing just enough mental discipline to scrape me through the carnage without submitting to the drink entirely. A tightrope I'd walked with a few wobbles on the way, but walked nonetheless. Still, I hadn't been enjoying it.

I'd forgotten just how good enjoying this place felt.

I'd forgotten just how good enjoying Anna felt too.

With her dirty panties in my pocket and my eyes intent on Keith Clarke as he gave his monthly roundup, I was far more in my groove than I'd been in months. My mind was full of strategy ideas I'd been searching around the dregs of my brain for that entire quarter.

So, I did them justice. I took the full reins of my directorship and I presented them. I thanked Keith for his input, but I was right up and on point, laying out the team plan for the next round of our security development project.

It worked.

Keith was full of nods and affirmatives, and so was Ralph Jacobs beside him. Amy, Beth and Dan were scribbling notes, and even Moose – our introverted genius who barely contributed to anything – was rocking along with the positives.

"Anything to add?" I asked at the end of the session.

"Yeah," Ralph said. "What the fuck happened to you this weekend, Pierce? You're bouncing off the walls this morning."

I smirked and winked, and grabbed my coffee mug along with my paperwork.

"My trade secret," I said. "Entirely confidential."

"Keep doing bloody more of it," Keith added. "And dish some out to the rest of us while you're at it."

I laughed out loud as I made my exit from the meeting room. I wouldn't be dishing any of Anna's pussy out to anyone this lifetime.

I was back at my desk in the quiet of my office when I dared to tug her panties out into my lap. I debated firing her off a picture of that filthy lace stretched tight around my dick, but I decided that Monday morning would maybe be pushing the communication channels, even by my crappy standards.

I had my legs stretched out under the desk and my head tipped back, balls pulsing deep and cock throbbing hard when the distinct trill of my phone sounded out loud and clear.

Maya.

I knew it would be Maya.

I cursed as I grabbed the phone from the desk top, panties still tight around my dick.

Millie needs picking up from school on Wednesday, she has swimming club after. And don't even think about letting her around those dogs again. She said they were jumping all over her last time. I could smell them on her coat.

My gut did its usual lurch as I checked the team diary and found a presentation meeting with the rest of the management team on Wednesday afternoon.

I'd usually panic over the fallout of refusing Maya anything, but not this time.

I'm busy at work on Wednesday. Can you rearrange what you have planned?

I could already imagine what she had planned. A bitching session with her friend Dawn over a coffee, in the guise of a *therapy* afternoon.

I was right.

Dawn and I are working through our self-development plan. She can only do Wednesday.

I shoved the panties back in my pocket and gave the phone my full attention. Usually I'd be scrabbling around trying to rearrange my own itinerary, dropping everything of mine to keep Maya amicable. But not the fuck today.

I can't rearrange my meeting, Maya, sorry. I'm sure my mother will pick up Millie from school.

I held my breath at the impending punishment. Sure enough, it came.

Fine. Put your work before your daughter. You can put your work before her next weekend too.

I cursed out loud.

What do you mean I can put my work before her next weekend too?

I knew the answer before it came.

She can stay with me next weekend. I'll make plans to see Dawn then. Millie can play with Phoebe to keep them entertained.

My reply was pointless, but I sent it anyway.

I already have plans for Millie next weekend. We're going to Sea Centre to see the sharks.

And so it came.

I already had plans for Wednesday. I guess we both lose out, don't we?

I threw the phone on the desk, gut twisting. All these months since Maya upped and dragged Millie away from me, she'd been nothing short of dangling puppet strings. I was a pathetic piece of shit, dancing to her tune, bending over at every whim of hers for the sake of seeing my daughter.

Fuck, how she'd made me fucking bend.

I didn't even know why she was so determined to kick me in the gut at every opportunity. I didn't know why she still wanted to hold our little girl as a chess piece in her game of fucking me over into submission.

Even then, sitting at my desk with my whole work week mapped out in front of me, I was tempted to get on the case of bailing out of my Wednesday responsibilities, but I didn't.

I knew what was coming next before it arrived.

Mother. And once again, I was the asshole.

Will you get your priorities right for once? Maya needs your support.

My fingers were hovering over the screen as a flash of *fuck you* zipped up my spine. Because that's what it deserved. One big *fuck you.*

A fuck you for Maya holding our little girl as a weapon for every time she didn't get her own bastard way.

A fuck you for my mother always taking that self-righteous cow's side of every stupid battle.

A fuck you for the whole sorry spectacle of having to jump through hoops every time I wanted to spend time with Millie.

I was done with justifying myself for every breath I took without their seal of approval. So, I didn't. I forced aside the pain of losing Millie over the weekend, because I'd already stomached plenty of that pain over the past few months. I dug down deep and finally accepted that this situation wasn't ever going to be resolved by jumping through higher and higher hoops until I was nothing but a show pony, parading around with that spiteful bitch on my back and my mother whooping her cheers from the sidelines.

And finally, with one glimpse of my real self shining up at me from the swampland of Maya demands, I decided that both she and Mother could go fuck themselves. I called up Maya's message and typed out my response.

Millie is coming with me to Sea Centre this weekend. We're seeing the sharks. Rearrange Dawn for next week. Self-development afternoon can go fuck itself, Maya.

I tossed the phone amongst the meeting minutes and calmed my breathing until my twisting gut opted to untwist itself.

No. Fucking. More.

I forced the fear, and the hurt, and the self-doubt behind me into the shadows where it belonged. I resolved to sort my fucking life out and find my spine again in the jelly of what I'd become for that bitch.

I pulled those panties back out of my pocket and wrapped them tight around my dick and thought of Anna Blackwell's pretty little mouth as I fucked her spit out of her.

I thought about her hungry asshole and the way I'd made her take it so fucking rough.

I thought about her dirty little smile and how that made me burn deep.

I thought about her sweet whimpers as she took whatever I gave.

Then I came in that filthy lace with a grunt and a curse, like every bit the filthy man she knew so well.

Unfortunately for Maya, that man was nothing like the version of me she'd come to know so well. Not in the wake of the pathetic little shell of the man she'd worked so hard to pound into nothing.

And *that* man wasn't ever coming back.

Chapter Thirteen

ANNA

So much for my intention to avoid drama.

I'd been such a moron for letting my phone run out of battery and scare Vicky shitless.

She'd messaged my parents and Nicola and told them exactly what I'd been doing, and now three of my most solid supporters were armed with the most solid lashings in my direction.

I felt like a criminal ploughing through my week and trying to keep the confrontations at arm's length, and maybe I was a damn criminal. Maybe I'd disrespected everyone who truly gave a shit about me, as well as disrespected myself, but it was a bit too late for that.

Nicola had been a wave of solid attack for days on end. Message after message telling me what an idiot I was for venturing anywhere near Lucas Pierce and demanding she get an evening in my presence to tell me so in person.

My parents had been worse. Not only screaming down the phone about how insane I was for daubing my self-respect in lighter fluid and setting myself in flames, but screaming about how ridiculous I was for casting aside the perfect Sebastian Maitland, with his perfect consideration for my wellbeing.

Yeah, yeah, yeah. I knew it.

I'd already had months of the same scathing mantras on loop. *What the hell are you doing? What the hell are you doing? What the hell are you doing?* Only this time they were far more frantic. More cursing and hissing and telling me what a stupid idiot I was for selling out something so good for something so bad.

I was torn up with the whole sorry lot of it. So torn that my mind felt severed in two, jagged and savage on the edges.

On one hand, I believed their disgust. I felt the concern behind their criticism. I agreed with every curse and scream of Lucas Pierce's name.

On the other, there was so much more. A scream of a very different kind inside me every time I heard his name.

I was a hamster on a wheel as I threw myself into my work that week. Meetings and minutes and consultancy calls taking up my time. Distractions that were short-lived but essential. Projects piling up, colleagues reaching out for extra insight, and hell, I gave it.

I gave it all, just to save myself the stress of working through my own fucked up headspace.

I gave it all, just to save myself the stress of realising just how much I wanted Lucas Pierce.

Friday was a long time coming after those busy days in the office. I should have been looking forward to a couple days off, long lie-ins and chocolate in front of the TV. But the looming weekend was nothing but a pang in my gut, knowing that the onrush of people wanting to shout at me was imminent.

I cleared my desk into some kind of order as the afternoon drew to a close, then waved goodbye to Stacey and Lucia as I headed out through reception and made my way home. I hadn't given much thought to anything other than the Kirby Project that day, and was happily pushing my concentration onto what I wanted from the local supermarket as I dashed on in with a basket.

Broccoli, beetroot, some salmon fillets. Orange juice and makeup wipes and a big slab of milk chocolate. Nothing particularly exciting. Nothing stressful. Nothing whatsoever that should've led to the swirl of senseless thoughts that marked the onset of my seizure.

Boy needing a sharpener. Again. Again. Kicking. Month reports. Boy. Again.

It took seconds. Barely more than a breath. No warning for me, and no warning for anyone around me.

My debit card was hovering by the machine, the attendant grinning over as my brain let me down and went blank to the world.

There was sickness as the seizure slammed in hard. A horrible wobble of nausea as the woman's face in front of me started speaking an alien language.

I didn't understand her. Couldn't understand her. Couldn't understand myself. Didn't have a clue where I even was.

It was terrifying, just as it always was. I was lost to everything in the world, but most of all me.

I must have stumbled on my feet as I tried to come to my senses. I must have spoken nonsense and turned pale and wide-eyed and every bit as fucked up as I did every other time I had a seizure in public.

I must have moved blankly when they led me off by my arm and forced me to a seat in the customer service booth. I saw them offering me a bottle of water but couldn't understand what they were saying to me. I tried to focus on their language but got nowhere, swimming in a sea of confusion and panic and nothing whatsoever I could form any sense from.

And then my brain came back to me. Slowly.

I heard words and understood them in fragments. I heard the woman in front of me asking about people she could call, but couldn't find the words to reply.

Her blonde hair looked so fair. Her eyes looked so clear. I couldn't stop staring.

She pulled my phone from my handbag and asked me about contacts. "Husband? Mum? Dad?" she asked, but I shook my head.

"No," I managed. "No. Please don't."

"No?"

I was shaking my head, pleading with the blonde angel.

"Okay, don't worry," she said, tapping at my phone. "We'll find the right person for you, don't worry."

I hoped they hadn't called an ambulance. I tried to tell them so, but my words were still jumbled.

She waited until I managed to make a scrap of sense, and when I did, I focused on my phone in her hand.

"Not Mum," I managed. "Not Mum. Please."

She nodded and squeezed my arm. "Don't worry, sweetheart. Not your mum if that's not what you want. We'll find someone else. Can you give me a name?"

I closed my eyes and urged my thoughts to come back to me, but the only thing coming was the heavy drag of exhaustion. I hated it when it took this road. Hours of having to recover in a stupor while my brain got a grip of itself.

Even in my dazed state, I expected the woman with my phone to call my mum, or Vicky, or Nicola. Even worse, I expected her to dig deep through the backlog and find Dad, or some random workmate, or even Sebastian.

I got a rush of panic when the bleep of a message sounded out and she took a gasp of a breath.

"Wow. I'm sorry!" she said, and her cheeks blushed pink. "I guess you do have a boyfriend. I'll give him a call."

There was a laugh. A laugh and a shake of her head, her cheeks blooming even brighter as she digested whatever message had come through.

I didn't understand the laugh until she turned the screen towards me and I saw my dirty lace knickers stretched over Lucas's throbbing dick.

Oh. My. God.

It was Lucas's throbbing dick on my phone screen.

I'm sure my cheeks must have been burning pink too as I tried to read the words along with his photo. I was still trying when she cleared her throat and read them out for me.

"Been thinking about you all week. Fancy a rematch tomorrow?"

I was still nothing like capable of a proper conversation when I saw her raise the handset to her ear.

Oh God, she was calling Lucas.

I leaned back in the seat and tried to gain control, but I was still spinning sick. My mind zoned out of the words around me, picking up just snippets on the nauseous ether.

Yes… Bath Street… right here… pale, but breathing fine…

I opened my eyes on hers when she leaned in close.

"He's coming. Don't you worry, sweetheart. He'll be here soon."

She winked as she put my phone back in my handbag. I tried again to gain control of my speech but the exhaustion was too much.

So I breathed.

I leant back in the seat and let the world turn around me… until I heard a voice in the chaos that cut through it all.

"It's epilepsy, yes," I heard him say, and then I smelt him. I smelt the scent I loved so much, earthy and warm. I felt him beside me, kneeling close, my skin tingling and crying out for his. His eyes were fierce on mine. His breaths were hot on my face. "Anna, it's Lucas. Are you okay? Do you need a doctor?"

I managed to shake my head, my hand reaching out to grab for him and landing on his shoulder. He was wearing a suit. His tie was purple.

My brain was still coming back to itself, but I knew I liked his purple tie.

It was a relief when my voice came out solid.

"No," I said. "No doctor, thanks. I'll be okay."

I knew Lucas would likely do a Sebastian on me and insist I headed to the local hospital for them to poke and prod me and tell me I needed my meds reviewed. I was fully prepared for him to bundle me up in *ill, so ill* considerations and look on me as an invalid who'd fucked up with bright lights, or eating bad, or not sleeping enough, or just about anything else he thought could bring a seizure to my door.

But he didn't do any of it.

"I'll get your shopping," he said, and got to his feet.

I watched him follow the blonde angel to an aisle with my beetroot and chocolate in tow, and watched her flash me a smile over her shoulder. It was weird as all fuck. She'd seen my knickers around his cock, for fuck's sake.

It was just a minute or two before he returned, coming back to me with a bag of shopping and an extended hand.

"Can you walk? My truck is right outside."

I nodded, grabbed hold of his fingers, and he pulled me to my feet. It felt the most natural thing in the world to lean into his side and let him hold me tight on our way out of the supermarket.

"I'll be alright," I told him once he'd helped me into the passenger seat and dropped into the driver's side. "I can go home now."

It was at that suggestion he pulled a face and buckled himself in. "And who is going to be at home?"

I shrugged. "Vicky, I think."

"Vicky? Vicky Mason do you mean?"

I gave him another nod, shocked to remember just how associated our social circles used to be. "Vicky Mason is my housemate."

"And she's definitely home?"

My stomach lurched at the thought of her horror at me coming through the door fresh from a seizure with Lucas on my arm. She'd be onto Mum and Nicola in a heartbeat, and then I'd have a whole mountain more exhaustion to contend with.

"No," I told Lucas. "I'm not sure she's home."

He turned the key in the ignition. "Fine. In that case you're coming back to mine."

I didn't have the energy to protest.

At least that's what I told myself as he drove us away.

Chapter Fourteen

LUCAS

She was barely with me on the way home, drifting in and out as I headed away from the city. I kept looking at her, a wash of relief flooding over me that she was safe in my care.

I'd been petrified when I'd first seen her there, slumped in that booth by the customer service aisle. Her eyes had struggled to focus as I knelt in front of her, anything but herself as she battled with conversation. She seemed to be so tired now that it was hard to know just how back to herself she really was.

I took the journey as steadily as I could, but my foot was firmly on the accelerator as I headed out onto the Lydney back roads. She was quiet all the way, head leaning towards the passenger window and her hands clasped in her lap. She was moonlight pale and her hair was ragged, but it was well and truly my beautiful minx Anna resting beside me.

My whole body was twisting with need. The need to hold her tight and make it ok. The need to understand. The need to run my fingers down her fear and promise her I was there.

But I could only drive.

She barely came to her senses when I pulled up on the drive and climbed out of the truck. She stirred, and her eyes opened with a flutter when I arrived at her side, but she was so exhausted she barely murmured a word as I lifted her from her seat and helped her inside the house.

"Almost there," I said, and headed straight through to the living room with her held tight at my side.

I eased her down into the big comfy armchair and kept the dogs away, then went back out to grab her shopping bags from the backseat. I dropped them on the kitchen counter, casting her a glance en route, and then I went back to her, stocked up with juice and chocolate.

She looked even more captivating than usual in that chair in the lamplight.

She'd gathered her legs up in the seat, and she was sleeping soundly, breaths steady. Hell, she looked so tiny against the leather like that. My little magpie with her thorny barbs all hidden deep.

I did my best to make her more comfortable. I slipped off her heels and pulled one of the fluffy woollen throws Maya had left behind down from the back of the sofa. I wrapped her up and she snuggled down on instinct, murmuring so softly as she settled.

I guess it was at that moment I realised all over again just how much I loved that woman.

I sat down on the floor in front of that chair, resting back against the base with my hand squeezing her knee, and I waited.

Waited and thought.

Waited and wished.

Waited and remembered everything we used to be.

She woke with a jolt when she finally came back to me. Her eyes were wide, flitting around the room before they landed on mine.

"You were sleeping," I told her. "I got you from the supermarket and brought you home."

"Seizure," she said. "Yeah, I remember."

There was something about the self-consciousness in her eyes as she threw the throw to the side and slid a hand between her thighs. A vulnerability that punched me in the stomach with the need to make everything alright.

"Sorry," she said, and breathed a sigh. "It's just sometimes I…" Her voice trailed off.

"Sometimes you what?" I asked, but she shook her head.

"Let's not talk about it."

"Tell me about the seizures," I said. "Tell me what they're like and how they work. How do you make them better? Can you make them better?"

She kept on shaking her head. "Seriously, Lucas. It doesn't matter. No point talking about it."

"How often do they happen? Are some worse than others? Tell me."

But she wouldn't. She shook her head all over again. "You can take me home now, honestly. I'm really sorry they called you. I'll make sure it doesn't happen again. Big mistake on my part."

But it wasn't a big mistake. It was nothing like a mistake. I was still thinking of the words to express that when she let out a groan.

"My God, Lucas. She saw a photo of your dick."

"My dick and your panties. Your *very* dirty panties. I'm sure it'll burn itself into her memory. She'll be blushing every time you head in there to get your beetroot."

"Damn," she said. "I'll have to get my vegetables further afield."

I didn't move and neither did she. I sat cross-legged on the floor in front of the armchair and she stayed huddled up in it, both of us staring at each other in the lamplight.

"How long have I been asleep?" she asked, and I shrugged.

"I don't know. Wasn't keeping track."

"Sorry," she said again. "For taking up your Friday evening. I would've called someone else, but I couldn't speak."

"I'm glad you didn't," I told her, and her eyes dropped from mine.

"Don't say that, Lucas. I shouldn't be here and you know it."

My cold rational head might have known it, but the pang in my gut certainly didn't. I cleared my throat and shunted closer, reaching out for her bare feet and pulling them into my lap.

She'd always liked that.

She let out a moan like she always had, eyes closing tight, and I got to work, kneading those toes on a mission.

Her toenails were red. I loved them that colour. Still, I'd love them any fucking colour, just so long as they were attached to her.

"I'd forgotten how good you are with foot massage," she whispered.

I circled my thumbs on the arches and upped the pressure.

Her eyes flashed open, twinkling as she smirked. "Still, I'd forgotten just how good you are at a lot of damn things."

"Ditto," I said. "Pleasant surprises all round."

"Pleasant surprises we can't take advantage of."

I didn't let up from her feet. "Why not?"

"Why not what? Take advantage of how well we fuck?"

I nodded. "I'd say that's quite a good thing to take advantage of."

She pulled her feet away from me and scowled. "Not when everyone in the world is screaming at you for how much of a moron you're being. And especially not when you agree with them." She paused. "Really. You should take me home. Thanks for coming to rescue me, but I shouldn't be here and we both know it."

I'd always been direct, so I came right out with my proposition.

"Stay," I said. "Stay here for the weekend with me."

She scoffed at me. "For the weekend? Are you crazy?"

"Maybe," I replied. "But fuck it and stay anyway."

Her mouth was open as she digested my words, legs bunching back up in the chair.

I gave her time to think, easing back to quiet until she spoke again.

"Even if I wanted to stay for the weekend, what about your daughter? Don't you see her at the weekends?"

I shook my head. "Usually. But not this weekend."

"No?"

I rose to my knees and handed her a juice. "No."

She must have heard the frustration in my tone, and didn't let it rest at that. "How come not this weekend?"

I leaned in closer, my hands on the arms of the chair. "Don't ask questions if you're not prepared to answer them."

Her eyelashes were so dark as her eyes blinked on mine. She paused and I paused, both of us scorching bright in the silence until she broke it.

"Fine."

"Fine," I replied, and got to my feet. "Alternatively, you can start talking. I'll be making dinner if you want to fill me in on life, the universe and epileptic seizures."

She ignored me as I made my way through to the kitchen, and I wondered if she was really going to opt for insisting that I take her back into the city. I'd fed the dogs and let them out into the back yard by the time she appeared in the doorway, looking considerably more steady than earlier, with the throw still wrapped around her shoulders. The fluffy purple suited her, just like everything else.

I didn't say a word as she stood there staring, just kept chopping mushrooms, and she stepped closer, coming to rest against the counter I was working at.

"I have temporal lobe epilepsy," she said. "It's weird and it's horrible and it means my brain screws up and goes blank and I can't understand what anyone is saying."

I didn't stop chopping, but raised my eyes to hers. "How often do you have the seizures?"

She shrugged and tipped her head. "How long is a piece of string? They are trying to control them with lamotrigine, but they've been on and off for years. Sometimes hardly any for months, other times they are every few days."

"And what starts them?"

She let out a sad little laugh. "If only I knew I'd avoid it. Could be anything. Foods, lights, stress, lack of sleep. A whole barrel of them mashed together. The brain can be a fickle bitch."

"Don't I know it." I paused. "What happens when you have one? What can I do to help?"

Another shrug. "Just be there." Another pause. "People panic and try to get me an ambulance, or a doctor, or lecture me on what I may have done to bring one on."

"An ambulance and a doctor don't make any difference?"

She shook her head and brushed some hair behind her ear. "No. No difference. And I'm panicked enough without everyone else doing it around me. Makes it worse."

"Ok. So calm and support is what you need?"

"It's not your place to have to worry about it," she said, but her eyes were heavy. So much unspoken.

We both knew that statement was a pile of shit.

We both knew I'd be worrying plenty about it.

I don't know who moved first, but the knife dropped from my hand with a clank and the mushrooms scattered from the chopping board. I reached for her and she reached for me, lips open and crashing hard.

The throw dropped from her shoulders, and her arms wrapped around mine. My fingers took her hair and held her tight.

"Stay with me for the weekend," I managed between kisses.

"We both already know I'm going to," she breathed back.

Yes.

Yes, we fucking did.

I lifted her up onto the counter, her arms still wrapped around my shoulders. She laughed as her butt squished the mushrooms and I laughed right back.

But it was us.

We were there. We were right.

We were everything.

"This is going to be a disaster," she said. "People will never let me do this. Not in a million years."

"People can fuck right off, I'm done with trying to please them," I said, and kissed her hard.

She hooked her feet behind my back and pressed up tight to my chest, both of us straining for contact. I couldn't get enough of her. I'd been in a drought of closeness for so long I'd forgotten just how desperate I was for a taste. Every scrap of me was screaming for every scrap of her.

"I can't stop this," she whispered. "I can't stop wanting you. I must be fucking crazy for it, but I can't stop."

"Then be fucking crazy," I said.

"Like I've got a choice."

"Like I've got one either."

Her mouth was wet and hungry. Mine was starving.

Her fingers were shaky on my shirt buttons. Mine were a frenzy on her blouse.

I tore her skirt down her thighs, and pulled her closer to the edge of the counter.

She yanked my tie and tugged my face down to her chest. Fuck yes, I wanted that.

I ate those pretty little tits through her bra, teeth nipping hard, and she moaned like the dirty bitch she'd always been.

"Yes," she hissed. "More. Give me more! Like that!"

But I was wary. That niggle of concern in the back of my mind bleated loud enough to be heard.

I pulled away, forcing some hint of composure.

"Should you be getting more rest? Are you well enough for this?"

"Yes!" she snapped. "Yes, I'm well enough for this. My brain works plenty well enough to know what the hell I'm well enough for, thank you. I'm always saying the same damn thing."

Oh, there was challenge in it. Defiance. The need to be heard.

Fuck, my heart was beating to the same tune. Fuck, I'd spent years wanting my voice to count for something.

I heard her plenty loud and clear.

And I sure as fuck didn't need telling twice.

Chapter Fifteen

ANNA

It was beautiful madness and I needed every bit of it.

He wasn't gentle. He wasn't calm. He wasn't wrapping me up in cotton wool and telling me just how careful I should be with every little thing.

He was rough.

Fierce.

Craving for more of me just as I was craving for him.

And he was absolutely fucking incredible.

He bit and sucked at my tits until I squealed and shuddered, his fingers teasing my clit just right through my knickers. I was a mess on that kitchen counter, hands crushing mushrooms as I gripped for balance, and just as I thought I was gaining it, he had me rippling a whole lot harder.

My body was out of my control all over again, but it was a whole other dance and a whole other tune. He didn't pull my knickers down as he kissed his way down my stomach, his breath met wet lace and had me begging.

He delivered.

Tongue and teeth and rhythm. Grunts and shunts and heaven.

He was heaven.

His hands were brutal as he spread my thighs as far as they would go. My shoulders were back against the wall, fingers seeking out his scalp to hold him tight.

And then the dogs started barking at the back door. I felt his smile against my pussy and I couldn't stop the giggle.

"Hold that thought," he said, and I nodded, taking back hold of the counter as he pulled away.

"I don't think I could lose that thought if I tried."

The dogs were a flash of fur as they bounded on in, and Lucas was a picture, half naked and grinning like a beacon as he guided them into the room to the side.

"Where were we?" he asked as he presented himself back between my legs, but I didn't want this. I didn't want teetering on the edge while he was out of my grip. I wanted all of him. Every inch of him on every inch of me.

My eyes swallowed his up as I dropped from the counter and took his face in my hands. His mouth was so close to mine as he spoke.

"I guess you aren't holding out for mushrooms," he said, and that sparkle in his gaze set me on fire.

I dropped to my knees and he cushioned my fall, pulling me close. I tasted myself on his lips and kissed him harder. Deeper. But it wasn't enough.

Our fingers had lives of their own, seeking out spit and skin and deeper, deeper, deeper. I sucked his thumb, his mouth still open on mine, and he grunted for more.

My fingers were twisted in his beard, claiming hold as he lowered us both flat to the floor. The wood was hard against my back, and harder still as he dropped his weight on top of me. My thighs wrapped around his waist and he freed his cock from his pants, and then he was inside me.

I bit his shoulder as he thrusted, and he slammed harder as he groaned, and the lace of my knickers was stretched so tight to the side of my pussy that it cut into my skin.

"I've been thinking about you all fucking week," he hissed.

"I've been doing everything I could not to think about you all fucking week," I hissed right back.

"Give it up," he said, and fucked me deep.

Holy crap, I gave it up. My whole mind was on him, thoughts spinning wild as he drove me to a whole other round of exhaustion.

He pushed my legs up high and slammed his hips so hard it made me curse, and then he had it. Oh fuck, he had it.

"There!" I squealed. "Don't stop, Lucas. Don't fucking stop!"

He didn't stop. It was a frenzy of an explosion, my back arching off the floor so far he caught my ass in his hands on the buck. He forced me back all the harder and I cried out with the need, my shoulders taking the brunt of the strain.

Not once did he hold back or ask me how I was feeling. Not once did he look at me like some kind of weak little china doll who needed putting to bed.

"Fucking take it," he snarled.

"I'll take whatever you've got," I moaned. "Just fucking give it."

I came again, one long shudder in silence, blowing too hard to even breathe. My ears were ringing as he spat on his thumb, and I knew what was coming as soon as he pulled his dick free.

It was his thumb in my ass first, and I cried out, gritting my teeth. He circled it wide before easing it out, and then he was climbing up over me, straddling my face with his cock angled down.

"Spit," he grunted. "Make it wet enough to slide right in."

Jesus, I'd try.

I spat over and over, slicking that dick up as slippery as I could as my heart raced fast.

I was already whimpering as he moved back into position, twisting my face to the side and tensing hard.

He pushed two fingers in, and then a third. Just a few slams before he pressed his dick up tight.

"Take it," he snarled again, and I did. I took it all the way.

It fucking hurt, but I fucking wanted it.

He held my thighs up high, and I watched him, his stare on his thrusting dick as he fucked me. But it was more than that.

I knew exactly what it was as his stare darkened and his jaw tensed.

My hand knew what to do before I did, sliding down to tease that stretched lace and tug it even tighter.

"It's so wet…" I whispered.

"Wet and fucking dirty," he said, the rhythm as he fucked my ass was so good. So perfect.

"How dirty did you make my last pair?" I asked him.

"I'll show you, don't worry."

"Make these just as dirty," I told him. "Make *me* just as dirty."

I cried out loud when he pulled out, and he was rough as he tore my wet knickers down my legs.

"Oh God," I whispered as he stretched them over the head of his dick and lined back up. "Fuck, Lucas…" I began, but he was already pushing in.

He got the head of his dick inside my ass, cloaked in sopping lace, but it was tight. So tight.

I loved the slick jerks as he worked his dick with his hand, the tip still inside me. His breaths turned ragged and I spread my thighs all the wider, straining for a view.

"Holy fuck," he grunted, and he was gone, trembling with the spurts.

It was absolutely fucking filthy.

He came over my dirty knickers, stretched tight inside my asshole. He cursed and groaned and told me what a dirty little bitch I was, and he kept on spurting and kept on working his dick until I was a dripping mess right down my butt crack.

But not as much of a dripping mess as my knickers were when he pulled them from his cock and held them up to his face.

"Nice," he said. "So fucking nice."

My clit was screaming again, knowing he was going to work that filth against my pussy before he did it.

Our bodies knew each other even better than our minds.

It was so slippery. So warm and wet and noisy as he worked my pussy through that fabric.

I came all over again with his cum against my slit, and I loved it.

I loved *him* for it.

Loved *him*.

I stared up at him as I shuddered and I saw it loud and clear.

I loved him.

My heart burst along with my pussy, and the world set alight all over again as I lost myself to Lucas Pierce.

It was still thumping hard from the orgasm as he dropped on top of me, breaths to breaths, those dirty knickers pinned slick between us.

I wrapped him in my arms and pressed my mouth to his shoulder as I caught my voice, and I wasn't sure I would ever be able to let him go. But I didn't say it.

It would have been the most natural thing in the world to say those three magic words. But I didn't.

Couldn't.

"That was amazing," he whispered and I nodded, but kept quiet.

I was glad when he eased up enough to press his mouth to mine. Grateful that he took away my ability to speak.

His back was clammy with sweat, and between us it was baking hot. It felt like pure bliss as we lay there.

And then he moved.

My skin screamed for his the very second he rose up and pulled me with him. He took my knickers and put them on the counter behind the mushrooms along with my blouse and got back to work on chopping, and I took the throw from the floor and wrapped myself up as I watched him.

I didn't want dinner.

My body was crying out for so much more than food.

It was crying out for him.

"I think maybe omelettes rather than steak," he laughed, and I nodded.

He cooked as I stared, a smile on his face every time he flashed me a glance, and I smiled back but it was all a veneer.

My soul was churning. My mind was chewing. My body was calling. Just trying to make sense of it all.

I shouldn't want him. Not one tiny bit.

I shouldn't be there. Anywhere else in the world but there.

I should be checking out my phone and telling him to take me home to my regular world, but I didn't want my regular world. I wanted his.

He served up my omelette with a *"Ta-dah!"* and I accepted with a thanks.

We didn't even bother sitting at the table, just chowed it down with a fork at the counter, and I sought out the emergency tablets from my handbag and tipped them back with some juice.

And then we went to bed.

It felt ridiculously natural to slip under the covers beside him, and worryingly natural to snuggle up close. The crook of his shoulder felt made for my head, and his chest was beautifully firm under my arm.

Beautifully firm and beautifully solid and beautifully safe.

"Thanks for coming to get me," I whispered, and his lips pressed to my hair.

"I'll always come to get you," he told me, and my heart panged at the truth in his words.

If only there had been as much truth in them a decade ago, before he ripped that same heart to pieces.

"You asked me questions about Millie," he said, and his voice was so quietly serious it made my tummy flutter.

"Yeah, I did."

He took a breath. "I've been arguing with Maya all week. She's keeping her away from me because of a bullshit demand I couldn't live up to. It's her way of punishing me."

I didn't know quite what to say, so I didn't say anything, just held him tighter. It worked. He kept on talking.

"I was supposed to have her tomorrow. We were going to see the sharks over in Chester. But she said it's a no go. She always does. It's the same crap whenever I don't give her what she wants."

"What demand couldn't you live up to?"

I felt the tension in him as he found the words.

"I can hardly live up to *any* demand she bitches out to me. As soon as I've tried to deliver one she raises the bar and kicks me down another. She wanted me to get Millie from school on Wednesday, but I had meetings all afternoon."

"Surely that must be alright with her? If you have work?"

He laughed a bitter little laugh. "Nothing is ever alright for her. Nothing is ever good enough for her to consider me good enough for Millie. Everything I do is a failure. Judged. Commented on. Scoffed at. It's like my whole life is under a running commentary. Don't do this, and must do that, and don't even think of thinking that, you piece of useless shit."

I tensed up alongside him, feeling his pain.

"So she's kept her away from you?"

He nodded. "Because this time I told her no."

"I'm sorry."

"Not as sorry as I am. I should be the one apologising," he whispered, and I knew where the conversation was turning all over again.

But no.

No.

"Don't…" I said, and he held me tighter. "I mean it," I said again. "I can't listen to the past. I don't want to listen to the past. It won't get us anywhere."

He breathed out. "And what about the future? Can you listen to that? Is there ever going to be one?"

But no.

I couldn't go there either.

I reached my hand up to his face, ran my thumb across his lips, and he was serious and sad, and I knew his expression by heart without even seeing it.

"Maybe the future has no place, either," I whispered. "Maybe all we've got is the present. Maybe that's all either of us can work on right now."

He sighed and pressed those sad lips to mine and held them there for long seconds.

"Then let's make the most of the right now," he said.

Chapter Sixteen

LUCAS

Waking up next to her with the morning sunlight streaming through the window was a stunning start to a Saturday. I soaked in the sight.

The bedsheets were crumpled around her waist, her hair fanning out on the pillow. She was still sleeping, peaceful with butterfly snores.

I settled back down, easing up close to her side and I admired the view.

I don't know how long I was watching her, but when she woke it was with a stretch and a yawn, starting just a little as she registered me beside her. Once again, she tensed and plunged a hand down below, but she relaxed in a beat.

"Morning," I said, smiling wide as she smiled at me.

"Morning, stud."

She didn't come to her senses and jump out of bed and demand to be taken home. She didn't scowl and reinforce that this was a *no way* situation she owed it to herself to escape from. There was nothing but sweet quiet as we lay easy and breathed together.

And then she broke the silence in the best possible way.

"My ass is really sore from the pounding you gave me." Her laugh was a dirty giggle and I loved it.

"My dick is really hard for another round," I told her, and laughed right back.

She sighed. "I need meds, and juice, and the bathroom before your dick gets another go."

"Make yourself at home," I told her, and meant it. I wanted her to be at home here. I wanted this place to be warmer to her than any other place she belonged in.

It had been cold enough for a lifetime these past few months.

She nipped my nose before she got out of bed, and I pinched hers back before she escaped me. It took every scrap of restraint to let her escape me at all.

I was down in the kitchen before she was, standing in the open back doorway watching Bill and Ted peeing in the flowerbeds when she headed on in wrapped up in my robe.

"Where are the mugs?" she asked, and I gestured to the cupboard by the fridge.

She took down two and put the kettle on to boil, and I noticed how she made my favourite tea from memory.

I was still butt naked when I joined her for my mug. Her eyes scoped me out, that smirk of hers blooming as she clinked her mug to mine.

"Happy Saturday," she said, and I smirked right back.

"Happy Saturday indeed."

It would have been tempting to bundle her back upstairs for another round on that sweet pussy of hers, but I didn't want the weekend to be all about the flesh. I wanted smiles and chat and laughter. I wanted her at full natural radiance as we enjoyed much more than the filth.

"What do you want to do today?" she asked, reading my mind.

I leant back against the side and took a sip of tea, running through the options.

"I'm easy. Tennis? Meal out? Vintage movie day?"

She looked past me through the window at the glow of the morning countryside and gave me a fresh smile.

"Show me this place. It looks amazing."

I raised an eyebrow. "You want to check out this majesty of an abode?"

She nodded. "I want to go exploring. I haven't been out of the city properly in ages. Sebastian didn't really like it that much out of town."

It felt strange to hear his name in such a natural tone. Everything about her life outside of mine felt strange.

"We can go exploring," I told her, then remembered her clothes from the night previous. Her heels, specifically. "You might want to stick to village exploring though. Anywhere off road is going to be muddy."

She tipped her head, eyes mischievous. "I can handle a bit of mud, Lucas. Don't worry. I'm not that much of a city chick."

I laughed. "This is more than a bit of mud, Anna. It'll be a swampland."

But still her eyes were mischievous. "Show me."

I wasn't going to argue with her.

"Fine. Let's get to it. Breakfast first."

She took her meds as I put the toast on and got to work, and I was still naked as I served up eggs and bacon at the kitchen table. We had a dog staring up at each of us as we munched away, but we were mainly staring at each other, smirks and giggles and the afterglow of a good hard fuck and a night in each other's arms.

I'd lost sight of that priceless spark that feels so good between two people who truly want each other. Flutters and soaring smiles and toes touching under the table. We had it all.

I'd forgotten how it felt to have someone truly listening to your voice, without judgement. I'd forgotten how it felt to talk freely without that frost of nerves, worrying how every word you speak is going to be fired back at you with spite.

I'd forgotten a lot of things.

We talked about work, and our distantly connected social group, and snippets of good in our time together. Painting orc figures and repotting aloe vera and the crazy time we trekked around all-night emergency dentists when she bust a tooth on toffee.

We talked about everything but what I'd done to her. It was aching in my ribs, the desperation to slam it out there on the table and tell the bitter truth and beg forgiveness, but I daren't. Not with her smile so sweet and her message so clear.

She didn't want to know.

Maybe she never would.

She cleared the plates before I could protest, finding the dishwasher and loading it up. She downed the rest of her juice and gathered her blouse from the counter top, where the slices of mushrooms were still scattered.

"Maybe you can try thick socks and some of my boots," I suggested, but she laughed at me.

"I'll wipe my heels down from a bit of mud, Lucas. I'm sure they'll survive."

I wasn't, and I told her so, but she was giggling determined.

"It'll be my mission," she said. "To navigate the swamplands in my work shoes."

"Whatever you want," I responded. "You can have one of my coats, at least."

We got ready upstairs, standing in harmony at the bathroom sink. She used my toothbrush after me and bundled her hair up in a band from her handbag. I found her a warm sweater that swallowed her up and she looked thoroughly swamped in my coat. And it was cute. So fucking cute it warmed me right through.

I whistled the dogs from their room and they bounded on ahead and out into the truck. Anna's heels were ridiculous, but I couldn't tell her all over again, so kept my mouth shut.

"I've left my phone in the house," she told me when I'd pulled out of the drive. "I sent a load of messages, but I don't want to hear anything back from the world today."

"Ditto," I said. "Mine's on silent."

I parked up at the pull in at the start of the hillside track and it was already muddy as we set off. The dogs bounded off into the distance and I stepped on firm, but Anna was already a picture, taking such neat little steps around the puddles that the grin burnt my cheeks.

"Sure we can't head back to the house and get you into some wellies?" I paused. "Or even into town to get you some?"

She shook her head pretty sharp at that. "No, thanks. I'll manage just fine."

Once again she was being insanely optimistic, but she always had been a stubborn little minx, so I let her be. We kept going, mud turning to grass but still squelching underfoot. She breathed deep and commented on the view all the way, at the surrounding hills, and the woodlands and the villages down below.

It gave me an appreciation of it all through fresh eyes, and it was a powerful thing, gaining that sense of life around a place I loved so much but saw so often.

I knew we were coming to the swampy ascent before we reached it. I told her we could turn around, but she ploughed on regardless, heels already caked in mud. Bill and Ted were waiting for us at the top, and they were covered in mud too, tongues lolling excited as they leapt around and watched us approach.

"We can stop," I said again, but she shook her head again.

"I can do it, I'll be careful."

She started laughing as she took her first step into the heart of it. Her heel sank in deep and squelched loud, her teeter becoming a slippery stumble before I reached out and grabbed her steady.

I adored the giggle that came out of her. "It seems your idea of mud and mine are two very different things."

I was laughing along with her. "Maybe bring your wellies next time."

Her eyes were straight on mine. "Next time? That's not focusing on the present."

"Cut it out," I said. "There will be a next time. I'll have you slopping around this path in better footwear, just like I'll be taking your ass on the kitchen floor all over again."

She didn't argue, just took another tentative step into the mud bath. I kept hold of her arm, but I was squelching too. I'm not sure whether it was the mud or the laughter that made me slide around alongside her, and I didn't care. It was absolutely fucking hilarious to watch her drowning in my coat, with the sleeves too long for her, while trying to navigate a ridiculous footpath in ridiculous heels.

"Stop it," she said, but she was laughing as hard as I was, pausing with her feet buried deep in a puddle with her legs splattered brown. "We'll both go flying if we don't get a grip."

Fuck my life, I felt like me as I watched her being her, right there in that moment. It was magic. Magic and stupid giggles and the wind in our faces.

We were only about halfway up the bank when she slipped a whole load harder and dragged me back a few steps along with her. I managed to keep my balance, and enough steadiness to keep her upright, but it was a losing battle and we both knew it.

"Back down?" I asked, but she was shaking her head as she laughed.

"I'm pretty sure back down is going to be even harder than the way up."

"I'd carry you if I wasn't certain I'd go tumbling with the both of us."

"Can you even begin to imagine how hard we'd go tumbling?" she asked, and she was doubled up at that, pissing herself laughing so hard it was the most contagious thing in the world.

Another few steps and she tried to keep to the side of the track, but it was too steep. She slid back into the depths, but her legs slipped wider and she braced herself for the fall. I made a grab for her waist, and I thought I had her, but then Ted sealed the deal by racing on down.

What a fluffy little prick.

I shouted him to stop but the wagging, barking idiot goofed right on up, skidding close enough that Anna recoiled a step backwards.

Backwards down a particularly squelchy divot in the path.

Backwards down a slurp, and a slip and a tumble that moved in slow motion, her heels finally bailing out of the climb and bailing her legs out with them.

I watched the scene unfold, arms flailing, hands reaching out and closing on air, and down she went, slapping down onto her front with her tits into a slop of a puddle, and it was classic.

So classic that I couldn't breathe for the laughter, and she was struggling too, laughing so hard she had to roll onto her back, caking herself even further in the brown gloop.

She was hilariously beautiful and her eyes were sparkling with so much fun it would have taken my breath, even if the laughter wasn't already on the case. I stepped back down to her and reached for her hands and braced myself to pull her to her feet. But it was too much. Too much and too damn stupid for the both of us.

So I went tumbling too.

Chapter Seventeen

ANNA

He was on his ass in the mud alongside me, and I felt like such an idiot for even thinking I'd be up to this in stupid heels. But I was glad I was an idiot. I was glad we were there, wallowing in the puddles, because it was hilarious.

I couldn't remember the last time I'd laughed as much as I was laughing there in the country winds with the fresh air filling my lungs. I reached out for him when I was finally breathing steady enough to attempt the rise, but he was still roaring and held me tight. Mud to mud through the coat that was stupidly big and the stupid skirt that was riding up my splattered thighs.

And then the dogs came bounding, just as muddy as we were, leaping all over us and barking loud. I held them just as tight as I was holding Lucas, my hands in their damp fur as they licked my face, and it was perfect.

I gave up on my feet and opted to crawl, and he came with me, on his knees like I was. He took my hand, slopping them joined together in the mud on every shunt forward, and slowly we made our way to the top. He pulled me to my feet when we got onto firmer turf, and then he hugged me tight. I hugged him tight right back and breathed deep and free.

I was free.

"Your shoes are fucked," he said, laughing fresh while stating the obvious.

"I don't give a shit," I said. "It was worth it."

We walked along the brow of the hill in the most stunning silence, and it was so rich with green, and rustling leaves and the dogs racing at full pelt. I'd never get enough of this and I knew it. I'd never get enough of him and I knew it.

I guess that's when I decided the future was inevitable.

And if the future was inevitable then so was the past.

I was scared. Staring up at him and wondering how the hell we'd ever get beyond that pile of hurt he'd slammed into me, and how we'd ever get beyond the repercussions that had cost me so much.

But I was more scared of how anyone else would get past it, even if I did myself.

"What are you thinking?" he asked, but I didn't tell him. Not there in that moment. I shrugged and smiled and pointed out another crazy big oak on the horizon and he told me how it was Millie's favourite.

He looked at me for a few long seconds before he pulled his phone from his pocket and unlocked the screen.

He pulled up a video and handed it over, and there was his little girl running around that very tree with her palm flat to the bark. Her giggle was beautiful, her eyes sparkling and so much like his it knocked me sideways. Her hair was like his too, the exact same shade of dark, her colouring a perfect match as it blew behind her as she ran. I couldn't speak. The pain was in my throat.

Because that should have been us.

She should have been mine.

"Let's play tag, Daddy," she giggled. "Bet you can't catch me."

"Smile for the camera and I'll be right there."

She poked her tongue out and did a dance, and the image shuddered as he laughed too loud to hold it steady.

"She's beautiful," I managed to say as the recording came to an end.

"She is," he agreed. "Maybe one day you'll meet her. She'll love you."

That brought the pain up fresh. I took his fingers in mine and kept on walking and kept on breathing, and he raised my damn hand to his mouth and kissed my knuckles, and I knew then I was doomed.

He whistled the dogs when we completed the circuit and got back to the truck. I was trying to wipe some of the splatted mud from my butt before I got in, but he told me not to bother and got right in himself.

We rumbled our way back to the house and my heart was thumping, knowing full well we had to confront the place I'd been avoiding.

He pulled onto the drive and I took the final steps on my trashed shoes, kicking them off by the door and stepping on inside the warm. I shrugged off his coat and he hung it up to dry off, and then we were back through into the kitchen, and he was starting up the kettle and asking me what I wanted.

I sipped on a fresh glass of juice and watched him making tea, and wondered if there was any way on earth we'd make it through this.

He laughed again as he scoped out my legs. "Let me run you a bath," he said, and I nodded. But that's when I opted for another round. I undid my blouse and dropped it to the floor, unclipped my bra and slid my filthy skirt down my thighs.

One final high before the low.

His eyes darkened with fire when he saw what I was wearing.

I'd been feeling them all the way, the filthy knickers I'd sneakily taken from the counter top earlier when he wasn't looking. They'd been the most slippery damp between my thighs all the way round that walk.

"You dirty bitch," he said, and I slipped my fingers right on down.

He didn't give me a second. A few long steps and he was down on his knees, his mouth pressed to that filth and sucking hard and his hands gripping my muddy thighs so tight I was his prisoner.

I wanted to be his prisoner.

"You're a filthy beast," I whispered, and he moaned against my pussy.

"Takes one to know one," he said.

He didn't pull my knickers to the side and I didn't want him to. I loved him like this.

I didn't know if my legs would hold my weight as I shuddered, so I gripped the counter to the side. My eyes were closed and my body was burning up and the waves took me like I was drowning in the thrill.

Filth.

It was filth.

His mouth was so wet when he pulled away, staring up at me like I was some dirty dark angel.

He pulled those filthy knickers down my legs and sucked them into his mouth, and my tummy did the dirty flutter only he could give me.

And then he got to his feet and he kissed me.

God, I wanted him to.

I wanted to lap up the filth from his mouth and taste his fetishes. I wanted to kiss him so hard we never stopped.

He was the one to break it. I was panting as he pulled away.

"Yum," he said, and dropped those sopping knickers back onto the counter. "Let's run you that bath."

I hovered in the kitchen to finish my juice while he headed on up, and by the time I caught my breath and joined him the bath was already full. Full and bubbly. I stepped on in and sighed as I dropped into the water, and it was heaven.

The whole thing was heaven.

Heaven teasing at the looming hell.

And that's when he fucking said it, hand splashing in the water as he sat muddy at the side of the bath.

"I love you, Anna."

It hit so hard I couldn't face it. I splashed the bubbles and pretended

I hadn't heard him, even though he was right by my side. My brain was spinning with what I could possibly say to that statement beyond confessing the same three words right back at him.

"Seriously, Anna, I love you so fucking much it hurts."

But not as much as it hurt me.

Finally, I confronted it. I looked him in the eye and I summoned the words, and I said them.

"Then why the fuck did you fuck me over for Maya Brooks? Why the fuck did you fuck her behind my back and spit in my fucking face, Lucas? Why the fuck did you love her so much fucking more than me?"

He was silent, his eyes almost as pained as mine must have been. If that was even possible.

"I'm sorry," he said, but my head was shaking.

"Sorry doesn't cut it. Sorry will never cut it."

"I know," he whispered. "Believe me, Anna. Nothing ever destroyed me as much as seeing you hurting like that."

"Fuck off," I snapped, and recoiled in the bath. And it was there. That hurt and pain and spite spewing up fresh inside after so many years of burying it. Burying everything. "You know nothing about being fucking destroyed. You ripped my fucking heart out, and you laughed. You fucking laughed at me."

He couldn't look me in the eye, and I was glad because mine were welling up, and I hated it, I hated that the tears were coming when it should have been the rage.

I pulled myself straight up from the water, and pushed him away as he tried to take my arm. I grabbed the first towel I could see and wrapped myself up before I headed on out of there, and he followed me. He still couldn't look at me as I searched through his wardrobe, trying to find anything that would cut it on my frame since my own clothes were trashed to hell.

"Seriously, Anna," he tried. "It's not like you think it was."

"Really?" I spat. "Because it seemed pretty clear to me when you were tearing my heart out and laughing about it, Lucas. It seemed pretty fucking clear to the rest of the world, too."

"I know," he said, and his voice was so fucking heavy it brought the tears.

"This was supposed to be one night…" I managed. "Shit, Lucas, it was supposed to be one night. Because I didn't want this. I didn't want any of this."

"I know," he said again, and then he was right there, on his knees in front of me as I tried to put one of his shirts on. I stopped halfway through, my arms giving up and my hands reaching up to my face to hide the tears.

This man was my heaven. He'd always been my heaven. He'd been every scrap of sugar syrup my body ever craved, and my heart craved just as hard along with it.

But he was my fucking poison too. I could feel it running through me. Toxic.

Fuck what he'd given my body, he'd poisoned my very fucking soul.

"I told you I didn't want to do this," I said through the sobs. "I didn't want to go there."

"We have to, Anna," he said. "We have to and I'm glad."

"I'm not."

"Please just hear me out before you say that," he said.

Chapter Eighteen

ANNA

Ten years ago.

I was fidgety on the train, much more so than I should have been. I should've had the bliss of calm and retreat and everything I'd been striving for those past three weeks.

But I didn't.

I'd tried Lucas three times already but he wasn't answering. Shouldn't have been that much of a big deal, but I hadn't had a bank of messages through from him like I expected once I switched my phone on. Nothing bar a drunken bleat on night one with typos saying how much he missed me.

I looked out of the window and tried to summon the inner peace, but I wasn't feeling it.

The messages had bleeped through when I got my phone back after the twenty-one day sanctuary up in Perthshire. Mum and Nicola and Dawn and Kelly from work. *Hope it's going well* and *missing youuuu* and *can't wait until you're home.*

But nothing from him past that one drunken text.

I tried him again, but still I got voicemail. I would have called someone else, but it was just a niggle down deep and I didn't want to worry them over something I was probably making out of nothing.

The train got closer to home and I tried to enjoy the journey. Towns and countryside and a whole world out there to view, but my mind just wasn't on it.

I'd always been a self-help kind of girl. I'd always believed in the power of the mind and the soul and all those amazing ways to heal yourself from life's challenges. They'd said it was stress at the doctor's. The weird flashes of sickness and the waves across my head and the freaky feelings of déjà vu I was trying to make sense of.

Stress, they said. Too much on at work, which was likely. Not enough calmness of mind to rest easy, which was likely. So when the retreat came up advertised, with a thousand testimonials singing praises about how much three weeks of seclusion and meditation and therapy had cleansed their souls, I'd thought it was a good bet.

I'd cashed in three weeks of holiday from work, and Lucas had told me it seemed like a good fit, and I was off on my mission.

I thought it had been a good thing. I'd been through so much meditation that my mind had flown free. So much therapy that I'd have sworn there was a rose quartz permanently attached to my forehead. Hands-on healing, and hypnotherapy, and circles with drumming. All great stuff, with no weird stress flushes for a couple of weeks. Success.

And here I was on the train ride home.

Holy crap, how I'd missed Lucas. I'd missed my man so much.

I expected him to be at the station when the train finally chugged onto home turf, but he wasn't there. I braved the rain and found a taxi at the rank and directed the driver to mine, but my heart was really racing by then. I was so worried, I felt sick, even though the rational part of me was still insisting it was nothing.

We were home in minutes. I paid the driver and grabbed my case from the back and then I was straight up our driveway, pulling my key from my handbag and letting myself inside with a smile.

But that smile was soon gone when I saw the state of the place.

Everything was different.

Pictures were gone, and the living room looked bare without his books and chair and coffee table. I was reeling as I stepped on through to the kitchen and found him there, standing at the island.

I dropped my case, only just realising it was still in my hand, and I should have been running up to him with kisses, arms open wide, but I was rooted to the spot, a horrible lump in my throat, even though I didn't know what it was for.

"What's going on?" I said, and my voice sounded distant.

His eyes didn't look like his as they met mine. They were cold. Colder than I'd ever seen them.

"I'm leaving," he said. "I wanted to wait until you got home to tell you, but I'm done. We're over."

I was shaking my head, not even beginning to fathom what he was saying.

It was insane.

So insane I didn't even know where to start trying to interpret it.

Over?

How the hell could we possibly be over?

We were fine when he left. Hugs so tight and whispers of how much he'd miss me but how much he hoped I'd enjoy my trip.

Normal.

Normal and good.

Normal and us.

"What?" I asked, but it was weak. Pathetic.

He took a step closer but was still at a distance. "I'm in love with Maya Brooks," he told me, and there was no care in his words. "I was waiting until she was ready before I left you, but she's ready now. I'm with her."

I pictured Maya Brooks standing there. Her pink lipstick and high boots and the way she always flicked her hair like she was an angel amongst sinners. I'd known her for years, on the outskirts of our friend group. I'd known she liked him. She'd always hugged him that second too long when we crossed her at socials, and I'd always seen that glint in her eyes.

But he was mine.

He loved me.

I'd never questioned that in all the time we'd been together.

"But it's Maya…" I began. "You hardly know her…"

He smirked at me. "I know her pretty well, Anna. I've been seeing her for months, I've just been waiting to let you know."

No.

It couldn't be.

No. It just couldn't.

But he was so sure standing there. So solid with his shoulders so tall in his coat.

Fuck, he was already dressed to leave. He had his coat and shoes on.

It finally hit me. The tears came hard and fast, hands on my stomach as I struggled with the sickness.

"WHAT THE HELL ARE YOU TALKING ABOUT?!" I was screaming. "I DON'T GET IT!"

"Get it," he hissed. "I'm sorry, Anna, but I don't love you. I don't think I ever have."

I was shaking my head, because it couldn't be real. Please God, it couldn't be real.

But it was.

It was real.

And it was agony. Pure agony.

He watched me crying and I didn't know what to do. I stumbled backwards into the wall, and I hated him and hated Maya and hated myself and the whole fucking world.

"Why?!" I whispered through the tears. "Why do you love her more than me?!"

I didn't expect him to answer, but he did.

"Maya is amazing. She's so fucking smart, and so fucking funny, and so fucking hot. I've known it for years, I just wasn't sure she wanted me back, not while she was with Paul Slater."

I couldn't see it. I really couldn't. But his eyes said it all.

"How long?" I asked, and he shrugged.

"Plenty long enough, Anna. Plenty long enough to know my future is with her."

I retched. Retched and doubled up and my vision was blurry and my ears were ringing.

He didn't even try to come to me.

And then he laughed.

He fucking laughed at me.

"Chill out, Anna. I've put three months' rent in your account until you find a new place. You'll get over it."

Jesus Christ, I wouldn't ever get over it.

It was crushing, like my whole heart had been ripped out and stamped into nothing. So physically fucking painful as I struggled to ride the hurt.

"Don't do this, Lucas," I managed. "Please, Lucas, don't…"

It sounded like I was begging, my words were so weak, and I hated myself for trying. I hated how the anger wasn't anywhere near close to the pain.

He dropped his key on the counter and came up close.

"I'll see you around," he said. "Thanks for a good few years, just a shame it wasn't good enough."

But he wouldn't see me around.

Not ever again.

I'd rather kill myself than share another breath in the same room as that cunt and his poisonous fucking soul.

He shut the door behind him and I sank to the floor, and I retched and spluttered and sobbed so hard I couldn't see. There was nothing in me that understood. Nothing in me that could really believe it. Nothing in me that could believe the man I'd left behind had shrivelled and died and become the evil monster who'd just ripped me apart.

He should have been kissing me, hugging me, slamming me over the island and fucking me wild.

He should have been happy, laughing. *We* should have been happy, laughing, a mess of filthy catch-up sex. But I was alone, a mess on the floor for all the wrong reasons, his smirk on loop as that door closed behind him.

I scrabbled for my phone and my hands were trembling so hard I could hardly call up Nicola's number. She answered with a *heyyyy*, but I responded with a retch, and she was asking me what the hell was wrong, what the hell had happened, and I struggled to tell her through jagged breaths.

It was a scream of a sob when it came out of me.

"I need you. Please, God, Nicola, I need you. Lucas has gone. He's gone!" And then I said it. I said it and made it all real. "He's left me for Maya Brooks. He's in love with Maya Brooks."

She sucked in a breath of her own. "What the fuck?!"

I could only meet her with fresh sobs, and I could hear her walking on the other end of the line, hear her grabbing her keys.

"I'm on my way," she said. "I promise, I'll be there soon!"

I hung up the call and rested my head back against the wall and begged the universe that she would be with me soon. I begged the universe that this was some sick joke and I was asleep on the fucking train caught up in a nightmare.

But it wasn't a nightmare. It was real.

The man I loved with all my heart and soul had laughed in my face that he was in love with Maya Brooks, and left me alone in the carnage, and I'd never hear from him again.

And that's when it happened.

That's when my mind gave up along with my heart as I failed to ride the pain.

That's when I had my first seizure.

Chapter Nineteen

ANNA

Back in the present.

I couldn't believe how much I'd truly blanked out the pain those past few weeks. I'd blanked it out and held it back like some kind of amnesiac on some stupid perpetual fairground ride.

I was sobbing all over again as it rose up from the ugly depths of my soul and I remembered just how much the man before me had hurt me all those years ago.

It was supposed to be one stupid filthy fuck. Nothing more than a decent orgasm that I was a total fucking joke for even considering.

I'd been a disgusting asshole to myself for even having his number on my phone, let alone texting the vile prick.

But here I was, crying for Lucas Pierce, in love with him all over again.

I don't think I'd ever stopped being in love with him. Not even for Sebastian who'd picked me up from the floor and given me a whole new world.

I hated myself and I hated the prick in front of me all over again. I remembered his cold expression as he'd laughed at me, his smirk as that door closed behind him, and with that I tried to step away, but I couldn't. He held me there, his arms wrapped tight around my thighs.

"Please, Anna," he said, and his voice was choked. "Please just hear me out."

"Hear what?" I hissed. "The way you fucking destroyed me? The way you laughed at me? The way you didn't even say fucking sorry?!"

"I couldn't," he said. "I couldn't say sorry because I'd never have been able to leave you if I had. I'd never have been able to stay away from you if you'd have even tried to fucking forgive me."

"What the fuck are you talking about?!" I screeched. "What the fuck do you mean you'd never have been able to leave me?! You were in love with Maya fucking Brooks! You fucked me over for Maya fucking Brooks!"

He was shaking his head and he was crying too.

I'd never seen him like that.

I'd never seen him cry, and never seen him hurting just as bad as he was hurting right then along with me.

I gave up. I fell to the floor and pulled my legs up and I rocked back and forth as I tried to catch my breath. He collapsed too and sat so close, pressing his forehead to mine, even though I wailed for him to go.

"I'll never be leaving you again," he whispered through the tears. "I swear to God, Anna, I'll never be leaving you again."

"Why?!" I cried, and it came out so weak and so hurt. "Why did you leave me the first time if it was so fucking hard?! Why were you seeing her for so fucking long behind my back without giving the slightest shit about how much it would fucking destroy me?!"

"I wasn't," he said. "It was one stupid mistake, Anna. One stupid, drunken, cuntish fucking mistake on one cuntish night you were gone."

My mouth dropped open, and I couldn't believe it. It didn't make sense.

"What the hell are you talking about?!" I snapped. "You were in love with her!"

"I never fucking loved her," he told me, and he was looking straight in my eyes so raw and so real, I believed him. I believed him and I felt it in my stomach. "I loved you. I always loved you. It was just one fucking mistake after two many fucking drinks, and I paid for it. Jesus Christ, I paid for it. It's been an acorn rolling down fucking Everest every fucking step of the way, gathering up so much fucking snow that it's a fucking avalanche that's fucked up my whole fucking world."

Yet again, I didn't get it.

I couldn't get it.

"Then why?" I asked him. "Why didn't you tell me so?! Why weren't you honest with me?" I paused and held back another sob. "I mean, I would have hated it, and it would have hurt real fucking bad, but if it was one mistake, Lucas… if it was just one mistake, then maybe we could have worked through it… maybe I could have forgiven you…"

"I know," he said. "I know you would've tried."

"So, why?" I pushed again, and my tears were streaming. "Why the hell did you leave?"

He took a breath, and his tears were streaming too as he gathered his voice to speak.

"Because she was pregnant," he said, and his words were choked. "My God, Anna. She was fucking pregnant."

Chapter Twenty

LUCAS

Ten Years Ago

Three weeks didn't sound all that long, but it would be. I'd miss her like hell.

She'd been struggling with stress for a few months, that pissing job and that jackass boss of hers putting so much pressure on her, having her working late every night and so wound up with deadlines that she was barely sleeping.

I'd hoped that requesting a whole chunk of time out like that would have them saying it was unviable and she'd have to make the choice to hand in her resignation, but they didn't. They'd been working her so bloody hard that she'd barely taken any annual leave, so there was a whole stack of days backed up to use.

So use them she did.

I've never been a fan of New Age bullshit. Anna was one of these meditation and visualisation and dream interpretation types who believed in the universe mapping out a road ahead. Whatever.

She stopped at the Neptune fountain in the centre of town every time we passed the thing, pulling a coin from her purse and tossing it in with a wish.

Every single time she would ask if I'd make a wish alongside her, and every time I replied with the same statement.

"The universe isn't responsible for my road ahead, Anna. I am."

Yes, I fucking was.

And responsible for the mistakes I made along the fucking way.

I'd waved her off from the platform with a thousand kisses and a lurch in my gut. She'd mouthed *love you* before she disappeared from view and I'd mouthed the same right back.

That first afternoon was boring. I flicked through TV channels and tried to flick through a paperback when they didn't hold my interest, but still I was bored.

I didn't drink all that much around Anna, I didn't head out and hit club nights every weekend until I was staggering home, like I had so much of the time before we'd got together. A couple of glasses of wine while we were talking about our day while we made dinner. A shot of whisky before bed when we'd had a particularly crazy fuck fest of an evening, but nothing more than that.

I figured it would be a good time for a splurge, and called up some friends and hit the town. We trekked around a few bars and I downed the beers and laughed the laughs and started up on the shots. I messaged Anna from the bar at Casey's Casino down on Broad Street, telling her how much I fucking loved her, and then necked back a couple more whiskies.

I think it was at Casey's we first met some more of our friends out on the town. I didn't know them so well as the others, they were mainly Dave and Kyle's regular hang out girls. There was Dawn Richards, and Yasmin Boyle and Hannah Ames.

And Maya Brooks.

There was Maya Brooks standing there at the bar with a large glass of white in her hand.

I barely spoke to her, keeping my laughter on Dave and Dawn for the most of it, but those shots kept on coming. We moved onto Bar Royale down the street and I could barely walk straight.

I think that's when Maya first giggled and came up to my side to keep me steady.

She smelt like Anna.

Same perfume. Black cherry and sea.

"Where's your sweetheart?" she asked, as if she'd read my mind, and Dawn answered before I could.

"She's up in Perth at that twenty-one day retreat. Sounds fucking ace."

"Right," Maya said, and I should have registered the smirk sooner.

I didn't. I was already too fucking gone.

There was already another triple shot waiting for me at the bar at the Ocean, courtesy of Dave. I looked at it through hazy eyes and should have opted for a taxi home.

I didn't think Maya was that close to me, just hovering. I didn't really notice her looking at me, just kept on laughing with the guys and checking my phone for messages from Anna.

I knew they'd taken hers off her at this bloody retreat thing, but still I kept checking it, and still there was nothing.

Another triple shot and it was madness.

I remember heading to the toilet and propping myself against the wall on the way, and then it all went blank. Blank until Dave was slapping me on the back goodbye and dropping himself into a taxi and Maya was clinging onto my arm and saying we'd share a ride in the next one.

She pulled a small bottle of whisky from her handbag in the backseat as we were setting off, and I remember laughing as I took it after her, swigging some back.

Idiot.

Stupid fucking idiot.

And then there was nothing.

Not until I woke up the next morning in a bed that looked nothing like mine.

My head was pounding, and my mouth was bone dry, and the room was spinning as I tried to get up. And there she was, grinning at my side, propped up on her elbow. Topless and loving it, and enough to send me reeling.

Maya Brooks.

I was in bed with Maya Brooks.

She tossed her brunette curls like some kind of porn star and acted like this was the most regular event in creation, and I was lost to the whole craziness of it, bleary-eyed and still barely sober.

"What the hell?" I asked her with a croaky voice. "What the hell happened?"

She gave me a giggle. "Plenty happened, Lucas. You were amazing."

I didn't know how the fuck I could have been amazing after that much drink. I didn't know how the fuck I could have even got it up.

She reached out for me and I forced myself to my feet, staring down mortified as she rolled onto her back and pulled the covers down.

"Come on, then, in for another go."

Another go was the last thing I wanted. Thoughts of the first go were enough to turn my stomach.

"I can't believe I did this," I said, and I hated myself. I hated every fucking cell in my body.

"Oh, you did it," she told me. "You couldn't keep your hands off me once we got through the front door."

I tried to walk away but had to prop myself up on her bedside table. I had to fight back the sickness as I gathered my clothes from the floor and struggled my way into them.

"I need to go," I choked, and she let out a groan.

"Don't be so boring," she said. "Now we've had one ride, you may as well dive back in for another."

I shook my head and the room was spinning. "I need to go," I said again, and headed for the door.

"You said you had feelings for me," she told me. "You said you always had."

"Then I was lying," I said back without hesitation. "Anna is my world."

She laughed. "Clearly not."

I got out of that room as fast as I could, storming straight across to the bathroom where I puked my guts up. I was a wreck, a guilty pitiful wreck of the man I'd been when I'd waved Anna off on that platform.

Maya was propped in the doorway while I was still retching.

"What do you want to do?" she asked, like it wasn't fucking obvious.

"Go home," I said, and my mouth tasted of puke.

"I mean it," she told me. "I'd love another go. Maybe we could have something..."

I burnt her eyes with mine, and I could barely fathom it, how she was so keen to continue with something that meant so fucking little.

"I've liked you for a long time," she said with a shrug, like that was an explanation.

"I'm in love with Anna," I said again.

"And I said that clearly you're not," she scoffed. "Seriously, Lucas, you weren't in love with her last night when you were fucking me senseless."

There was something so calm about her, so sure of her words and her stance and the rightness of this fucked up situation that made me feel sick on top of sick. I flushed the toilet and pushed myself to standing, and I was out of there, down the stairs and finding my phone on her coffee table.

No messages.

For once I was so fucking glad there were no messages.

She was wrapped in a satin slip of a thing when she joined me downstairs, and I felt like a prick from all angles.

"I'm sorry," I told her. "Fucking hell, Maya, I'm sorry. I'm sorry for the whole fucking lot of it."

I didn't hang around to hear a response, just threw myself out of there and stumbled down the drive. I squinted and recognised the road and knew I was just a few streets from mine, so I ran.

I ran like a skidding stumbling mess all the way home, and when I got there I fell through the door and hit the floor in the hall, and I hated myself. Our home smelt of us and our life and our future and I hated myself for ever being such a drunken prick.

I called up Anna's number and thought about hitting dial, but I knew she wouldn't answer. I pulled up my emails and the emergency contact details of the venue, but couldn't bring myself to wreck the retreat she was counting on so much just to give her a whole load more stress.

So I didn't.

I decided I'd stomach the guilt and the self-hate and the serious fucking regret and wait for her to get home. And then I'd beg forgiveness. I'd get down on my knees and confess my stupid sins and beg her to give me another chance at our world.

But I couldn't.

I couldn't, because after two weeks of hating myself and struggling into work with ashen features and an ashen heart to go along with them, I got a call from an unknown number.

Maya Brook's number.

I had no fucking idea how she'd got mine.

She needed to see me, and her voice was strained.

I told her I didn't want to see her, but she cried and said I had to.

I think I'd known right then. Known it could only mean one thing.

I met her at the Crown Inn on the city outskirts and I sipped on mineral water while she sipped on the same, and then she pulled a white plastic wand thing from her bag and handed it over.

And there were two blue stripes on it.

I could've passed out from the shock.

"I'm pregnant," she said. "You've got me pregnant, Lucas. And I won't get rid of the baby. I'll never get rid of the baby."

My eyes must have been terrified ghosts with no soul as I stared at her across that table.

"You're sure it's mine?" I asked and she rolled her eyes.

"I'm definitely sure it's yours."

I retched at her pause and she looked so hurt.

"You're going to be a daddy, Lucas," she told me. "I hope you'll live up to it. Please live up to it."

I didn't want to live up to it.

I didn't want to live up to anything to do with Maya fucking Brooks now or forever, but I couldn't not.

I couldn't not and I knew it.

"I need to get my head straight," I told her.

"Sure, I get that." Her eyes were so hard as she stared over, but there was a flash of fear in them too. It hurt to look at them.

"I'll be in touch," I said.

"Please don't mess up twice, Lucas. Please be there for me. I need you."

I left her in the pub and was in the same daze I'd been in for weeks, and then I was sick all over again, only this time it wasn't from drink. It was all from me.

I had to face up to it, and I was scared. I was a scared excuse for a soul watching his world fall away, and I needed someone to tell me I could get through this.

I called my mother and I struggled to speak, and she struggled to speak right back at me. I headed over to hers and she was waiting, as pale as I was, holding me tight as I walked through the door.

My words were a jumbled mess, asking her to please help me work out how I was going to get through this with Anna, but she shook her head.

"No," she told me. "You won't get through this with Anna. You've made a pit for yourself and now you have to climb on in."

I was shaking my head, but she was nodding hers.

"You listen to me, Lucas. I was Maya once. I was the scared woman with a baby growing in her belly and no idea how she was going to exist in this world."

I'd heard this before. I'd felt this before.

I'd hated the man who'd left her to bring me up without ever knowing my name.

And I couldn't be him.

I couldn't be that man.

She carried on talking and I was listening. I couldn't not.

"You aren't going to be your father," she hissed. "I didn't bring you up for that. You're going to be the dad your father never was, and you're going to make it work. You're going to make it work, son."

I was shaking my head and the tears came.

"I can't," I cried. "I can't do it. I love Anna!"

"And you'll love the baby you've created with Maya. Believe me, Lucas. You'll love that little soul more than you love your own. You just have to try your best now and leave your mistake behind and make a brand new start."

I was still shaking my head, but she didn't stop.

"You'll make a new start with Maya," she said. "Or you're a worse man than your father was, Lucas. You'll be a pitiful excuse of a man who isn't worthy of either of those women."

I believed her.

I believed her because it was true.

I was a pitiful excuse of a man who wasn't worthy of shit in that moment.

I definitely wasn't worthy of Anna.

It was killing me inside as I opted to take the course that would rip my heart in two and Anna's along with it. I called Maya up and met her the very next day, and I told her I'd try to be there and try to be the man she needed and the father I'd sealed the deal to be.

She was so happy as I told her I'd give us a go that I was sick to the stomach all over again. She threw her arms around my neck and once again she smelled of black cherry and the sea, and that acorn kept on tumbling down the mountain and it was already so caked in snow that my fate was well and truly sealed.

I was waiting for Anna when she walked through the front door after her trip away, and my stuff was already gone.

I knew she was forgiving, and loving, and everything I didn't deserve, and I knew I couldn't give her a hint of how broken I was too.

I needed her to hate me and carry on living her life, and curse my name whenever she thought of me.

I needed her to run away from me and never even try to reach out and ask me why.

So I choked it back. I choked it all back and pretended this was what I wanted. Pretended I'd been thinking it out and it was so much more than one stupid night and one stupid mistake.

Even through her broken screams her eyes were full of love, and I had to hold it back so fucking tight and get out of there before I begged forgiveness so hard I'd never make it through the door.

Never make it to Maya.

Never live up to being the man my mother had made me into.

I knew it needed to be bad, and unforgiveable.

I knew I needed to be the biggest cunt who'd ever lived.

So I laughed.

I laughed at Anna's pain as she broke in front of me, and I swore I'd hate myself as long as I lived.

And then, when I was sure I'd destroyed our world beyond all repair, I walked away.

Chapter Twenty-One

ANNA

I listened to his words without interrupting.

I felt his pain and regret and cried along with him and let it all sink in. It was a beautiful hurt, but it was tragic. It was so tragic, it broke my heart in a thousand new places.

"I'm sorry," he said and his forehead was pressed to mine all over again. "Please believe me, Anna. I'm so fucking sorry, you'll never know."

I did believe him, and it didn't make what he'd done hurt any less, or make it any more okay, but I felt it all as the truth.

My mind was piling up the questions, letting them spin, and I hated Maya just as much as I'd always hated her, but I had forgiveness for her predicament.

"What happened after that?" I asked. "I mean, Millie is only five… what happened to the baby?"

He didn't pull his forehead from mine.

"She lost it. Miscarried."

I sobbed fresh and he wrapped me tight in his arms and rocked us both.

"Then why did you stay with her?!" I begged to know. "Please, Lucas, you have to tell me why the hell you didn't come back and tell me the truth."

He let out a sob as he eased away from me, and wiped his cheeks with the back of his hand.

"Because she was broken, Anna. She was absolutely fucking broken."

And I screamed. I screamed in his face as the pain reached its peak.

"AND SO WAS I! I WAS ABSOLUTELY FUCKING BROKEN!"

I put my face in my hands and struggled with my own story, knowing it was time to lay it all out on the table, and trying. Just trying to let it out.

"I can't make it better," he said as I was still finding my voice. "I can only say I'm sorry. I thought you'd move on. I thought I'd be such a prick that you'd leave me behind and find someone better. And you did, right? You found Sebastian Maitland and I heard you were happy."

"I wasn't happy! I was just trying to find what the hell happy was again!"

We took a minute to get our breaths back to some semblance of steady, and then I cleared my throat.

"When you left me that day, I couldn't even begin to handle the pain. I loved you so much, and I wanted you so much, and I thought we had our whole world right there."

"We did," he said. "We did, I just fucked it up."

"And fucked *me* up," I continued. "I didn't know where to even start with it. I was crying like a wreck and couldn't speak, and I felt like you'd sliced me into pieces and stamped them into nothing. I tried to call Nicola and she was coming over, and I was trying to think, but I couldn't."

"I know," he said. "I know how broken you were. I saw it."

"BUT YOU DON'T!" I shouted, then struggled to calm my voice. "I was on the floor retching and sobbing with my brain fucking broken, and then it did break. It broke right there and then. I got a wave across my head that felt like I was falling out of myself, and I went so blank I didn't know where I was, and I couldn't speak, or think, or understand what the hell was going on." I paused to breathe. "I was so scared, Lucas. I was so scared and alone until Nicola came through the door and found me there. And that was the start of it. That was the start of the seizures, and they were so bad, and so cruel and I was terrified. I WAS TERRIFIED!"

"Jesus Christ," he choked, and his head dropped. "Jesus Christ, Anna, I didn't know. I'd never have left you there like that if I'd have known."

"You wanted to know about the epilepsy," I said, "You asked me to tell you about the seizures and I'll tell you about them now."

I did tell him.

I told him how they started with me going so blank at random points I didn't know where I was or where I was going. How I got so scared of having them I wouldn't go out on my own. How I became such a state before I was diagnosed that I lost my job and ended up back in my room at my parents' house too afraid to look for another.

I told him how the daytime ones turned into night time convulsions that had me chewing my tongue so bad I couldn't speak in the morning, and how I'd wake up in my own soaked sheets from where I'd pissed myself.

I told him how my temporal lobe got so asymmetrical that they picked it up on the EEG reading without me even having a seizure, and how, when I was waiting for them to give me a diagnosis, Sebastian first came into my life and said he loved me regardless.

I told him how I lost so much of myself when my mind was that fucked that I forgot just who I used to be, and Sebastian helped me find myself again so slowly it was an uphill battle that lasted years to truly find my feet again.

I carried on and told him how everyone was so worried about me there was a constant fear in their eyes every time I stopped speaking for five seconds straight.

How that fear turned to sympathy.

And that sympathy turned to pity.

And I stopped being Anna and started becoming the invalid who needed to take care of herself and stop taking any risks or living any kind of life for herself.

"But it wasn't just that," I said. "It wasn't just the epilepsy that hurt so bad. It was more than that. The seizures had already started before you left me, they were in the sickness and those weird feelings of déjà vu and everything they told me was stress. It was more than my brain and the bullshit it sparks when it feels like it, it was the pain of losing you. And everyone knew that. Everyone knew what you did to me. Everyone knew how much I loved you and how much you'd broken me into the mess of who I was before."

"You've been having seizures that long?" he asked, and his voice was as broken as mine.

I nodded. "Yeah. They've been better and worse, but they've always been there. They helped loads with the lamotrigine, and Sebastian tried to help by controlling everything I did, but they never went away. Not completely."

We sat for another round of silence, both of us staring at the carpet between us and trying to find our thoughts. We were both lost and knew it. Both broken and knew it.

I had no idea how the hell we would ever find the way up from that spot on the floor, both of us stuck in this pit of pain. Neither of us tried to attempt it, just sat and breathed.

Sat and breathed and cried.

Sat and breathed and remembered just how hard the whole sorry wreck of our life was in the aftermath.

"Did you love him?" he asked me. "Did you love Sebastian? I thought you were happy. People said so."

"I was trying to love him," I said. "I thought I did, and I wanted to, and I was so grateful for everything he was being to me."

"That's what I was doing with Maya," he said. "I was trying to love her, and wanted to love her to at least drag some scrap of good from the carnage. And she was trying so hard. Trying so hard to make me love her."

I nodded. "Sebastian was good to me. If I had any sense, I'd love him back and would still be there."

"That's what my mother is telling me about Maya."

"But I can't," I choked. "I can't love him, because he's not you. I've never loved him like I loved you."

"And that's what was happening with me," he choked back. "I can't love her, because she's not you. I love Millie. I love Millie more than life, but I can't love Maya, and she knows it. That's why the trying so hard turned into so much spite. Because she knows I don't love her, and she wants to punish me for it, and I don't blame her, not really."

I gave up at that point and let myself fall to the floor. I lay on my back and stared up at the ceiling, cried out of tears. And he joined me there, at my side, staring up at the ceiling along with me.

"What the hell do we do now?" he asked, but I didn't have an answer.

"I don't know what we can do. Nobody will ever accept we're together. My parents are still screaming for me to get back with Sebastian, and Nicola would slit your throat before she'd sit in your company."

He sighed. "I wouldn't blame her."

Neither would I. She'd watched me through the very dregs and cried with me through every second of it.

"What about you?" I asked him. "Is Maya still trying to make it work?"

It took him a few seconds to answer. "She says not. She says she's done and over and never wants another night with me, but my mother says that's bullshit and I should be busting my gut to make it right again. Mother says she still bleats on about *the destiny of souls having a higher purpose together* every time she gets five minutes."

"Do you want to make it right again with her?"

"No," he said, without even a hint of a pause. "I hate how I'm away from Millie, and I hate she uses it as a weapon, but I don't want another shot at it. I think it does Millie more harm than good to see us together like that. Unfortunately, my mother doesn't agree with me."

"This is tough," I said, stating the obvious.

"Yeah, it's fucking tough. It's a fucking joke how fucking tough this is.

I don't even know where we go from here."

But I did.

As bitter and painful and fucked up as it was, I knew where we went from here.

My fingers reached out for his and squeezed, hands holding tight on the floor between us.

"I love you," I told him, and meant it. "You are a cunt and a monster and you destroyed my whole world, but I love you. I never stopped loving you."

"I love you, too," he said. "I was a cunt and a monster and I destroyed your whole world for one stupid mistake that cost us both everything, and a whole host of stupid decisions on top. But I never stopped loving you, Anna."

"So, what now?" I asked. "What the hell comes after this?"

His sigh was all out of tears, just like I was.

"Dinner," he said. "Dinner comes after this."

I let him pull me to my feet right up after him. And I let him hug me tight before we went downstairs.

Chapter Twenty-Two

LUCAS

We stood in silence in the kitchen, the world so heavy between us that we were both out of words. I made lasagne and she was standing there, swamped in my shirt, looking so fucking beautiful and in so much pain it tore me apart all over again.

There was no way out of this.

There was no way Maya would let me out the other side of this with Anna in my arms. Not without holding Millie to ransom.

There was no way my mother would ever hear me out and understand just how much I needed a fresh shot at my old life.

There was definitely no way Jim and Terri would ever accept that their daughter was ditching Sebastian Maitland for the jackass who ripped her to shreds and gave her seizures and stole her soul.

And I couldn't even begin to imagine how Nicola Henshaw would handle me back on the scene. Probably by doing a lifetime in prison for decapitation.

I felt split in two. On one hand, I was so insanely grateful for the chance to tell her the truth that the relief was burning bright. On the other hand, I was deeper than ever in the pit of self-hate, cursing my own piece of shit mistake all over again with a whole new understanding of just how much I'd fucked her up.

Epilepsy.

A decade of fear, and pity, and her brain hurting so bad she couldn't live her life anymore.

And I'd done that.

I'd done that to her.

I looked her in the eyes once I'd put the lasagne in to cook, and my self-loathing must have been so visible it didn't need words.

Her cheeks were still streaked from the tears, and her voice was still wobbly when she spoke, and she still had the ability to read my thoughts without asking questions, even after all this time.

"You didn't cause the epilepsy," she told me. "I was already having seizures, they just weren't that severe."

"Stop," I said. "I don't deserve it. I was a cunt, and I caused everything."

"You were a cunt, but you didn't cause everything. Just made it worse."

I wanted to hold her tight and never let her go, but we were both paper thin and barely capable of standing, and we'd never manage it. Not another round of rocking and sobbing when we didn't have any tears left to cry.

"I can't see how we fix this," she whispered, and it twisted the pang in my ribs a whole load harder.

I didn't want to say I couldn't either, because I couldn't give up. Her stare was a pool of cold, dark misery with only a sliver of hope. I only wished mine had a sliver of hope staring right back at hers.

My fingers were weak as I pulled the cigarettes down from the shelf, and I didn't even ask if she wanted one, just handed them over.

"I've never quite needed one like I need one right now," she said, and managed a laugh.

I pushed a laugh out of me right back. "I'll be to blame for this too. Your fresh smoking habit."

"Add it to the list."

"It's quite a fucking list."

"Yes, it is."

She should hate me with every inch of her, but she didn't. She was still in love with me. It was shining right through her, and it was the greatest gift I could have wished for. Maybe that was the universe's ultimate form of karma, if there was such a bloody thing. Giving me a taste of something that meant so much, just to snatch it back away. And I'd live with that, because I'd deserve it.

But she'd never deserve it.

Anna would never deserve a breath more of this misery.

She stubbed her cigarette out on the plant pot tray where I'd stubbed mine, and it was her who closed the distance, resting her head against my chest as her arms gripped my waist.

"We only have the now," she said again. "Let's make the most of it."

I kissed her head and squeezed her back. "I'll always make the most of it."

I wasn't expecting it when she headed over to the fridge and pulled out a bottle of prosecco. I definitely wasn't expecting it when she looked through three of my cupboards until she found the right one for glasses.

She popped the cork and poured out two, and I clinked hers to mine as she handed it over.

She took a swig before she smiled. It was still a butterfly kiss on a broken heart, but it was enough to have me smiling right back at her and taking a swig of my own.

"I'm so used to everyone pulling faces at everything I do," she told me. "People would be wrestling this glass from my hand and bundling me off to bed before I'd even got a taste back at home."

"You know your own mind," I said. "You're perfectly capable of knowing what you do and don't want to do, Anna. If you need my help or my opinion you'll ask for it. I'm more than happy to give either."

"It's because they care," she continued. "But I'm so tired of not living."

"I care too. I'd walk through flames if it saved you from a single seizure, but I can't." I sneered at myself. "Plus, it would be the biggest hypocritical shit show in creation if I advised you not to drink anything."

She put her glass down on the counter after just a few sips, and then she wrapped her arms around my neck all over again.

"Let's live the now," she whispered. "I'm done with thinking and crying and wishing for some kind of miracle answer to this crazy." She paused. "Please God, can we try to forget it, just for one night."

"How?" I asked her, but I already knew. I ditched my glass on the side, and my hands tugged my shirt up over her ass and grabbed tight.

"Fuck me," she breathed. "Fuck me hard enough to take it away."

My answer was a kiss, and it was deep and dirty and wet enough that she gasped against my mouth. I pushed my thigh between hers and the horny minx in her shone bright. She rubbed herself against my leg, and her mouth was on mine, open wide.

I managed to stumble back and turn off the oven, and her hands were busy freeing my cock and jerking hard.

Holy fuck, I could have blown my load right there and then. But no.

No fucking way.

I didn't lead her upstairs. I opted for the living room, guiding us through the door and down onto the sofa without pulling my mouth from hers.

"Make me forget," she breathed again.

My smile was all for her. "I'll make you such a dirty little bitch, you'll forget everything."

I tore my shirt off her so hard a few of the buttons pinged off, and her tits were straining ready. I was rough. Really rough.

She begged me for rougher, and I gave it. I gave her even rougher.

"Make me a dirty bitch, Lucas."

I'd make her the filthiest little bitch she'd ever been.

I slammed three fingers inside her deep and she wanted more. My thumb was against her clit, circling hard, and I spat on another two fingers and pushed them into her ass. Her back arched and legs spread wider and she took it with a curse.

"That's it," I hissed. "Believe me, Anna, it's going to get dirty. I want it, Anna. I want you, so fucking dirty."

"Do it!" she hissed, then moaned as I pulled away.

She knew exactly what I was going for as I headed out to the kitchen, but still her eyes opened wider as I held up the filthy white lace we'd already made so dirty.

"Oh fuck," she whispered, and I was already there, rubbing the panties against her clit.

"Watch," I said, and she did. She propped herself up on her elbows and stared down at my fingers strumming her through the lace.

I made her come over and over, working so hard on that horny little nub that her thighs were trembling as she took it. I played her body better than ever I played my own, mouth watering as those panties soaked right through.

Once again she knew what I was doing before I did it. I positioned myself between her legs and took my cock in my hand, stretching that lace across her slit. I told her to keep her hands away and she gripped the cushion behind her head, pinning her lip between her teeth like my filthy little angel ready to play. I cast off my clothes between jerks and she watched me, moaning fresh as my flesh came into view.

That much adoration made my cock all the harder.

My balls were aching, needing to blow, and my hand was slick with precum. My breaths became ragged, eyes fixed on that beautiful pussy as she ground it back up at me. I stretched those dirty panties tight over that delicious pouting cunt before I jerked a final thrust and unloaded, spurting thick cum all over them, and then I was right up and at her, slamming her flat onto the sofa with that sopping wet lace ready and waiting.

"Open your mouth," I told her, and she whimpered as she did it, opening up nice and wide.

I pulled that dirty white lace tight between her lips, and her tongue came out to meet it.

I told her to suck on that filthy lace and she sucked on it with the most adorable lust in her eyes. She had me. She fucking had me, legs wrapping around me, pulling me into her hot cunt.

I pinned her down and fucked her fast and fierce as she sucked on those filthy panties, teasing me so sweet that I was soon ready to fucking blow again.

"You'd better keep fucking still," I grunted as I pulled free and moved to straddle her pretty face.

It was bliss. Both of us fixed on my cock as I jerked it fast.

"Open wide," I hissed. "And don't even think about fucking swallowing."

She did what she was told, opening her mouth all over again with that lace sopping slick between her lips. My cum splattered even thicker this time than before, spurting over her tongue and lips and those dirty panties like a seedy fucking fountain.

"Don't fucking swallow," I hissed again, and she managed a sharp little nod.

My cum collected at the back of her throat, panties still tight, and I was straight back down at her pussy, sucking on her clit as she squirmed.

I knew it was sensitive as all hell.

I knew it would take every scrap of restraint for her not to swallow hard and catch her breath. But she was a good girl.

She was *my* good girl.

She was the filthy little angel that never failed to drive me insane.

Her body was a shuddering wreck as she exploded again, and I pushed my fingers back deep into her ass to ride the waves. Her moans were gargled and bubbling, and my balls were aching fresh, mind lost to everything but that moment.

"Don't fucking swallow," I said again, and she nodded. I pulled my fingers out of her ass and was straight up in front of her as I sucked them clean. Holy fuck, how hungry I was when I sucked them clean. Her eyes fixed hard, and she tipped her head back ready. Oh fucking yes.

I stretched her lips apart and stared right inside her mouth with those soaking panties still spread tight.

"Suck," I said, and shoved my fingers in deep, pushing the lace all the way to the back of her throat, and she retched, then sucked and swallowed, moaning hungry.

Fuck, she was my world. My match. My everything.

I pulled my fingers free but she kept on sucking that lace clean, and then she opened back up, to show me how well she'd done.

And I kissed her.

I kissed her with those panties still between our wet mouths, tongues crashing and twisting as we tasted. I lifted her up from the sofa and she wrapped her arms around my shoulders, as keen for the kiss as I was.

Dirty,

Oh fuck, it was dirty.

It was me who finally pulled the lace free and kept on kissing her.

I don't know how long we were holding tight. I don't know just how long that kiss ate us up and wouldn't let go.

I do know that my dick was aching with the throb as I got hard all over again, and I do know it was her who hitched herself up and took me inside her.

It was a beautiful rhythm. Slow and steady. Neither of us wanting it to end.

"I love you," she whispered, and her lips were puffy with kisses.

"I've always loved you," I whispered back. "I always will."

It was dark outside by the time I came inside her. She took it with a smile and held me tight, and I didn't let her go. Couldn't let her go.

We breathed together and lay together and lived in the moment. And that moment was bliss.

It was everything I'd ever wanted.

Chapter Twenty-Three

ANNA

It was a stunning release. Enough to obliterate the confusion and hurt and tragedy, even though it was just a flash of calm in the storm.

I fired the oven back up and took care of the lasagne while Lucas took care of the dogs, and it was good. Just what we needed as we munched at the table and soaked in the high.

I was determined to keep the high going as long as possible, finishing up my glass of prosecco before moving onto juice while Lucas finished the bottle. We smoked, and laughed, and remembered old times, and it was magical. Truly magical.

So was going to bed in his arms and sleeping, flesh to flesh.

Unfortunately the storm of life's carnage was back in full force when we woke the next morning. We were both heavy with what was looming as he fucked me one final time in his bed. It was slow and steady, and everything we could do to delay what would be coming just as soon as we got ourselves up and dressed and facing the day. It was just a blink before

Sunday was motoring ahead and I had to state the obvious.

"I need to go home. I have my parents to see, and Nicola is screaming to head over to mine, and I need to face this. I can't keep holding it off."

He nodded. Because he was in the same space, and I knew it.

He had his mother, and Maya, and Millie to face up to.

I put my clothes into quick wash and dry, minus filthy knickers, and presented myself in some kind of order in muddy shoes, then said goodbye to Bill and Ted while they wagged their tails like I was their lifelong friend.

Then Lucas took me home.

It was on the way that I made the dumb decision to head into the garage shop for a pack of my own cigarettes while he fuelled the truck, and it became dumb on top of dumb when we saw Hannah Ames in the opposite queue while me and Lucas were standing there together, clearly too close to be just friends.

Hannah Ames, matter of factly right there with her three kids bustling around her and asking for sweets from the counter.

Hannah Ames, one of Maya's closest friends.

She smiled but it was fake, and we smiled back, but it was mortified.

And that was it. The storm reached a new high. Our days of secrecy were truly numbered.

There was a fresh round of heaviness in the truck as we reached my street.

"What now?" he asked, and I shrugged.

"We think, I guess. Think and hope for a miracle."

He kissed me before driving off, and I made my walk back to my apartment feeling like a criminal, even though my heart was soaring high.

Vicky was scowling when I hit my living room, asking me a round of questions I struggled to answer. She had her gym clothes on and her hair scraped back, a big pot of yoghurt in her hand while she watched vintage comedies.

She put the TV on mute when I sat down next to her.

"You're going to be in so much shit when people get hold of you," she said, and I shrugged.

"I guess I face it, then," I told her.

She muttered something damning and put the sound straight up again as I headed on through to shower.

One confrontation down.

A fair few harder ones still to go.

I replied to my parents saying that I was on my way for lunch, and I replied to Nicola saying I'd see her that evening, and she messaged back with nothing but a thumbs-up.

And then I did it. I dressed myself up, and put on my makeup as something vaguely like a mask, and I headed on over to my parents' place on the other side of town.

Mum answered the door with a horrified expression, eyes full of nerves at just how the hell I was doing, and I felt like a criminal all over again, trying to soothe her with a smile as we made our way through to the living room.

I took a breath and started with my blurt of an explanation, but she hissed at me to shush and gestured on through to the dining room, through the double doors. And there he was.

Sebastian.

Laughing with my dad, while my dad patted him on the back.

Holy fucking crap.

I hadn't seen Sebastian in weeks, and my stomach tumbled when I saw him smiling over at me, and I didn't want it. I didn't want even a hint of him on my criminal Sunday, bad on top of bad.

I bit my tongue as we sat at the table to eat our Sunday roast, and every mouthful was hard as I battled to keep my nerves in check. And there it started.

Make sure you go steady with your chicken, Anna. Did you sleep last night? Make sure you drink enough water, you don't want to bring on a seizure. Don't want to bring on a seizure. Don't want to bring on a seizure.

Underneath the thin smiles and overflow of instructions to take care of myself, there was such a thrum of disapproval and rage it raced my heart in my chest. In some ways I was glad Sebastian was there smirking across at me, just to stop the explosion from Mum and Dad, but the line of crap was still pretty tight between the two.

I made sure to leave before he did, bailing out with a happy fake goodbye while they scowled and said I should stay. I used Nicola as a welcome excuse, and air kissed Sebastian from as great a distance as possible before giving my parents a hug and saying I'd be back to see them soon.

And then I bailed.

I dashed back to my apartment after giving a *no need, thanks* to Dad when he offered me a lift, and I took advantage of the walk. Another little burst of calm in the storm.

Time for round three.

I was braced in my living room when Nicola knocked at the door. I was already through three of my cigarettes with the stink disguised by mouthwash and plenty of perfume when she headed on through to the sofa with me, and her expression was so dark it was scary.

But still, she held it back.

I must have been visibly surprised when she held it back.

"Talk to me," she said. "What the fucking hell is going on with you, Anna?"

I wasn't expecting anything like a scrap of calm from her.

So, I was honest.

As honest as I dared to be.

I told her it had started as a one-off and was never meant to be anything more. I told her that Lucas and I always got on crazy well, and I was enjoying seeing him, even though it was carnage, and I knew it.

I told her that I was feeling the glow of life around him and was taking advantage of it for all it was worth. And it was good. Really good.

I held back that I loved him, and that I would give anything for another chance in his world, because there is only so much someone can take when they are in poor Nicola's shoes and want to slice right through Lucas with a chainsaw. And still she was calmer than I expected, clearing her throat before she came back with a response.

I realised all over again in that moment just how much I loved Nicola Henshaw, and how come she had always been my best friend.

"Don't hide back the obvious, Anna. I know you love him," she told me. "I know you always have, and I think it's bullshit, and I hate his fucking guts, and I'm praying you'll come to your senses if you just give yourself a chance to see reason."

She had optimism I didn't, that was for sure, but still I heard out her logic.

She leaned on over and squeezed my knee, and her eyes were bursting with sympathy and worry and the wish that I'd sort my fucking life out. And it was harder that way. Harder than her screaming at me, because there was more guilt to feel from her support than her rage.

"You need more of a life," she said. "You walked out on Sebastian because you think he held you back somehow, so just bloody think about it. All you've done since rushing out on him is work, work, work and stay holed up in this place."

She had a point. I hadn't exactly thrown myself into socials, not outside of finding randoms to attempt to give me an orgasm and the odd night out with work friends. Fear, I guess. That constant concern of having a seizure out amongst a load of people having a good time, and trashing a hole in the middle of their fun.

That and not being able to drink while they were downing plenty.

"Alright," I said. "You're right. But what am I supposed to do? I'm not exactly ditching offers all over the place."

She scowled at that.

"Bullshit. There's a school reunion down at Casey's in a few weeks you haven't signed up for, and Lisa had a birthday drink down at Oscars last Saturday and you didn't bother coming."

I nodded, because that was true, but she kept on going.

"You haven't replied to Amy Miller's wedding after party invite, and that's two weeks off. And I've got my bloody girls' night next Friday and you haven't even told me you're coming to that. Plus, Emma Staplow has some makeup sales party at hers on the nineteenth. Do I need to tell you any more?"

No. She didn't need to tell me more.

Vicky came through the front door with a *hello* at that minute and headed on through, and Nicola brought her up to speed with her lack of socials assault on me.

Predictably, Vicky was all nods. "Don't say you can't get over Lucas Pierce if you don't even try to have any fun in your life."

"Alright," I told them. "And if I try to have fun in my life and bundle myself along to all these socials, and I still don't get over Lucas Pierce, does that mean you'll give us another try?"

They looked at each other before they spoke, but it was only for a second before their response came out in unison.

"No."

"No," Nicola repeated. "I'll never give you and Lucas Pierce another try. He's a cunt and a prick, and I can't stand the sight of him. You're worth a whole lot more than that waste of space, Anna."

"No," Vicky added. "He's a cunt and a prick, and I can't stand the sight of him. Get back with Sebastian."

So, I shrugged.

I shrugged and brushed it aside and sank back into the sofa cushions and accepted the storm was still raging as hard as ever.

And then I agreed to their onslaught of *fun*, and watched as they signed me up to the bank of socials and told everyone I was coming.

At least it was worth a damn shot to get them on side eventually, even if it took another whole damn decade.

I'd be praying.

Chapter Twenty-Four

LUCAS

I tried to find a scrap of optimism through Sunday afternoon, but it was a pointless exercise. I knew Hannah Ames would be straight onto Maya with the gossip just as soon as she had the chance, and I knew Maya would be straight onto my mother.

I tried all over again to get some time with Millie before the weekend drew to a close, but Maya wouldn't answer my calls, and when I turned up at her place to try harder in person, her car was gone from the drive.

So I cursed her for her vile bout of punishment all over again, and I went home.

It already felt empty without Anna. The rooms felt bare, and Bill and Ted already looked behind me to see if she was following me through. I gave them a decent fuss and extra treats and played ball in the garden, and it was a regular day in my regular world minus Millie, but that whole world felt so much shitter without Anna's smile.

I kept looking at my phone for messages, but none came through. I ate another portion of lasagne, staring hard at the empty space opposite me at the table, then handed a chunk to the dogs. And then I opened a bottle of wine, and smoked cigarettes, and stared out at the night sky over the horizon.

I only wished Anna was there to see it with me.

I wished she was there to open her mouth nice and wide to take a fresh round of dirty panties, and then smile her filthy smile as she watched me jerk my cock over tainted white lace.

But she wasn't.

She wasn't there and I'd better get used to it.

There was still nothing from Anna, or Maya, or my mother before I showered for bed. I sent off one final text to my bitch of a co-parent asking for time with my daughter, but this time it didn't even show as delivered.

The night made it even worse of a contrast without Anna there in my arms.

I slipped into bed and the covers smelt like black cherry and sea. I pulled her pillow over from her side and held it tight. Breathed her in. And I prayed.

I prayed for another shot at another life.

I prayed that we'd make it through to the other side of this hell with our hands holding tight.

I prayed that Maya wouldn't use Millie to destroy my world beyond repair.

But still, I also knew that prayers never go answered. At least not when they're coming from me. I smiled before I finally drifted to sleep, remembering the sparkle in Anna's eyes every time she tossed a coin into the Neptune fountain, and I wondered if she'd already tossed one in there and wished for us.

I'd sure be grateful to be proved wrong and that fountain to fucking deliver.

I held onto that thought until the night finally sucked me up into the darkness.

There were still no messages the next morning. I went about my usual business and suited myself up smart. I put Anna's filthy panties back in my pocket and let the dogs out before setting off, and made my way into my working week.

It was a busy Monday, and busy Tuesday to match. Keith and Ralph had a shit ton of reports to push on with, and we had to drag Moose in on Wednesday, which was always a whole fresh round of a battle. Anna and I texted, but it felt distant, no matter what we said. It was never a substitute for having her in my arms. Plus, we never had an answer. Not anything that sounded truly positive to make it through this with everyone on side.

I jerked off into those filthy panties every night of the week, and several snippets of afternoons on top. It was a welcome relief, sure, but not anywhere near enough for thoughts of my dirty minx not to drive me fucking crazy through every fucking lousy minute.

It was Thursday evening when I first got a message through from my mother. I was already churning sick without a response back from Maya, with the inevitable pang of fear stabbing every time I weighed up what options I had to take.

Her message was short and sharp and unforgiving.

Sort yourself the hell out, Lucas. Don't you dare lose Maya and Millie.

Like I wasn't fucking trying to see my fucking daughter.

I was back in my office and feeling the pressure by the time my Friday afternoon took a turn for the better. A parcel landed on my desk from one of the reception team, and looked quite a strange little spectacle.

I turned it over in my hands, puzzled to shit as I wondered what the hell it was. It was hand scrawled with nothing but a simple *Lucas Pierce, Director of Security and Cryptology* on the front, and my heart leapt as I recognised the scribble.

No. Fucking. Way.

It had already been opened to check it passed through security clearance, and I laughed out loud when I tipped the contents out on my desk.

Pink lace, still wet at the crotch, a perfect gift on a dull as hell work day.

I checked there was nobody lurking outside my room before I unzipped and worked that fresh pair of panties up and down my cock. I was rock hard and throbbing in barely a minute, well on my way to shooting my load by the time I called up my phone camera and fired her a photo message.

Nice present, you dirty little minx.

I added a tongue out emoticon, and she sent one right back.

And then she sent kisses.

I didn't know how the hell she'd made it over with the parcel without racing through her lunch break at lightning speed, but I was equally quick in my response, calling up her name online and finding her photo and title in the PR section of Lewton's Consultancy.

I scrawled down their address on an envelope of my own, then grunted hard as I shot one hell of a fucking load onto those filthy fucking panties and wiped up every fucking drip from my cock.

Oh yes, Anna, my sweet fucking love. Take this.

I was smirking as I summoned a courier via reception, and still trying to hold back the grin under a guise of professionalism as they came to collect my package.

"Anna Blackwell, direct into her hands, please."

My instructions were clear, and I reclined in my chair until the ping came through, barely twenty minutes later.

OMG, Lucas. Just OMFG!!

My reply was sent in a heartbeat.

Send me a picture of you enjoying the gift. I'm waiting.

I hovered around my desk for another few minutes, dragging the wait out as long as possible considering I had a meeting to head into. It seemed she was in the same predicament as I was.

I can't, her message read. *I have a team discussion about Kershaw's.*

My mouth was watering as I typed.

Fuck Kershaw's. Go to the bathroom and send me that pic.

Another tongue out smiley came through and I waited as long as I dared before I joined Ralph in the meeting room and waited for the rest of the security management team to make their appearance.

The seats were full and conversation was buzzing heavy by the time my phone next vibrated in my pocket. And I couldn't stop myself sneaking a glance at my photo message. Not for a second.

Oh fuck.

It was fucking glorious.

She had her head tipped to the side, eyes on the camera as she held those panties up nice and high against her open mouth. Her tongue was stretched out and lapping at the filthy crotch, and she was smiling. Smirking. Loving it. Her eyes were twinkling damn fucking bright enough for my balls to ache at the sight.

I need to see you, I typed before the meeting got off to its full start. *Fuck this hell, I need to fucking see you.*

I'd done my overview of the month's project and Ralph was onto his presentation by the time my phone buzzed again.

I need to see you, too, she told me. *Seriously, Lucas, I couldn't stay away if I tried.*

I forced myself to concentrate through the rest of the management session but my mind was focused on a whole other tune when I arrived back at my desk. I pulled up Maya's number and mustered up a whole new round of strength as I typed out another new message.

I needed this hell to move forward.

I needed to sort out my damn schedule.

If you don't tell me when I can see my daughter, I'll have to find another way to gain access. I mean it. I'm done with this utter bullshit.

I wasn't expecting a reply so quickly. Not after so much radio silence.

I'm done with this utter bullshit too, Lucas. How about you ask Anna Blackwell what time she can fit Millie in? Oh, except you can fuck off. Millie is busy with me this weekend. We're going away.

I tossed my phone across the desk.

Thank you, Hannah fucking Ames.

Just what this situation fucking needed.

I caught my breath and thought out my options before I opted for another message.

I'd play hardball. I was out of choices with no pot to piss in. Not anymore.

I fucking mean it, Maya. I'll find another way to gain access. I'm not staying away from Millie.

Whatever I expected in response was nothing as simple or as bold as the text that pinged back through.

It said it all, and I was scared as I read it. Really fucking scared of what lay ahead.

You can try, Lucas. Stay away from Anna Blackwell, or I'll see you in court.

Jesus fucking Christ.

The stormy sky just got a hell of a whole load darker overhead.

But still, I couldn't stay away from Anna Blackwell. No matter how hard Maya lashed out at me.

Anna's was the number I next called up, and my words were as just as needy as my thoughts.

I'll be wherever you want me to be, sweetheart. Just tell me when. And make it damn quick.

Chapter Twenty-Five

ANNA

It had been a long week. Seriously long.

I'd been playing smiles and trying to avoid tough conversations with just about everyone who would tell me that Lucas was the world's biggest prick over and over. I'd been trying to keep myself in line, and sleep, and eat, and do well at work without going crazy, and I'd managed it. Just one little blip of a seizure while I was waiting to go into a meeting on Thursday. I could cope with that.

But over the top of it all, I'd been trying to survive on nothing but a stream of text messages from Lucas as the days wore on.

I was totally sick of it and needed more.

But it wouldn't be that night, not while Nicola was hosting her girls' night at hers and I'd promised I was going. I dressed up in one of my decent red dresses and styled my hair in curls. Vicky and I stood side by side in front of the mirror as we both applied our makeup, and she was waffling on about just how much fun it was going to be.

I made sure my cigarettes were buried deep in my handbag while she was grabbing her two bottles of wine, and then we set off, piling into the taxi and heading across town to Nicola's.

I expected quite a gathering in her living room, because that's how Nicola works. She loves crowds, and laughter and stupid party games after too many wines.

But not me, especially not that night.

I was anything but excited as I stepped on through her front door, knowing full well how she would likely get preachy after a couple of glasses and I'd be sitting sober at the sidelines taking it all.

That's what I figured was coming, and I was fine with that. I could handle that.

What I wasn't expecting was for Nicola to have stocked up on Maya Brooks-now-Pierce's best friend club. There they were, sitting around the coffee table along with the regular crew. Dawn Richards, and Yasmin Boyle and Hannah Ames.

Great.

Just fucking great.

My level of cringe just reached a new high. Awkward didn't even begin to cut it.

Hannah shot me an evil stare as soon as I stepped on through, and Dawn sneered as I took a seat opposite. Thanks, Nicola. Great show.

Not only had Dawn and Hannah clearly organised the evening around their kids and work shifts and everything else just to be there, but I hadn't seen Yasmin Boyle in years, so Nicola must have gone to some seriously exceptional lengths to bring her into the crowd. She'd moved up to Newcastle years ago, and rarely came back around these parts. Not that I'd ever heard of.

Even better. Thanks.

Vicky smirked from my side, and I realised then that she'd been in on it. Another winner.

The cigarettes were already screaming from my handbag, but I kept my seat as Nicola handed me a juice from the kitchen. She clinked her glass to mine and looked triumphant, and sure, I could get her sense of victory. If that seemed like a way to drag me out of my madness, then I had no doubt she'd have jumped in on the strategy at any cost.

But getting Dawn Richards along? Surely that was stooping to a whole new low.

She was Maya's wing woman. People had said over the years that they were constantly whispering in each other's ears like the Bitches of Eastwick. I was just lucky Nicola hadn't opted to invite Maya along herself in person.

It was only Yasmin Boyle who looked awkward amongst the scowls. She was already deep into her bottle of sparkling, and we shared a *whoa, great* glance as Amy Miller started up another one of her looming wedding conversations.

I was grateful for the distraction. I'd talk about bridesmaid dresses for the next twenty-four hours straight if it meant even two minutes clear of the Maya posse.

But we didn't talk about bridesmaid dresses for all that long. Even Amy Miller stopped talking weddings once the wine got truly flowing. I sank into the sofa and kept quiet, smiling as blandly as possible while Maya's bunch kept up their scowls.

And then they started talking.

Dawn was the one to bring it up, telling the room just how much Maya had been struggling in recent months.

"It's so hard on her," she said. "I mean, Lucas usually bails when things get a bit tough, but this time he's really being a dick about it."

I wanted to say so much, but I didn't dare, just kept quiet and sipped on juice while the rest of the girls tuned in to the gossip.

"She's waiting for him to go back, of course," Dawn continued. "I mean, she has Millie there crying for family life back together, and Maya's trying, but this time Lucas just doesn't seem to want to sort things out. Not yet, anyway."

"But he will," Hannah chipped in. "I mean, of course he will. He has Millie to get back to, and they'll sort it out. They always do. Just so long as nothing else gets in the way."

Oh yeah. The tension was savage, and I hated it.

I hated how every pair of eyes in the room were fixed on me, and I carried on sipping my drink, craving a cigarette and cursing Nicola's fantastic wisdom in all of this.

"He needs to get his act together," Dawn went on. "Sure, Maya left. But that's because he was being such a total asshole, drinking and watching disgusting weirdo porn late at night, and doing just about anything other than being how he fucking should be."

And that was enough.

I put my glass down on the side and grabbed the box of cruddy party games from the bottom shelf of the coffee table and cleared my throat.

"Time we got this out," I said. "Let's get this party started and stop with the bitching."

"It's not bitching," Hannah said. "It's talking about friends and their problems."

"Oh, it's bitching," I said, and took the lid off the box. "Let's just play a game and forget about it, shall we?"

Several of the girls edged forward to get involved in the box unveiling, and Amy Miller even mucked in and pulled the snakes and ladders out, but it seems Dawn wasn't quite prepared to let it go.

"Truth or dare, then?" she suggested with a swagger, then downed her wine as everyone cheered their approval.

Except me.

I didn't cheer my approval, because I knew exactly where it was headed.

Disaster.

That's where it was headed.

Like watching a car crash unfold while you're in the front seat.

Ellie Borthwick jumped in first with a *would you rather fuck Ricky or Jason* question for Amy, and the girls laughed as she weighed up her options.

I wanted that cigarette more than anything, just to bail on the stupid game as everyone kept on pouring out drinks, but I didn't dare show myself up for yet another bad habit while I was already being crucified for my life choices. So, I kept my mouth shut and listened to their sneaky blurted truths and watched their stupid dares.

People doing handstands against Nicola's fireplace. People doing stupid stripteases like they were in some Amsterdam show routine. People singing songs at the top of their lungs to cheers and whistles.

And then it was my turn to pick my truth or dare.

Of course it would be.

Everyone knew what was coming before Dawn opened her drunken mouth and shot me the evils.

"Exactly what's going on between you and Lucas Pierce, Anna? Truth or dare?"

I wouldn't lie, because I don't. I never lie, especially not when the room is full of people who know me for myself, and value my self-respect and honesty.

"What's the dare?" I asked.

Several girls were weighing one up, but Dawn was already prepared with the impossible. She poured a pint glass full of white wine and slammed it down on the table.

"Down that in one, or answer the question."

Nicola and Vicky were horrified, I could see them about to make their move before I opted to take my own fate in my hands and show them all that I'd do whatever the hell I wanted.

I picked up the pint glass and slugged back that wine so fast that a trickle ran down my chin.

Stupid.

It was stupid.

But I was past giving a shit about any of that.

I slammed the empty glass back down on the table and smiled over at Dawn, and she was absolutely seething as the room whooped their cheers at me.

"You shouldn't have done that. You're not allowed with epilepsy medication," Dawn said, stating the obvious.

"No, you fucking shouldn't!" Nicola hissed and raced on over. "What the fuck were you thinking?!"

I shrugged amidst the horror, and she was screaming about my stupidity, Vicky in tow, with so much force that I reached into my handbag without even breaking a sweat.

"I'm going for a cigarette," I told the crowd and got up from my seat, and they were all still bitching or staring on open-mouthed as I pushed my way through and out into the damn back yard.

Fuck it.

I lit up and took a drag, and I could feel the wine burning in my belly. I was grateful for it, even if it caused me some bullshit in the aftermath, because it was warming. Warming and heavy and nice.

I expected it to be Nicola storming after me when the back door swung open, but it wasn't. It was Yasmin Boyle with a cigarette already hovering in her mouth.

I braced myself for another bitching session, but it didn't come. She looked at me with a strange glance as she started smoking and then she stepped up closer.

"Don't listen to that lot in there," she whispered. "You don't owe Maya Brooks anything."

I smiled back at her, thankful that someone finally remembered how Maya first stole Lucas from behind my back in the first place.

"I know that, don't worry," I said, but she stepped up even closer.

"You don't know the half of it," she told me. "Believe me, you owe her fuck all, and it's not just about her fucking off with him. She was a sly little bitch way beyond what people know."

"I know it wasn't exactly the lengthy process it seemed to be," I said when it looked like she was in on the secrecy.

"I know how it started," she said. "I was there on the night she did it. He was a wreck, you know. Too trashed to even remember his own name."

My stomach lurched at the knowledge that someone else really knew what happened that night. It burned deep, that fresh bout of knowing just how much of a mess that one shitty night turned into, and I was summoning up more questions to ask her when that back door opened all over again.

This time it nearly swung from its hinges.

"What the fuck are you doing now?!" Nicola spat, and pulled the cigarette from my fingers. "Drinking *and* fucking smoking?! More greatness from Lucas cunting Pierce, no doubt!"

But I was done. Truly, I was done.

I wanted nothing more to do with Dawn or Hannah or any of the bystanders feeding on my humiliation. I forced Nicola into a hug and checked I had my keys in my handbag and then I was out of there, calling up a cab as I made my way onto the main street.

I heard Nicola shouting after me but didn't turn around.

"SORT YOURSELF OUT, ANNA! FOR FUCK SAKE, SORT YOURSELF OUT! THAT CUNT IS WORTHLESS. HE'S FUCKING POISON!"

I thought she'd finished, but the rant started up again before I was out of earshot.

"UTTER FUCKING POISON! HE'LL TEAR YOU APART ALL OVER AGAIN! I'M NOT WATCHING IT NEXT TIME!"

Once again, I was grateful for the wine. The shards of panic were dull enough under the surface that I didn't flinch with this fresh round. Thumbs-up to Dawn and her bullshit dare.

I was smoking a fresh cigarette as I waited for the taxi, and my phone was back out in my hands in a heartbeat summoning up Lucas's text history.

Tomorrow, I told him. *This time you can come to me. I'm sick of hiding.*

I had a sickening pang of concern as soon as I sent it, scared I really was being a total bitch who was fucking things up with his daughter, but his message came back in a flash before I could truly rethink myself.

Can't wait to see you there, he said. *I'm sick of hiding too.*

Chapter Twenty-Six

LUCAS

Nobody was ever going to accept us, so fuck it. I was done with all thoughts of trying to make them.

I called up Beth from my work team and she was happy to dog sit with her boyfriend, and take advantage of house sitting the countryside alongside it.

I waited until they'd arrived before I finished getting ready, putting on a smart blue shirt and garish red and gold tie for the fun of it, and trimming my beard into order. I chose my finest tailored trousers and laced up my finest brogues, and my heart was thumping hard at the thought of seeing Anna there in town.

I fussed goodbye to Bill and Ted, and thanked Beth and Wes all over again, and I was churned up with pure waves of want as I set off to meet her.

I opted to take the truck, and parked up overnight in Broad Street car park before walking on through town to our agreed location.

And there she was, my Anna, right there and waiting – standing on the lawn right beside the Neptune fountain. Her usual sweet spot.

The water was tumbling down in a torrent and she was framed just perfectly by the orange glow of the lighting, and she looked divine.

Absolutely fucking divine.

Her heels were high, and her legs were bare. Her dress was silver satin and her hair was swept up in curls. Her eyes were dark and her lips were pale, and she was enough to stop my breath, as well as stop me in my tracks along with it.

Holy fuck, how I loved that woman.

She closed the distance between us, and her smile was shining bright.

"I missed you so much," she said, and her arms were straight around my neck.

It felt so right to be there standing next to her that I didn't give one single shit about any potential onlookers. The whole world could go fuck itself. I belonged there.

"Ditto," I whispered. "I missed you so much it fucking hurt."

She kissed me, and it was soft, but it said more than a thousand words. The way she took breaths, and the way her body pressed so tight to mine, and the way she ran her hand down my tie with a grin once she pulled away.

"You look great," she told me. "I love it."

"You look incredible," I told her back. "I love *you*."

We didn't head into the nightlife straight away, just walked closer to the fountain and hovered there. Her eyes were fixed on the statue at the top, and they were glittering.

"Gonna make a wish?" I asked, but she shook her head.

"Just did before you arrived."

I turned her face to mine. "And what did you wish for?"

"The impossible," she told me. "And how about you? Going to make a wish this time? I've got a coin."

I shook my head, holding on to my mantra.

"The universe isn't responsible for my road ahead, Anna. I am."

"Then let's try to make it a good one," she whispered.

We took it slowly as we walked hand in hand through to Oscars, pointing out the constellations overhead, just like we had a thousand times before.

Orion, and Sirius, and where's the Big Dipper?

Is that Venus? Yeah, that's Venus.

I hadn't expected Anna to make even the slightest social event out of our evening out in public. It hadn't occurred to me for a second that anyone on this whole planet would want to join us. But I was wrong.

There was a small crowd waiting at the bar that she walked right up to. She held me tight to her side as she made the introductions, and there was a bloom of pride in her smile that took me aback.

I hadn't seen anyone proud of me in years.

"Lucas, this is Lucia, and Stacey and Melissa from my office."

I said hello to all three and they shook my hand, and behind them were Peter and Jamie from *finance*.

I said hi to them too.

Then we hit the social. I bought a round of drinks, but went steady on my beer. Still, one turned into two, and two turned to four, and the stilted introductory conversations morphed into laughter and office jokes and embarrassing stories between co-workers.

I soaked in every single one, grateful beyond belief just to have a single taste of normality with Anna on my arm.

She'd finished two proseccos by the time the girls wanted to move on to the dance floor, and nobody had said a word about her alcohol consumption. She was grinning up at me as they dived into the beats, wrapping me up in her arms all over again.

"Dance with me," I told her, and she laughed.

"This isn't your kitchen, Lucas. This isn't bopping around with nobody watching. I haven't danced out in public in years."

"No," I said. "It's much better than bopping around with nobody watching. Live in the moment."

She answered with a grin and I took her hand.

It was a stupid tunes night, retro pop and disco tracks blaring out loud. I led her on up and then spun her around, and she ground up against me through her giggles like we were the only ones in the room.

Fuck, it was classic. Songs that had us exploding with laughter as we grabbed each other and hit the beat.

Better the Devil You Know and *Let's Go Round Again* and *Love is a God Damn fucking Battlefield.*

It felt like we danced for hours.

I don't know when the fun and laughter turned into the sizzle of pure fucking lust burning deep. I don't know when she started looking at me like she wanted to eat me alive, and I was growling back at her over the music with the promise that I was going to eat her up first.

I do know that we were at the side of the dance floor with my mouth hot and wet on hers while her friends were still partying, and I do know that I hitched her back against the wall between a few of the seating booths with quite a slam to pin her tight.

Oh, how she fucking laughed. She laughed so hard she clutched at her ribs and struggled to catch her breath.

She was staring me in the eyes, lipstick smeared across her lips from my kisses, when she told me just what the hell she was laughing about.

"It was here!" she said. "Oh my God, Lucas! This was what started this whole entire shit storm in the first place!"

I must have looked puzzled to hell, but she pointed to a seating booth across from her.

"I was sitting right over there, with a load of Sebastian's work crowd, and there was a couple over here who just couldn't keep their hands off each other. And I couldn't hold it back, not once I'd seen it, just how much I needed more." She paused. "Just how much I needed *you.*"

"You saw a couple getting it on and you realised you didn't want to stick with Sebastian anymore? Was he really that crap in bed?"

She was tipsy on those two proseccos, and she giggled. "We don't share a whole load of interests, Seb and me."

"I guess I owe that couple one hell of a thank you then, don't I?" I said, and kissed her even fucking harder, and we were at it. Hands and breaths and heat. Enough tension that we could explode the whole room along with us just for one sip of this madness. Enough tension that her eyes were scorching mine, lips swollen just right to suck them all the harder when I finally pulled away.

Hell knows where her work friends were by then, but she sure wasn't looking for them.

"I'll never get enough of loving you," she said. "I could kiss you for a whole damn lifetime, Lucas Pierce, and it would never be enough."

"If your fountain finally lives up to its bullshit and cuts us a break, then I *will* be kissing you for a whole damn lifetime, Anna Blackwell."

She ran her hands down my chest through my shirt, and it took everything I had not to tear her dress from her tits and take her right there and then.

"I think it's time we went home," she said, feeling my dilemma, and I smirked, mouth just an inch from hers.

"I think you're right," I told her, but I made her push me away before I'd free her, just to feel the contact.

It was only when we were heading for the front exit that I noticed a gaggle of drinkers at one of the far tables, with one of the girls staring over at us wide-eyed.

And there it was.

The crossover of two parallels on opposite sides of the spectrum. Another bystander staring at another couple, watching them heaving desperate for a single taste of each other.

Her blonde hair was tied back tight and her lips were bright red and her necklace was a chain of sparkles, but she was anything but a burst of sparkles herself.

She was a dead light on a dull day.

A pretty shadow under cloud.

A shiver of the laughter around, lost to it all.

It seems Anna noticed her too, and also seemed to notice the guy facing away from her – his arm just casually resting over the back of her seat.

Disinterested.

Bored.

Empty.

I had Anna's hand held tight in mine as I led us on out, but she tugged back with a pause as we passed by the woman's table. I stayed still as she leaned into blondie – who was still staring right at us – and pressed her lips right up to her ear.

Anna spoke.

Just a short little whisper, mouth to ear.

And then she smiled.

She smiled up at me with an even brighter grin as we left, and she was at me as soon as we were onto the street outside, her fingers dancing a tune with my belt as we edged down the pavement.

"What the hell did you say to her?" I asked with a smirk.

She shrugged, but I pushed her all the harder, nipping her bottom lip as she giggled.

"I told her to ditch him," she whispered. "I told her to ditch that guy next to her and find the man who really makes her orgasm."

"And that's advice you'd give yourself all over again, even if you knew what a shit storm was brewing ahead?"

She nodded. "I'd give myself that advice a thousand times over, just for one little moment with your magical tongue on my clit."

My cock was raging. It was raging and desperate with nowhere to go, and I'd never make it to her place. Not without pinning her against the wall ten times over and fucking her brains out en route.

Instead, I shunted her down a side road, and she squealed and giggled as I bundled her along in my arms.

"Where are we going?!" she laughed at me. "What the hell, Lucas? My place isn't this way!"

I kept on guiding, and grabbing, and urging us along, and she was still giggling and swaying as she joined me. And holy fuck, she was so much more than I'd let myself remember, even after all this time.

She was intoxicating. Addictive and irresistible and contagious, and horny enough to explode my whole world.

"I mean it!" she insisted. "This isn't the way to my apartment. I don't live this way!"

"No," I said. "But Neptune does. It's time to make another damn wish, Anna."

Chapter Twenty-Seven

ANNA

I'd stared up at Neptune over that tumble of water more times than I could ever hope of counting, but never like this. Never in an empty street in the middle of the night with Lucas's mouth at my neck. I'd never been moaning tipsy on prosecco, exposed and giggling and begging for more as he pulled my dress up. And I'd definitely never been so desperate to take him inside me that I didn't give a fuck for passers-by, or street cameras, or whispers of gossip eating us up in the aftermath.

He pushed me down onto the lawn in front of the fountain and was straight down on top, and it was such a stark contrast between the cold of the grass and the heat of him that my whole body was alive.

Magical.

It was magical.

Hell, we made the most of it.

We kissed, and we laughed and we enjoyed the breaths of each other. Timeless and free and fun. Hands grasping and grabbing and wanting.

Until wanting turned to needing. And needing turned to knowing.

I stared up at him and he was staring right back, and I guess it was there, in that stare that the laughter truly changed and turned. Our breaths were deeper and harder. That timelessness became an urgency. Because that was us – that urgency.

I felt it all at once.

As much as I wanted to believe we'd make it through this and come out as one, a quiet little voice down deep whispered that I was craving something that could never be. That we were a flicker of candlelight in an open window, doomed but alive, fighting the inevitable.

But still, my soul was sailing high.

I'd lived long enough to know that life has a rhythm – that this much of a high can hit the sky, but then ultimately peaks and tumbles. But maybe this time I was wrong. Maybe, amongst the chaos and the carnage and the disgust of the whole world looking on, just maybe we'd hit the sky and soar.

I could hope.

I could dream.

I could try.

We thrusted and writhed so hard across the grass that we reached the stone ledge of the fountain. I didn't care whether there were people passing by or watching from windows. I didn't care about passing cars, or CCTV cameras, or anything but the way he was touching me. The spray of the fountain soaked my hair, and my face and my tits through my dress. He kissed his way down my stomach through the satin and I moaned for him as he hitched my dress up around my waist.

Tonight I'd chosen red for my knickers.

"That's a good little dirty girl," he groaned as he saw them, and then he was at me.

My clit was alight, and his tongue was a-flicker, and I was already lost by the time he clamped his mouth through the lace and sucked hard.

"Please…" I managed, and I wasn't sure whether I was talking to Lucas, or the world around us, or even what I was truly asking for – release in that moment, or from the battlefield where we were taking fire from both sides, exposed in no man's land without a weapon.

Because that's what it felt like.

It felt like a battlefield.

It was the scowls over truth or dare, and the disgust of my family, and the videos of his little girl running around that oak tree, so innocent.

It was rocking together cross-legged on his bedroom floor as we sobbed over what could've been.

It was the pain, and regret and the desperation for another chance.

I exploded as his tongue flicked just right to set me on fire, back arching against the grass. *Fuck, oh fuck, yes.* I was soaked in water, writhing on the lawn as Neptune watched, crashing and sailing and panting for breath.

And then I was smiling. Smiling as a strange tide of feeling bloomed up from my stomach and up with it came tears at my eyes. I didn't get it, but I couldn't stop it. That crazy combination of the highs and the lows singing as one.

His mouth tasted of me when it came back up to meet mine, and my hands reached up to hold his face.

And then he fucked me.

Neptune didn't let up with his torrent, and this time we were both getting soaked underneath the spray, but it didn't matter. Lucas kept on thrusting until I was whimpering underneath him, building up a second time round. I turned my face flat to the stone as I reached a second peak. But no. He wouldn't let me look away. He forced my face back to his and his eyes were right back on mine, and we came like that. A mirror of explosion as we both crested and bucked and unloaded.

Vulnerable.

Exposed.

Perfection.

He caught his breath against my shoulder.

"I'd never have made it back to yours," he laughed, and I laughed along with him.

"Neither would I."

He raised himself up just enough to tug my dress back down, and I propped up on my elbows as he stared at me.

"You looked like you were about to cry for a minute back there. That must have been some kind of orgasm."

"Guess that's what two glasses of prosecco does to me."

"Would take a bit more than two glasses of prosecco to do that to you," he said, and helped me to my feet.

My feet screamed out pretty loud from the fresh assault of my heels, but I didn't care. I leant into Lucas as we took the correct route home this time, and we were happily back to constellation spotting, soaked through to the skin and wandering without a care until we were just a street away from mine.

That's when he stopped and turned me to face him.

"Don't give up on us," he said. "I know it's going to be real fucking hard, but don't ever give up on us, Anna."

"I couldn't give up on us," I said back. "I love you too much. But I guess that's why I felt the tears at the fountain. Knowing what's coming ahead."

"At least we get to face it together this time."

I took a breath and forced a lighter smile. "Well, this conversation sure got intense. So much for the giggle-dancing in Oscars."

"Yeah, maybe we need to fire up another round of *Better the Devil You Know* when we get back to yours."

That made me laugh. "We'd have to be mad to fire up a round of *anything* that would get Vicky out of bed at 2 a.m."

"Kylie Minogue will have to keep her mouth shut tonight then."

We held hands and swung them between us as we crossed the road and took the last steps to my front door. I stared up at the darkness of the windows. Thank God Vicky was definitely in bed.

I turned the key in the lock as quietly as I could and we made our way through the living room with careful footsteps. I started up making him a tea when we reached the kitchen.

"Nice place," he whispered as he looked around, and I shrugged.

"Not as nice as yours."

"If Neptune delivers your wish then maybe you can join me in the countryside. Bill and Ted would love to have you."

"And how about you?" I whispered. "Would you love to have me?"

He stepped across the kitchen and I abandoned his tea making to hold him tight.

"Nothing would give me greater pleasure than to have you in that house with me, Anna. You make it so much of a home that it's already screaming empty with you gone."

"And how about Millie, Lucas? Would she love to have me there too? And what about Maya? Will she ever swallow it down and let her come visit? Somehow I don't think it's going to be that easy."

He let out a breath. "She'll have to. Somehow she'll have to stomach it. Everyone will."

I let out a breath right back at him. "And are you sure you want to go through that? Because it could be one hell of a road, Lucas. She could tear you to shreds and you know it."

"She's been tearing me to shreds for years, she can just make it worse. And yes, I want to go through that. I want *us*."

Now wasn't the time for this, not after spinning and twirling and bopping to the beat for hours on end. I finished stirring his tea and handed it over, and then I let out a stretch and a yawn and said I was ready for bed.

He didn't disagree.

We made our way through to my bedroom, and it was so strange to have him there under the bedcovers I'd been alone in for months. Strange but beautiful.

"If anyone finds me in here it's going to be an even bigger shit storm than it already is," he whispered, stating the obvious, and I nodded.

"Yeah, well, the whole saga is one massive shit storm, one extra cloud of poop isn't going to make any difference."

"I haven't seen Vicky Mason in years," he said, and I smirked against his shoulder.

"I'm not sure these are the best circumstances for reacquaintance."

"I guess we'll find out in the morning."

I hoped not, but that would be a whole other wish for Neptune's fountain.

Crossed fingers and a wish at the moon would have to do instead. I gave both gladly.

He went to sleep before I did, and I stared at him in the darkness, until dreams found me too.

Chapter Twenty-Eight

LUCAS

I woke up before she did, her face still pressed to my shoulder and her arm stretched over my chest. Black cherry and sea and heaven itself.

I breathed in her hair and relaxed under the covers, and listened to the bustle of the street outside.

Until I heard the bustle of someone moving around the kitchen from down the hall.

Anna was still fast asleep, so I weighed up my options. On one hand it would have been an easy choice to sink back down into the bed and face the confrontation together, but no. If there was even a sliver of a chance I could save her from any of the fallout that was coming I'd happily head out there alone.

I was gentle as I lifted her arm from my chest. She wriggled and yawned, then rolled over, gripping her pillow tight before settling back down under the covers without waking up. I climbed out of bed and gathered my clothes up from the back of her armchair, as quiet as I could be as I pulled on my shirt and stepped into my trousers. And then I went out there to face the music.

Vicky Mason was in a fluffy pink dressing gown as she munched on a bowl of cereal by the cooker, completely oblivious to my presence as I approached. She had her phone propped up on the side, watching a gym video about push ups, well absorbed in the fitness commentary until I arrived in the doorway.

She leapt out of her skin when she saw me standing there, cursing as she dropped her bowl to the counter and slapped a hand up to her heart.

"Fucking hell, you made me jump."

Her expression of shock turned to one of disgust as she looked me up and down. I'd known this interaction wasn't going to be an easy one, but still, I wasn't expecting the simplicity of the greeting that came out of her mouth.

"You're a cunt," she said. "You can fool Anna all you want, you know, but you won't be fooling anyone else. No chance."

"I get it," I said, but she kept on going.

"Like you didn't fuck her up bad enough first time round. Why the hell are you fucking things up for her again? She's got Seb to get back to, you know. It's such bullshit you even being here."

"Yeah, I've been a cunt," I replied. "But I'll sure as fuck never be one again."

She laughed a hiss of a laugh at me. "I'm never going to be convinced," she said. "And believe me, I'll be the easiest person to talk to. Just wait until you see Nicola, or Jim, or Terri." She paused. "Or Dawn, or Hannah, or Yasmin for that matter. Seriously, Lucas, nobody on this planet is fighting your corner. Just give it up and fuck off."

I stared at her but didn't speak, because what could I say?

"Poor Maya," she continued and her stare was fierce. "I heard plenty about her at the girls' night on Friday. Great job you did fucking her over too. People were plenty keen to talk about how shitty she's had it. Just a shame Anna bailed before she could hear it." She shook her head and picked up her cereal. "Please, Lucas, just fuck off, will you? Fuck off and leave Anna alone. She's got a decent guy to get back to. What have you got to offer her? A few better orgasms? Big fucking whoop."

"I love Anna," I told her. "I've always loved Anna. I'll be giving her everything I can. I'd do anything to make up for what I did to her."

"Yeah, yeah," she said and her hand gave me the chatter gesture. "Like I said, no point in trying to convince anyone. It'll never happen. You're just a fucking prick."

It struck me right there in that moment, looking over at her and the way she despised me, just how far people's opinion of me was well beyond repair. There was no way Vicky Mason would ever look at me with anything other than a hiss of *fuck you*, and she was right – she really would be the easiest person in the crowd to seek forgiveness from. I didn't stand the slightest hope with anyone else.

I'd been planning to be a lot further along in the Vicky interaction by the time Anna came out of her bedroom, but no. She was at my side and wide-eyed before I'd even registered she was awake, staring from me to her friend across the kitchen then back again.

Vicky pointed at me as she first addressed Anna. "What the hell is he doing here? Nicola would've gone ballistic if she'd stayed over. And she nearly did. She was talking about watching the latest Apprentice episode and ordering pizza last night!"

The way Anna's mouth dropped open said it all. The very prospect of Nicola Henshaw being face to face with me in this place was enough that she paled.

"Seriously," Vicky continued. "Have you both gone crazy or something? Aren't you even giving a toss for the utter shit fest that's occurring right now? I thought you'd be at least trying to stop it, Lucas. You must be an even bigger prick than everyone thinks. Congratulations, that's quite an achievement."

I narrowed my eyes, having no idea what she was talking about, and seemingly neither did Anna. She piped up before I did.

"What do you mean, utter shit fest that's occurring now? We went out to Oscars last night, no biggie."

"You are joking, right?" Vicky asked.

Anna shook her head. "Uh, no. I've been pretty much avoiding everyone since girls' night. What are you on about?"

Vicky cursed under her breath before she answered. "Dawn was saying that Maya really does know you're back together now and is planning to run from all of it. She wants to move the fuck away from the mess and take his daughter with her."

The words were out of my mouth in a flash. "She wants to take Millie? What the fuck are you talking about? Dawn Richards was saying that?"

Vicky nodded. "Yeah. Dawn was telling everyone about just how much of a prick you were to Maya when we were all at girls' night on Friday, I mean she's her bestie, right? But then when Anna didn't answer the *what's going on between you and Lucas* question and downed that stupid bloody glass of wine it was obvious that things were a whole load more serious than some weekend fucking. Because that's what people were hoping it was… just some weekend fucking… and even that was bad enough…"

"But what the hell?" Anna said. "What's that got to do with anything today?"

Vicky actually looked uncomfortable, even though she hated my guts. "Dawn was pinging us all yesterday saying that Maya was upset. She said Maya wasn't going to have Millie seeing any of this shit, or seeing her daddy fucking some other woman, and she'd rather it was just them setting up together on new turf than having to talk Millie through this bullshit." She paused. "She's already been looking at properties over in Hampshire by her parents, or so Dawn says. Hannah says so too. They were pinging about it yesterday."

That was too specific to be made up, and I felt myself paling too.

"Let me get this straight," I said. "Dawn Richards was saying that Maya is upset I'm back with Anna and is looking at properties in Hampshire?"

"Yeah," Vicky said, as though it was obvious. "She said Maya's already planning an extended stay down there from this afternoon. She was helping her pack yesterday. She sent the group chat some photos of them in the garden over there... I mean, I guessed you knew..."

Holy fucking shit, I had no idea. I didn't even know where to start with the thoughts that tumbled.

Anna was staring up at me with a horrified expression to match mine, and my heart pounded as the full implication hit me.

If Maya was taking Millie down to Hampshire there was nothing I could do to hold her back. Not in the short term. She could drive on down and stay with her parents for as long as it suited her, and I could picture it being a damn long time. However long it took to get what she wanted from me.

No.

I couldn't lose Millie like that.

But I *could*. I *could* lose Millie like that. Maya could be getting in the car right there and then as far as I knew, and I should have known it. I should have seen it coming. I could picture her so clearly, bitching along with Dawn while she packed, revelling in just how much losing Millie would destroy me. Because that's what she'd do if she was hurting. She'd try to hurt me back harder.

I didn't know what to do, just stood there mortified as Anna squeezed my arm and shoved me towards the kitchen door.

"Go," she said. "Seriously, Lucas, just go. You have to. You have to get to her before she leaves!"

"Get back to her and stay if you have any sense!" Vicky snapped, but this time Anna snapped back.

"Stop!" she hissed across the kitchen. "Just stop a second. You don't even know what the true situation is. Nobody does. *I* didn't!" She turned back to me, and this time she pushed me harder towards the front door. "Go," she said. "Please, Lucas, you have to get there before she leaves. Please, just go!"

So I did.

I grabbed my shoes and my tie and forced myself into some kind of order. I gave her one quick kiss and a squeeze, and then I was out of there, piling out onto the street and launching myself across town to Broad Street car park as fast as I could go. I daren't have tried to message Maya ahead, just pressed my foot as hard as I could on the accelerator and tore through the lanes.

I let out a hiss of relief to see her car was still on her driveway. I threw myself out of the truck and raced to the door, and my fists were pounding on the wood so hard it shook the frame. Maya peered her way around the living room curtain to check out who was knocking, like she'd ever need to check who the fuck would be busting their way inside as she got ready to steal Millie to Hampshire.

"Open the fucking door!" I shouted, cursing myself when I figured that Millie must be able to hear me. Maya scowled and shook her head before she moved away from the window, and I forced myself to shut right up until I heard her on the other side of the door. It rattled, then opened an inch, and there she was, but the door was held tight on a security chain. There was no way I could bust my way in without creating one hell of a commotion.

"Oh, you want to come over now, do you?" she spat. "Done enough fucking Anna Blackwell for one weekend, have you?"

"What the fuck has any of this got to do with who I'm fucking?" I hissed. "We've been separated for months. YOU were the one who left ME."

"BECAUSE I THOUGHT YOU'D COME RUNNING!" she screamed and her eyes were wild. "BECAUSE I THOUGHT YOU'D SORT YOUR FUCKING LIFE OUT AND COME RUNNING!"

Holy fuck, I stumbled backwards.

"You can't be serious," I challenged and stepped back closer. "You haven't loved me for years. You've hated the sight of me for years…"

And that's when I finally saw it in her eyes, the pain under the rage.

The pain under the disgust. The pain under everything I'd ever been to her.

The shock was savage.

The shock was spiteful.

The shock tore me into shreds with a whole fresh round of guilt.

"You've never loved me!" she snapped, but her voice was weaker than I'd ever known. "I've been trying to make you love me for years, but you never have. Nothing I ever did was good enough, not even having Millie. So I wanted to show you. I tried to show you. Over and over and fucking over. Always trying to be good enough, but it never worked! Because you never *believe*, Lucas! You never believe there's a bigger fate than the one you see in front of your smug face!"

My heart was beating a crazy tune, and the ground felt unsteady as it all came crashing in.

"Never believe in what bigger fucking fate, Maya? You *hated* me," I countered. "You've hated everything I've done for years. I was the one who was never good enough!"

"Yeah, well, maybe I was trying to convince myself," she hissed, and that pain was right there again.

And the reality took my breath.

Maybe she was trying to convince herself. Maybe she always had been.

Maybe the whole thing was one fucking endless pit of utter misery and carnage and nobody ever being fucking good enough.

But I'd married her.

I'd put that ring on her finger and promised to try.

I flinched as I heard Millie's voice sound out from the hallway behind Maya. She called for her mummy, then she called for me, and my gut jumped right up into my throat.

"I'm taking her to Hampshire," Maya hissed up close to the gap in the door. "Don't even think about trying to stop me. You're a fucking wreck, Lucas. Drinking and making a state of yourself and fucking someone else. I'm not having her seeing that. I'm taking her away now. You need to get your shit together if you want us to come back."

"You can't take her!" I hissed back. "This won't solve anything, Maya. It's just a bullshit excuse to punish me." I paused. "You think I'm not hurting? You think I haven't hurt as much as you have with every bitchy little dig that's come out of your mouth for years?"

Her eyes flashed with rage all over again. "You haven't hurt like I have, Lucas. And you haven't hurt like Millie has as she's watched her father give up on us without a fight."

No.

Fuck no, that wasn't true.

Millie hadn't watched me give up on her without a fight.

I didn't just let Maya walk away like it didn't fucking matter. It was a battle that cycled over and over and over, one vile circle of hate and spite and pain that helped nobody.

I slammed up into the front door until my face was up close to Maya's. "Don't take Millie away from me. Seriously, Maya. Don't you dare."

"Then don't you dare think about playing happily families with Anna fucking Blackwell, Lucas. Make your choice. You get back with us, or we're staying away. You can decide while we're gone, but we're going this afternoon." She paused. "Millie already knows we're going, she's excited to see everyone back in Hampshire. Don't make this any harder on her than it has to be."

"Daddyyyy." Millie called again from inside, and it took my breath.

"I mean it," Maya said. "Don't make this hard on her. You decide what you want while we're gone, but we're going today."

She slammed the door back shut before I could say any more and I didn't know what the fuck to do. I pressed my forehead to the wood and knocked again but she didn't answer. I wanted to pound the door so hard it tore from its hinges, but I couldn't, not with Millie knowing it was me out there.

I heard her voice calling my name again from inside, and heard Maya shout something that sounded harsh. I pressed my ear tighter to the wood, close enough to hear the race of footsteps thumping up the stairs.

My eyes were already up at Millie's bedroom window when I stepped back from the porch, and that's where she appeared. Her favourite teddy bear was pinched tight under her arm as her hands pressed up at the glass, and she looked so sad and confused and scared that it tore me in two.

Please, no. Please God, anything but take Millie away.

I felt the sob catch in my chest as Maya appeared in the window behind our little girl. She tugged her away from the glass, but Millie's eyes were still on me all the way.

I was still staring up at the empty space, breaths ragged in my chest when my phone vibrated in my pocket. My hands were shaking as I pulled it out and called up the message.

Maya.

Us or that slut, Lucas. You decide!

But I couldn't decide.

How the fuck could I ever make that choice? How the hell could I ever face walking away from Anna all over again for someone I didn't love?

I couldn't.

But how the fuck could I put Millie through months of pain while I fought over her future with someone who'd never let me be happy?

I couldn't.

Jesus Christ, I couldn't.

For the first time in years I felt so torn apart that I retched my guts up all over the grass out by my truck. It was like reeling from that pregnancy test in Maya's hand all over again with no sign of a way out.

I didn't know what to do, so I went back up to the door and dropped down onto the front step. And I waited. I didn't pound and I didn't shout. I didn't do anything but sit there on that doorstep to stop her from driving away.

Stalemate.

It was stalemate.

She texted again after hours of sitting in silence.

Fuck off, Lucas. I'll just wait however long it takes until you leave.

We'll still be going to Hampshire.

Don't take Millie to Hampshire, I texted back, and her response came back within seconds.

Us or her, Lucas. You decide. We're going to Hampshire.

It was getting dark by the time I finally got to my feet and walked back down that garden path. My stomach was still twisting and my puke was still at the side of the truck, and the nausea was churning hard all over again.

And I needed someone. I needed someone to confess my mistakes to, and help me make sense of this madness, just like I had done back then with those two stripes on the pregnancy test.

Only this time it was different. This time it wasn't my mother.

This time it was Anna.

Just like it should have been in the first place.

Chapter Twenty-Nine

ANNA

The night was cold and dark as I waited for Lucas at the end of my street. My legs felt weak and my heart felt broken all over again, even though it was still waiting to tear in two.

Still, all of that paled into nothing once his truck pulled up alongside me and I slipped into the passenger seat.

Lucas was destroyed.

His knee was tapping nervous as he drove, and even in the flash of the street lighting through the window he looked ashen. Ashen and broken. His eyes were sunken and his lip was a tight line, like he was trying to hold himself back from teetering over the edge.

But I guess that's what you look like when your little girl is being torn away from you right across the country.

And I'd done this.

I'd done this with one random text message on one random Sunday morning. One random Sunday morning that may be costing him his daughter, and his family, and any shot at making this right again.

I waited for him to speak with my heart in my throat, because I just didn't know what to say. We were both silent, the tension heavy enough to slice, and the roads turned to lanes, and those lanes started climbing, and we were up on the hilltop when he pulled into an off road parking spot and turned off the ignition.

I felt physically sick at what was coming.

"I can't face going home," he said to me, and his voice was thick. "Beth and Wes left the dogs earlier, and I need to get back there tonight, but I can't face it. Not yet."

I waited for him to carry on.

"She's taking her," he said. "I tried talking to her, and I tried waiting, but it wouldn't matter how long I stayed there, she'd just pack her off in the car as soon as I left."

"So, she's gone?" I asked. "She's really taken her to Hampshire?"

He nodded. "I got a voicemail from my mother before I got to yours. She was screaming that Millie's on her way down there."

My own voice sounded so raw when I spoke again. "What happens now? Can you follow her down there? Can you ask her again to come back?"

He lit up a cigarette and put the window down before he answered. "She won't come back until I do what she wants me to."

I pulled a cigarette out of my own before I found the strength to ask the next question. "And what does she want you to do?"

I knew the answer before it came, but it still punched me in the heart.

"She wants me to choose, them or you."

I managed a nod, but that was all. It took me a while to speak, and he was silent too. Both of us staring ahead at the lights of Lydney burning oblivious down below, taking deep drags of our cigarettes as we battled with the words.

I forced down the tears as I summoned my final statement.

"Then we're done," I said, "and it's okay. It's okay."

He spun in his seat in a flash, shoulders hard in a way I didn't expect.

"What do you mean we're done?"

I was glad the night was dark outside so he didn't see how my eyes were filling. "I mean we have to be, Lucas. She's your little girl, and you can't risk it. And I get that, and it's okay. We survived losing each other last time, right? We can do it again."

He was shaking his head as I spoke. "No, Anna. That's not it. We can't be done." He stubbed his cigarette out. "There has to be another way out of this. Maybe I can talk to her. Maybe over time she'll be able to accept that we'll never work, me and her. I mean, she's hurting right now, and I didn't see that, and I should've seen that, and I should've seen so many fucking things and I didn't. But it doesn't matter." His eyes were hard on mine, even in the dark. "There's got to be another way. There has to be a way we can make it through this. I mean, people have to come around to us, at some point they have to accept we're together. Even Maya. Even your parents. Even Nicola fucking Henshaw. Right?"

I was shaking my head as the tears fell. Because there was no way out of this. There never would be.

"They have to!" he insisted. "Jesus, Anna, at some point they have to!"

But they wouldn't. I forced my breath to stay steady as I found the words.

I told him how I'd spent the rest of the morning trying to tell Vicky the real, full story of just how and why he'd left me all those years ago. I told him how she'd scoffed at me and told me I was an idiot for believing the bullshit. I told him how I'd called Nicola over after and tried again with her and Vicky in the same room and got the same response.

They didn't believe him, and they shook their heads at the fact that I had, and they didn't believe anything other than he was a prick and us being together was one massive pool of shit I was wading around in.

I told him how Yasmin had come out to join me at girls' night and was the only one with another opinion in the chaos, but even that didn't matter to my friends. I'd asked Nicola and Vicky to go check with her that what Lucas had told me was true, but they brushed it aside as nothing and said she was already back up in Newcastle and barely in contact. Another great help from the universe.

I told him how the whole world was against us, and people would never buy into us being together, and that was obvious. Especially not the woman screaming for him to choose his future, me or them, and taking his little girl across country.

"Maybe Yasmin will be able to help us convince people, if she knows the truth," he said, but I shook my head.

"That isn't what I meant. What I meant is, it doesn't matter that she does. It will never matter. Even if she screamed from the rooftops that Maya was a total bitch who deserved you coming back to me, they'd still be cursing and scowling and saying I'm an idiot and you need to get back to your little girl."

"Stop it," he said, but I couldn't. I wouldn't.

"We'll never make it," I told him. "Seriously, Lucas. You can't let her take Millie across the country. Whatever it takes. You have to make it right for Millie."

"But I can't!" he said, and his hands were right over on mine. "I can't walk away from this, Anna. Not again. I can't make that fucking choice!"

We sat in silence, because what could we say?

Maya and Millie were likely already holed up at her parents' place, and I hadn't even attempted to reason with my parents yet. Everyone was still determined I should get back with the man who'd pulled me up from the floor last time around, nursing me through nights of pissing in the bed and blanking out in random places and dropping down exhausted for hours. And even though my seizures weren't down to Lucas, that would never be accepted by the people who'd helped me through them in those early days.

I'd been having seizures before he made his idiot mistake, and I'd been the one to let myself wallow, and cry, and work every hour of the day or night just to try to forget he existed. But it didn't matter. They'd still be cursing him for plunging my brain into one long ping pong of misfiring.

But even that faded to insignificance with the other coal of doom burning in the fire.

Millie.

It was all about Millie.

He had a little girl who needed him to be there for her, whatever the cost, and she had to come first, no matter how much we wanted each other.

"You have to get to your daughter," I said, and saw him flinch in his seat. "You know it as well as I do. You have to get to her."

"There will be a way," he replied. "I mean, Maya can't keep her away from me without legitimate reason. Not in the long-term."

"But she'll try," I said. "She'll use anything she can, and it'll take months, and battles, and court, and so much time without her before you get it fixed."

He gripped the steering wheel and cursed, and I reached out to squeeze his hand.

"I can't choose," he said. "I can't walk away from Millie, and I never would, but I can't walk away from you either. Not again."

"So what are you going to do?" I asked him. "Threaten Maya with legal action if she doesn't come back? Split your time between Cheltenham and Hampshire? Do you really want it to get that aggressive between you?"

He didn't answer, because he didn't have an answer to give me. I forced my hand away from his and forced my breath into line, and then I straightened up.

"You need to think," I said. "You need to drop me back at home, and then you need to think."

He was shaking his head when I spoke. "No. Don't walk away. Please don't leave."

But I was shaking mine right back. "This isn't leaving," I said. "The last thing I want is to leave, but you'll never make a way through this while I'm sitting beside you. It's too clouded."

He slammed his hands on the steering wheel three times over. "This can't! Be fucking! Happening!"

Oh, but it could.

It most definitely could.

"Take me home," I said again. "Please, Lucas. You have to be objective in this, and that's never going to happen here."

My whole body was crying out to hold him tight and go back to his with him. I wanted to greet Bill and Ted, and lose myself in his beautiful filth, climb into bed in his arms, and count on the world outside coming around to us by some miracle, but it wouldn't. Seeing Nicola and Vicky scoffing at the idea of Lucas making one night's mistake and trying to be there for an unborn baby was more than enough to show me acceptance was nowhere near in sight. And that was without even beginning to comprehend how far Maya could hold Millie to ransom.

I said it again. "Take me home. Take me home and think."

Finally, he relented.

He started up the truck and headed down from the hillside. My stomach was fluttering with butterfly sick all the way back into town, and my heart was a wreck as we pulled up in my street.

He grabbed my arm as I opened the passenger door, and his eyes were full of so much hurt it took my breath.

"Don't leave me, Anna. I can't make that choice, and I won't. I'll figure something out. *We'll* figure something out together."

I nodded, and tried to smile, but it was empty.

"I love you," I said, and my voice hitched. "You know I love you, but you need to get Millie back and you know that too."

I left the truck before he could say anything more, and I didn't look back at him, just put my key in the lock and headed on in.

Vicky was in the living room as I walked on through, and she tried to talk to me, but I couldn't speak, just headed on through to my bedroom. She knocked at the door and asked to come in, but I told her I needed my space. I forced my meds down and wiped my tears away in my dressing table mirror and wondered how the hell I was going to make it through work the next day.

I'd have to try.

I waited until I was pretty certain Vicky had gone to bed before I showered. There were messages from Lucas and missed calls when I came back to my bedroom, but I didn't click to read them, because I couldn't. He needed his time, even if he didn't want it.

Sleep was hard.

Tossing and turning, and churning with nausea. I don't know what time I managed to drift into some semblance of rest, but it didn't do me any good.

My sheets were wet when I woke up, thighs drenched and tongue sore with how much I'd been chewing. I cried a fresh sob and stripped my bed, casting off horrible wet knickers and waiting, sitting in my own piss until the sound of Vicky's shower eased off through the wall.

And then somehow I got myself ready for work.

I tried to take part in my morning meetings, knowing full well my eyes must be nothing short of shadows underneath. I tried to smile and joke about just how great Oscars was with Lucia and Stacey and Melissa, and it stabbed me in the heart all over again – hearing how happy they'd been to meet him. A spiteful tease from fate at just how good life could be between us if we made it through.

I was waiting to talk with the Kershaw's project manager when I had to revisit the fun chatter all over again with Peter and Jamie from finance, and I was on the edge of breaking all over again. I was feeling my dreams crumbling a second time around and praying for a miracle when I got a summoning call through from Lucia back on reception.

I had a visitor.

My heart raced, wondering, just wondering, if it was Lucas coming to tell me he'd found a way through hell, but I should have known.

I should have known there was no way Lucia would have said anything more than 'your dance buddy is here and waiting', or 'here your hot guy comes' if it had been Lucas out there.

I should have known it was some more shit on top of the rest to face on a Monday morning.

But I'd never have known it was Margaret Pierce standing there in reception waiting for me, the first time I'd seen his mother in a decade.

I'd never have known her cheeks were lined with tears, and that she'd take my hands in hers and beg me to let Lucas go back to Maya.

Her brown hair was clearly dyed now and tied up in a bun, and she looked thinner and older, but she was still her as she called up a string of beautiful pictures of a smiling happy family and shoved them in my face.

Lucas smiling at Maya with their baby girl in his arms, and Maya glowing happy in her wedding dress.

A video of Lucas and Maya singing happy birthday to Millie over a dinner table and both of them holding her tight when the candles went out.

"Please, Anna," she said, and her eyes were so raw on mine I felt the sick bubbling in my throat. "Please, don't do this. Maya's a lovely woman who wants to try her best, and she's always loved him, and always will, he's just made it so hard for her to show it."

I couldn't speak, so she carried on.

"If you love him, then love his daughter too. Please don't make him choose. Please don't."

And that's when I knew it.

That's when I knew the answer.

The choice wasn't his to make, the choice was mine.

It stabbed.

Oh fuck, how it stabbed.

But it was there. And it was real. The answer staring me in the face through the shit storm, while we were still choking and trying to breathe in some semblance of an answer from the clouds.

This time around it wouldn't be Lucas walking away, it would be me.

But this time I'd be doing it for him.

Him and his little girl.

Chapter Thirty

LUCAS

I burst through the door at my mother's house and I didn't give a shit about how fucking fierce I looked. I was straight through to the living room where she was sitting in her armchair staring over at some mindless bullshit on the TV, and I closed the fucking distance like a fucking bull at a red rag.

I nearly threw the TV remote across to bust through the screen, but managed to hold my temper back enough to press the power off and toss it back onto the side table, and then I asked her the question. Yelled it out with a voice racked with pain, and rage, and pure fucking panic.

"WHAT THE FUCK DID YOU DO THAT FOR?!"

Her eyes were a mirror of fierce on mine, lips pursed as she glared back at me.

"Because somebody had to see sense, Lucas. Somebody had to see sense and solve this ridiculous situation!"

I leaned into the chair, my hands on the arms, and she pressed herself back into the cushions, with her eyes opening wider.

I hadn't been this close to her in years.

"IT WAS NONE OF YOUR FUCKING BUSINESS, MOTHER! IT NEVER HAS BEEN!"

It was then that she flipped back with her authority. She pushed me backwards and jabbed a finger straight at my face.

"It's always been my *fucking* business, Lucas. Millie is my *fucking* granddaughter, and it's *you* who's being a selfish idiot enough to watch Maya taking her away!"

"Selfish?!" I barked. "What's selfish about wanting to be with Anna? Maya was the one who walked away from *me*!"

"Because you were a selfish idiot to *her*! Right the way through your marriage, Lucas! She's had *years* of your selfish bullshit! *Years*!"

I stepped away from her and caught my breath, and there was that flash of guilt again in my gut. The whole world was spinning, reeling, driving me fucking insane, and there was still no way through. No fucking way at all.

My hands were in my hair.

My lip was pinned between my teeth.

My heart was thumping.

Mother used my silence to carry on speaking.

"Maya's a lovely woman," she said. "Loving and genuine and honest. She's always done her best with you, right from the beginning when you got her pregnant in one stupid night's mistake. She committed everything to you! But you don't, do you? You never make her feel like she's worth anything, least of all the mother of your child. The least you can do is commit to her right back. Just like she deserves, Lucas!"

Another pang of guilt hit hard, but there was more. A whole ocean of churned feelings battling deep.

My words came out in a hiss.

"I *did* commit to her right back. And I *did* always do my best with her, right from the beginning when I got her pregnant in my one stupid night's mistake. Why does that make her so much better than me?! *I* was the one who gave up my whole fucking world for one stupid fucking mistake! ONE STUPID FUCKING MISTAKE!"

"You gave up your *whole fucking world* to start a new one!" she hissed back. "To start a new one with a woman who loved you!"

"ANNA LOVED ME!"

She stood up from her chair and the finger jab was even stronger. "YOU DIDN'T GET ANNA PREGNANT THOUGH, DID YOU?!"

The atmosphere was toxic, both of us desperate and pained. Mother swallowed, and I saw the fear and the hurt in her eyes staring right back at me.

And I felt it. It was right there in me too.

"Millie needs to come back to us," she said. "Whatever the cost, Lucas, Millie needs to come back to us!"

I couldn't argue with that, so I didn't try, just stared at a picture of my beautiful little girl hanging above the TV, with her sweet little smile grinning bright as she held up a handful of daisies she'd picked from the garden. I wanted my daughter back enough that I'd have bled for her, but it wasn't fair. Surely it couldn't be fair to lose Anna. None of this could be fair for Anna and I to lose each other all over again.

"You are going to try again with Maya, aren't you? You are going to get your family back together and get Millie back here?"

And the pang of guilt in me said that I should. Just like it always had done, right from the beginning. It said that I'd misread everything about Maya and how she felt about me. That maybe all the spite and disgust and criticism she'd dished out to me over the years was because I didn't love her enough and never had. And maybe I should've seen it. I saw it as her not giving any more of a shit for me than I gave about her and being trapped for the sake of Millie, but maybe I was wrong.

Maybe I was every bit the cunt everyone believed me to be.

But even though the pang of guilt in me said that I was a cunt who should have seen things better and tried harder, it couldn't alter a thing.

Because I didn't love Maya.

I'd never loved Maya. I'd just been trying to create one sliver of good from a mistake so fucking bad, and it had never made any difference.

I loved Anna. I'd always loved Anna. I'd do anything to have her back.

But Mother had taken her from me with one disgustingly fronted office visit. Just like she'd been so keen to take her from me the first time around with her spouted advice.

She was still pointing the finger as she summoned up her next words.

"You'll thank me for this one day," she said. "Believe me, you'll thank me for this!"

My eyes were on fire as I stepped back up close. Her jabbing finger trembled when she saw how serious I was in my rage.

My words were a simmer of pure fucking venom.

"Believe me, I'll *never* fucking thank you for this, Mother. Stay out of my fucking life if you can't respect it."

I didn't bother saying goodbye, just stormed out of there and slammed the door closed behind me.

I lit up a cigarette before I was even clear of her driveway, heart still pounding hard as I drove out onto the Lydney back lanes and called Anna's number all over again.

Yet again it went to voicemail.

Yet again I begged her to answer me.

But she wouldn't.

Of course she wouldn't.

Anna was always sure of her own mind – it was one of the things I loved most about her. How fucking typical that it was now the main thing about her that would cost me her love.

There was no doubt about it – Anna's mind had told her loud and fucking clear, thanks to my mother, that I needed to be with my daughter, whatever the cost.

I called her again. It went to voicemail again.

I left another message and sent another text. But nothing.

She'd delivered her decision to leave me in a short, sharp, cold little phone call she'd been hiding back so much in, and it was pitiful, but I knew why.

I knew there was no way she'd have been able to tell me in person without both of us breaking from the pain.

I thought about driving round to her place and seeing her in person, because I knew it would be so much harder for her to stay fixed on her decision in the flesh. But she'd never answer the door. And neither would Vicky Mason, no matter how much I begged her to. Hell only knows what the fuck Nicola Henshaw would do if she was the one to answer.

I nearly leapt out of my skin when a text finally sounded through, fingers shaking around my latest cigarette when I saw it was from Anna.

Please God. Please fucking God, give me a chance.

But no.

I'm doing this for you. And I'm doing this for your daughter. Please don't make this harder than it is for me. I won't be changing my mind.

I tried to reply. I really did.

I managed to get a *we're supposed to be together, Anna, we've always been supposed to be together* message over to her and was typing out another when her next came through.

Maybe we will be together in another lifetime, she said, with a kiss, and then she sent a last little *goodbye.*

That was it. A goodbye.

I was typing another message as quickly as I could, begging her to listen to me and give me a chance to work this out, but when I tried to send it my number was blocked. I couldn't send a text and the number no longer went to voicemail when I called her. It went to a dead line.

My forehead was against my steering wheel and my breaths were nothing short of retches when another ping sounded out. It took me a few minutes to get my senses together enough to look at the text, and when I did it made me retch a whole load harder.

Nerves, and guilt, and regret, and fear.

And relief.

And pain.

So much fucking pain.

The message was from Maya, and it should have been everything I wanted.

We're coming home tomorrow, it said. *You can come and see Millie. We need to talk.*

But even now I slammed my forehead right back on the steering wheel as my guts bubbled higher.

Seeing Millie would be heaven. Talking to Maya would be hell.

Even if I did want to talk to her. Even if meeting up with Maya was something that made perfect sense on some *fated plane* out to kick me in the ribs at the cost of love, just what the holy fuck was I going to say to her?

Where the holy fuck could we ever – fucking ever – manage to go from here?

My heart was with Anna.

It would always be with Anna.

Chapter Thirty-One

ANNA

The days were long, and the days were shit, and work didn't cut it this time. Not for the distraction it needed to be.

I was quiet, keeping away from the friends who were determined to reach out and big me up about how *wise* I was being, putting pressure on top of pressure to give my *real life* another shot.

My parents were calling constantly, asking me to go over to dinner with Seb at their dining table. Nicola was inviting me out every evening for some *girl time.* Vicky was wanting to watch reality TV with me and bitch about the contestants.

I wanted none of it.

I wanted Lucas.

There was only one social that I couldn't shy away from, and that was Amy Miller's wedding.

I gave it everything I possibly could to enjoy the amazing experience of a friend I'd known for years, but it was impossible. Truly, it was impossible.

My heart was shattered into pieces right the way through.

The pride of her father walking her down the aisle to meet the man she loved. The way he was so proud of the life she was walking into.

The glow on her face as she stared up at her fiancé, knowing they were crossing that beautiful threshold into something more.

The nerves as she took the ring on her finger and how he was helping her keep her hand steady, squeezing tight.

The cute little bridesmaids holding their posies and giggling as they twirled around to see their skirts flow.

Fantastic.

Another big thank you to the universe for helping me feel so damn *great*.

I was sitting at a table at the reception party, once again fully ingrained amongst the usual crowd toasting my *great decision*, except it wasn't great, was it? It was necessary. Necessary and cruel and shit.

I was struggling to clap along to the speeches Amy's parents and their best friends were giving to the crowd – feeling sick at just how much support couples got for their love when the people surrounding them gave a thumbs-up.

I was struggling to keep a face on my hurt, smiling a fake smile while Amy and Dan took their first dance for the guests – when all I was thinking about was spinning in Lucas's arms in Oscars, dancing like the night would never end.

I was struggling not to bail out and shut myself away in the venue toilets to sob the makeup off my face. It would have been so easy, but so unfair too. Unfair to draw any attention to me on someone else's special day.

I guess that's why I was smoking. Smoking and drinking champagne. Smoking and avoiding every scrap of conversation that could stab me further in the gut.

I was still getting the scowls, and the shakes of the head, and everyone telling me how terrible it was for my meds, but it was the least of my concerns. Getting through the day was all that mattered, and staying outside as long as possible to soak up the nicotine was the best chance it had of happening.

That's where Yasmin Boyle found me – just like the last time round. She stepped outside to the smoking area just as I was lighting up one of mine, and there was that strange look on her face as she stepped up close. Just like I'd seen outside Nicola's girls' night shenanigans.

"I heard you let Lucas go back to Maya," she said.

I shrugged, champagne blunt. "I didn't have much choice. He needed his daughter and she needed him."

She shrugged right back. "I heard she stole her down to Hampshire and didn't give either of you a fair choice. Selfish cow."

"Yeah, well, it's done now," I said, and took a long drag. "He's probably back at home with her trying again. Whatever. She wants him, he's her husband. They have a decade together behind them to make it work and he owes her more than he'll ever owe me."

Yasmin let out a sneer at that. "If only you knew. She owes both of you more than anything, believe me."

But I didn't want to believe her and I didn't want to know, because what was the point? Even the thought of listening to what she was blatantly eager to tell me was stabbing me harder in the ribs that I could manage. I was dithering on the spot, hating life for all it was worth, and it didn't matter. Nothing Yasmin said to me could matter.

Maya had stated her case, and it didn't matter who she was or what she did, there was no way I'd go back on my decision now. Even if I wanted to run to Lucas over burning coals with open arms, I couldn't do it. I couldn't bear to stir up a whole fresh load of carnage, because he was back at home now. Back at home with his family.

I would never be his family again.

So I didn't hear her out. I said it was nice to see her and stubbed my cigarette in the bin and walked away. I went back into the venue, where everyone was dancing, and I watched the world having a good time with a fresh fake smile on my face for as long as I could stand it.

And then I left.

I bailed out of there and called a taxi back into town and I jumped out at the Neptune fountain. I let out all the tears I'd been banking up as I tossed a whole handful of coins into the water from the bottom of my handbag, and then I made my wish.

I made the same wish I made a decade ago, with the same tracks of tears down my cheeks and the same broken throb in my stomach.

I wish that I could forget about Lucas Pierce for the rest of my life.

But even Neptune would never be that strong.

He hadn't been that fucking strong last time around.

Nicola and Vicky stumbled into the apartment late that night, long after I'd bailed from the wedding. I heard them singing party songs and clattering around in the kitchen, and then I heard the inevitable rap of knuckles on my bedroom door.

I couldn't answer. Couldn't face it. I pulled the covers up and hid my face in the warmth and prayed they'd fuck off and leave me in my own pit of misery.

"Anna... Anna are you awake? Where did you go?" Nicola's slurred voice sounded out.

Like they didn't know where I'd have gone, and like they didn't know why.

"You know it's only cos we care, right?" Vicky called. "We care about you! That's why we're so bothered! Lucas Pierce is a cunt, and we're saving you! Believe us! We're trying to save you!"

"We love youuuu!" Nicola sounded out again.

"Come and talk to us!" Vicky said. "We spoke to Yasmin, you know... and we get it more now, and we'll talk. We promise we'll talk!"

"Yeah, come on," Nicola tried. "Do you wanna hear? I mean, you must wanna talk about Lucas, right? And he's a cunt, but we know you're sad, and we know you love him, and we care!"

I knew it was right. I knew it was true they cared. I knew everyone had nothing but my best intentions at heart when they were cursing and damning and calling for destruction, but it didn't matter. It couldn't matter.

My heart was broken. And my heart was failing.

The worst I could do now was talk about Lucas a whole load more, and chat about Yasmin, and Maya and what a bitch she was, and dredge up a whole new whirlwind of shit with people who wouldn't get it, no matter what.

I ignored the girls, and tried another shot at sinking into sleep, but it was another shit attempt at normality to add to the failure pile.

I felt so torn up and so lonely I felt sick. I was barely sleeping, and the seizures were coming back, and I didn't want to eat a bite.

I was missing Lucas so much it felt like round one all over again, and I guess that's why round one started repeating.

I guess that's why I felt like I needed someone to hold me tight and tell me it was all going to be ok.

I had nothing but the barrage of people telling me what they thought I needed, and nothing but the pain in my chest telling me I'd never have what I wanted, and it was blurring into one long, fucked up, miserable string of days that were going nowhere.

I pictured Lucas happy with his wife and little girl – just like his mother's pictures had shown me.

I pictured his mother grinning happy now he was back in his *real life*.

I pictured Lucas and Maya renewing their vows, and making it work this time, and making another little brother or sister for the treasure they'd created already.

And I couldn't stand it.

Not anymore.

I couldn't stand everyone on loudspeaker telling me just how much I should be back in *my* real life, to match his. I couldn't keep fighting it, because I wanted to believe it too, just to believe in something.

So when that regular text message came through on that regular

Monday morning, a few weeks after I'd been trying to do it all by my myself – through blanking out useless with my seizures in the meeting rooms at work, to waking up in pools of my own piss and tears, and the epilepsy nurses trying to insist I put my medication levels up all over again – I did it.

Have you come to your fucking senses yet?

I stared at the text message for three hours straight until I sent my reply to the man who'd picked me up from this pain last time around.

I was scared, and alone, and felt like maybe I was insane after all – just like everyone was so keen to convince me I was – and I sent that reply with shaking fingers.

One simple word in one simple moment at breaking point.

Yes.

I sent the *yes* I'd been avoiding for months.

And so he came back for me.

My *real life* in Sebastian Maitland came back for me, and the whole fucking world was cheering for it, waving their party banners and thanking the heavens.

If only I could too.

Chapter Thirty-Two

LUCAS

"Hey, Daddy, look what I drew for you," Millie's face was a beautiful smile, so innocent in her happiness as she held up her drawing for me to see. "It's us! You, me and Mummy!"

Three scribbled people, one in a dress, and one in a scribble tie, and one grinning little girl in between them.

I'd have given anything for it to work and be as picture perfect as she wanted it to be, but it never would. Never could.

"Let's have a look, sweetheart," Maya said and called Millie around the table, and I had to look away, across the kid's group Saturday art session to the other grinning families and feeling that same crushing pain in my gut all over again.

Failure.

Failure to be what I needed to be.

It was Maya's condition on coming back to Cheltenham – that I could see Millie, but only with all three of us together as one group, showing her just how great we were together as *Mummy and Daddy*. I was taking any opportunity, because I needed it. I needed my little girl.

I also didn't deserve any better treatment. I'd been enough of a prick to Maya for a lifetime already – so Mother had been so keen to tell me. *Poor Maya being so bound by life at your side, knowing you never wanted her from the beginning. Terrible, so terrible.*

Seemingly the rest of the world was certain this was life at its finest anyway, pushing us back into regular contact, regardless of what I was feeling. I was choking back my pain at Mother's dining table over far too many evenings to feel comfortable while she smiled smug over at Maya and Millie, shooting me knowing glances like she *told me so*.

I was keeping my schedule open to make the most of the potential time with Millie, but I wasn't doing any more.

Whenever Maya pushed me to stay on past Millie's bedtime to *talk* or *spend time together* I'd politely decline, and keep my message clear and true.

I'm here for Millie, but not for us.

There will never be an us, Maya. I'm sorry, but there will never be an us.

I'll do anything I can for Millie, but I can't do anything more for me and you.

She would shrug and pull faces, and cast me aside like I was still the selfish prick she was fighting against, but it didn't matter. I couldn't be anything else to her anymore. I'd be lying if I tried.

In my head I was still churning through potential miracle solutions on loop, but it was getting nowhere. Anna's phone still had me on block, and I couldn't see her listed on any other channels of communication, even though I looked.

Oh fuck, how I looked.

I was barely sleeping around seeing Millie. The dogs were getting their usual walks, but I was on autopilot, throwing balls and praising them like I was still fully engaged with the world, but even they knew the difference.

They'd stare at me from my feet at night, looking up at me with far more sympathy and care than I was getting from anywhere else in my life.

Work was doing fine, but I was back to the grey, bland version of me they'd come to know before I'd exploded in colour. I didn't give a shit for the projects I'd been throwing myself into with newfound zest, and I couldn't give a shit for socialising around work meetings.

It must have been desperation that meant I abused my position at GCHQ for the first time since I'd been employed there. I used the security surveillance potential to tune into Anna's communication channels and see when and how she was active.

It showed me nothing new. She was working long hours, and switching her phone onto standby for early nights, and at least that was a relief – that she was sleeping long hours, and taking care of her epilepsy and going about her regular life.

This grand *fate* that Maya and her friends were so keen to believe in was just a fucking cunt. Anna's regular life should have been with me.

I lost track of how many nights I'd been smiling fake at Mother's dining table, but I was taking our plates through to the dishwasher on one of them when she followed me through to the kitchen and closed the door.

"Well?" she asked, in a whisper-hiss. "When are you going to sort yourself out and make some actual progress? Millie needs to see you back with Maya. Maya needs it too." She paused, and I felt my stomach lurching. "And *you* need it, Lucas. Even if you are too *Anna Blackwell blind* to see sense, you need it too! Take some action, before it's too late!"

She was right on one score, at least. I was Anna Blackwell blind to the maximum. She had my heart, and my thoughts and my dreams snared in hers.

I tossed and turned in bed at night, craving her next to me. I was coasting through my waking life praying that some kind of crazy lightning bolt would strike and bring her back.

Losing her would be a nightmare I'd wake up from on loop, and she was everywhere. In everything. Lost from my whole fucking world.

I think I must have coasted for weeks on end, staring at the sky and hoping for a bizarre strike of fortune.

I must have shrugged myself into oblivion, buying into helplessness and accepting this bullshit outcome as the only one I was capable of living. But then it stopped.

I snapped myself back to reason one morning while sitting at the project meeting table at work.

I'd never once wished on fortune. Not once in my life had I ever dug into my pocket and tossed a coin into Neptune's fountain along with Anna.

My outlook was simple, and it was strong.

The universe isn't responsible for my road ahead. I am.

It was true.

I was responsible for my road ahead, and I was responsible for seizing my own destiny.

And so I would.

I wrapped up the project meeting ahead of schedule, standing up at the table to gather my notes and laptop while a host of confused faces stared over at me. I retreated to my office and got my coat, and checked straight out of the building with one eye on the time.

Lunchtime was busying in town when I closed the distance. I grabbed a bouquet of stunning red roses from the florist on the corner and headed across the final few streets with my heart pounding hard, because I had to do this. Fuck all the consequences and how I'd still need to find some miracle way ahead, I had to do this.

I kept my distance, holding back a little way from Lewton's Consultancy so as not to freak Anna the hell out just as soon as she stepped out through the front doors for lunch, but I was ready. My mouth was dry with nerves, and my whole body was humming with need, but I was ready.

I needed her.

I needed her to know that I needed her.

I needed her to know that she was my whole world and always would be, and this time I couldn't let her go.

But then I saw him.

Sebastian Maitland was crossing the street up ahead, dressed in his uber designer suit with his phone pressed up to his ear. I saw him head up to the Lewton's front doorway and heard him explode-laugh his snotty laugh at whatever pompous *associate* was on the other end of the line.

And then I saw her.

Anna.

Jesus Christ, I saw my beautiful Anna.

She came out of the front doors and she was smiling. Beautiful, and smiling, and enough to set my soul on fire.

That fire burnt me to nothing but dust.

She was smiling as she walked up to Sebastian like it was the most natural thing in the world, and she was smiling as she slipped her arm through his and they walked away up the street.

He was still on his phone, without giving a toss for even saying *hello* to the woman at his side, but that didn't seem to matter.

They were back together.

They were back together and she looked happy for it.

And I was done.

Reeling, and broken and done.

I handed the bouquet of roses to a sweet looking grandma on the way into the nearest shop, and I ran. I ran back towards GCHQ, not really sure quite where I was going until I ran out of breath down a side alley between two stores.

Once again, I was fucking retching my guts up as *fate* spat me out. I was sick and I was sobbing, and I was cursing everything I'd ever been and everything I'd ever done all over again.

But at least Anna was happy.

Thank God, she was happy.

And so was Millie.

So was my little girl.

That was all that really mattered. I deserved every fucking scrap of my pain, and I'd live it and take it, and stop fucking trying.

My own happiness was worthless anyway.

Chapter Thirty-Three

ANNA

It was one of his work social nights. Sebastian's.

I was sitting at our regular table, making the same regular small talk with the same regular group of other halves, twirling the engagement ring on my finger that was fresh on there for the past few days, ignoring my orange juice as the other women sipped away on their wine.

Bored.

I was so damn bored.

But it was more than that.

I scanned the club, our usual venue after the usual restaurant, the cycle swirling all over again, like it had done for years. My eyes glossed over the man who was supposed to be the love of my life as he stood in his usual pose, one elbow on the bar top, laughing along with his pompous work friends like their lives were the epitome of worldly success.

I should have been happy. Everyone had been trying to convince me I should be. Everyone telling me we were great, we were great, we were great. That Sebastian Maitland was the best future husband anyone could wish for. Attentive. Smart. Successful. Invested in our future.

My heart was a static flatline, even though I told myself it wasn't. I'd forgotten who I was – fading back into myself so hard after losing Lucas that I didn't recognise my own soul anymore.

I was trapped in my own glass box, with a fake smile and fake hopes and dreams.

But tonight I couldn't accept it. Tonight I couldn't accept that I was numb and lost and fading into the background.

I got up from my seat and made my way to the bar. I ignored Sebastian and his friends and ordered myself a prosecco and returned to the table to drink it.

The other women looked at me with horror on their faces, knowing I was breaking the rules of life by drinking alcohol on my meds, but I didn't care.

I didn't want to care anymore.

It was when Sebastian shot me a glance from his crowd, and he was glaring with that same horror and disgust as the rest of the party, that I knew I had to break away from it, even for just a few short minutes.

I finished my drink and made my excuses and headed out the back to slip amongst the rest of the smokers, and I sucked in that nicotine and tried to convince myself all over again that this was my life now, and it was good. It was great. It was everything.

Then, when I was done with my cigarette, I made my way back inside.

Sebastian was already waiting for me with my coat over his arm from the back of my chair. He would barely look at me as he told me we were leaving, and there was a taxi waiting for us outside.

We sat in silence on the way back to his, and my heart was in my throat, knowing full well that this was the final step in returning to our life together, and it was off to a terrible footing to match the terrible nerves.

I'd been stalling for days, telling him that we needed to find our feet together, and I was nervous and scared and wanted to take it slow – but this was it. The doorway to his was the final threshold, and we were about to cross it on terrible terms.

My fingers were twisting together in my lap, and I was desperate for him to speak to me, to say anything to make this feel better, because I wanted it to.

Please, God, I wanted it to.

We arrived outside his in a few short minutes. He paid the driver and headed up the front path, and I followed him.

He opened the front door, turned off the intruder alarm and hung his jacket up. He tossed the keys on the kitchen counter and I watched him. I watched him ignoring me with that same scowl on his face he'd had since I ordered the prosecco at the bar.

"Did you take your meds?" he asked.

"Yes," I said. "I took them before the club."

"No seizures?"

"None," I said.

"Well, that's a fucking blessing, isn't it? Considering you asked for one with your fucking drinking."

He poured me a glass of water, and slammed it on the counter. I sipped it as quickly as I could.

"Bed time," he said. "At least you can get *something* fucking right with your ill fucking brain."

I hadn't even taken my coat off, but he didn't notice, just stormed on by me and headed upstairs. My hands were shaking as I took off my heels and got ready to follow him. My legs felt bandy as I climbed the stairs, my heart still thumping as he finished brushing his teeth with the bathroom door open.

He jammed his toothbrush back in the holder and stomped across the landing to the bedroom, and I brushed my teeth with my hands still shaking, praying I could be the person I needed to be to make this work all over again.

He was still undressing when I joined him in the bedroom. He tossed his cufflinks down onto the dressing table and tugged his tie loose.

I watched him cast it on the floor.

"I'm sorry," I said. "I know you like me to be careful, and I know I shouldn't be drinking, but I like a prosecco now, just one every now and again. Just to loosen up a bit."

He sneered at me. "Sure you do. And I guess you need to puff on some filthy fucking cigarettes to loosen up a bit too, do you?"

I didn't have an answer to that, just stood hovering awkward and feeling disgusted with myself.

He stepped up closer, and sniffed at the air. "You smell revolting, Anna. What the fuck do you think you're playing at?"

I hated him like this, after too many drinks out at Oscars. I hated the way his ego grew, and his self-righteousness grew along with it. And it was sad, because he wasn't like this, not in regular life when he was caring, and trying, and wanting to save me from my own failing brain.

"I just smoke sometimes now," I told him, and shrugged to try to lighten it.

His eyes were full of rage, and I didn't blame him for that. I knew I was asking a lot for him to pick up the pieces. I knew I was asking a lot for him to treat me like the woman I used to be before I'd walked out and left him behind.

"This is his doing, isn't it?" he spat. "This is that piece of shit's influence on you all over again?"

I didn't have an answer for that, but I felt my cheeks burning up.

"Don't think I don't know about you diving right back into that filthy pit with that filthy cunt, Anna. I know all about what you ran back to, with those slutty little legs of yours spread wide and begging."

I shook my head. "It wasn't like that."

He laughed in my face. "Oh, believe me. I know what it was like. I pulled you up from the wreck of it last time around, remember?"

I did remember.

I remembered and I was grateful, and I would be again, but he looked so spiteful and so wronged that I couldn't find the words to tell him so.

"He ditched you for that other bitch again, didn't he?" he laughed. "Like you didn't learn your lesson first time around."

We'd had this conversation over a nice meal, and a heart to heart, and me offering a million apologies and telling him I was eager to try again. I thought we'd covered it. He'd told me we had. He'd told me he'd accepted that I'd had a blip in my sanity and was ready to try again.

He'd said he wanted that too.

"Please, let's go to bed," I said. "We'll talk about it in the morning."

I took off my necklace and dropped it on the bedside table, and tried to ease into our night time, but he was right up and at me, spinning me around by my arm and putting his face up close to mine.

"We'll talk about it whenever I fucking want to talk about it. We'll talk about it with your filthy fucking breath on the air and that vile, perverted cunt still coming between us."

"I don't know what you mean…" I tried. "Nobody is coming between us… we're starting again…"

"So show me you want me," he said, and his voice was low and cold. "If you're so keen to start again, show me how you want me so much more than him. You barely looked at me in the club, just like fucking always. People are laughing at me, you know? They're laughing that I'm pathetic enough to give you another fucking go…"

My heart dropped and thumped, right in my belly. Because I couldn't. I couldn't show him that I wanted him so much more than Lucas. I was still trying to show myself.

I knew people would be laughing at him, and I was sorry.

I was sorry, and I wanted to show it, but I couldn't.

I'd told him it would take time, building bridges and making a new life together before we could be what we were before, and he'd told me it would be ok. He'd told me we'd work at it.

"I can't show you anything just yet," I managed to say. "We need time…"

"Oh, right," he snapped back. "So, we need time now, do we? You didn't need time when you were diving into bed with that cunt, did you? I bet you were climbing the fucking walls to get to his dick."

"Stop," I said, but my voice was just a breath. "It wasn't like that…"

I hated how he squeezed my arm and yanked me towards him. I hated how his eyes glared harder and his fingers gripped tighter.

"Answer me one thing," he said. "What is it you like so much about that piece of shit? What is it about him that drives you so fucking crazy?"

"It wasn't like that…" I said again, and tried to pull away.

But he wouldn't let me. He gripped tighter, and sneered harder, and put his face right up to mine.

"You always were that dirty little slut, weren't you?" he hissed. "I tried to make you someone better, but it never worked, did it?"

"Stop it."

"I thought I was picking you up off the floor and leaving your filthy slut ways behind, but I wasn't, was I? You kept hold of them the whole fucking time."

I shook my head, because he was talking crap.

He rarely got like this, so spiteful and so bitter and so vile.

He was usually wrapping me up in cotton wool every second of the day, and making me promise to be good, and healthy, and take care in every little way he told me how.

"This is nothing to do with me and Lucas," I told him. "This is about us, and starting again. I want to start again!"

There was a strength in my voice I hadn't heard all night. I felt a flash of myself back in my veins, because I couldn't let myself slip back into those same old shoes. Not for anything or anyone. I couldn't let go of the very person I'd been so desperate to find in myself those past few months.

I thought he'd love that person.

I thought he'd love *me*.

I shrugged him off a whole load harder and looked him straight in the eyes.

"Let's go to bed," I said. "We'll talk in the morning, when we can talk properly again. It's been a long night."

I pushed past him to find my nightdress from my overnight bag, and was leaning over to sort through my things when his arms wrapped around my waist, clenched tight, and spun me off my feet. I was unbalanced in a heartbeat, and he threw me down onto the bed, and I stared up at him open mouthed, because I didn't get it. I didn't understand.

"I tried to do everything for you!" he barked. "I sort your useless fucking brain out when you're such a state you don't even know your own name. I pick you up from the floor when you're too fucked to take the most basic fucking care of your own piss, and this is how you repay me?! This is how you fucking repay me?!"

I'd heard this kind of rage from him before whenever he was in one of these dickhead moods over the years, but I thought we were done with it.

He'd apologised for his bullshit and I'd apologised back for mine, and we'd started over.

He'd said we'd started over.

"Please stop," I said, and tried to get up, but he pushed me back down.

"Is that what you say to him when he's trying to fuck you? Do you say stop?"

"What's that got to do with anything?" I asked, and I was getting angry right back at him, even under my fucked up nerves.

"It's got everything to do with fucking everything!" he raged. "Because I want to know. I asked you what is it you like so much about that piece of shit, Anna, and I want to fucking know!"

I shook my head. "It's got nothing to do with us! I'm here because I want to give us another go!"

"And I'm telling you, I want to know why you want his fucking dick so much!"

I felt sick inside when I met his stare.

He thought I was disgusting.

He thought I was seedy, and useless, and a pitiful excuse for myself.

But it was more than that.

He hated me when I was like this and always had done.

He hated me ignoring his *advice* and making my own choices.

He hated *me* being *me*.

"This is about me having a prosecco, isn't it?" I asked him. "Because I'll have one if I want one, Sebastian. Thanks for your advice, but I'll have one if I want one! You aren't my childminder!"

I really did try to get up from the bed this time, and he really did push me back down hard. I squirmed, but he kept me in position, and his eyes filled with a whole fresh round of rage.

"Why do you want his fucking dick so much, Anna?" he sneered, and his hand pinned my wrists above my head.

I squirmed and bucked, but the bed was soft, and it was hard to get leverage. And then he moved. He moved fast and hard, and managed tug my dress up and yank my knickers down my legs, and I spat and cursed and told him to stop, just fucking stop! But he kept on going.

And then those knickers were up in my face. They were up in my face and he was rubbing them hard against my nose and shoving them into my mouth as I tried to fight him off.

"Does this make it better?!" he grunted. "Is this what he does with your filthy fucking knickers to make it so much fucking better?! Don't think I don't remember what that filthy cunt used to do to you!"

I hated that he knew. I hated that he knew everything.

I hated that I'd shared everything about my past, and my fears, and my dreams, and believed that he was going to be so fucking much to me.

I kicked out, but he pressed down harder, and my knickers were still rammed in my mouth and held tight. I was retching, and trying to breathe and trying to protest as my brain screamed to a whole new tune, but I couldn't stop him. I didn't have the strength.

"I'll be the man you fucking want me to be, shall I?!" he snarled. "I'll be your next Lucas fucking Pierce and his cunting fucking perversions, you disgusting little slut!"

I tried to scream out again, but it was muffled.

"I made you more than this!" he spat. "I worked so hard to make you more than this!"

I couldn't cry out, just retched.

"Why won't you fucking love me?" he hissed. "I tell you what, Anna. I'll make you love me! I'll be just the man you fucking need! Just keep fucking still and let me fucking show you!"

I didn't keep still.

I didn't stop squirming and I didn't stop retching and trying to scream, and I didn't stop hating the man Sebastian became when I wasn't the woman he wanted me to be.

I'd forgotten this man.

I'd always blamed myself for this version of this man.

But not tonight.

I didn't blame myself tonight.

Not anymore.

I didn't stop wishing I was anywhere other than underneath the man I'd run back to because I was scared and alone and believed he wanted the best for me.

I didn't stop knowing what was happening as he pinned me down hard and forced himself into me.

Didn't stop begging him to stop as he slammed into me.

And I didn't stop crying when he was done.

"Oh, quit with fucking tears," he said, as I scrambled to tug my dress back down. "We both know you like it rough. You should be thanking me for showing you a good time for once in your sorry life."

I rolled onto my side and pulled my knees to my chest, and I couldn't look at him, couldn't do anything but try to catch my breath.

"Let's go to bed now, then," he scoffed. "We'll talk about it in the morning. Hopefully you won't need another prosecco over breakfast. I'll make you some eggs, just how you like them."

He laughed. He shook his head and laughed, and stared over like I was me and he was him, and we were us all over again.

And sure he was. He was Sebastian again, cool and calm as he finished his own undressing and got himself ready for under the covers, but I was anything but me.

I could never be cool and calm again. Not in the same room as the man I'd believed would take care of me when I couldn't take care of myself. Because he'd... he'd...

He scoffed again as he gestured me off the bed. "Oh come on, Anna. Calm yourself down now or you'll be having another seizure. You know how upset you get when you wake up soaking in the morning."

My head was spinning, and my nerves were jangling, and my heart was racing, and everything was confused and wrong and broken.

"Come on," he said, and held out a hand to help me up, but I shied away, scared, and so shocked that I didn't know what the hell I should be doing.

Except I did know what the hell I should be doing.

I should be getting the hell out of there. I should be anywhere but in the same room as the man who'd just...

Who'd just...

Who'd just...

"Don't be shy," he said, and there was that scoff in his voice again. "We both know you liked that. I should have made a dirty little slut out of you years ago, then you wouldn't have needed to run back to that filthy prick in the first place."

I was shaking my head, even though I couldn't find my voice, and my arms finally came to life, pushing me up and away from that bed, where my feet took up the mission and backed me to the door.

"Come to bed," he said, and he had that stare in his eyes that I'd seen a million times before. The stare that told me I was ill, and unwell, and needed him to make my decisions and take care of me.

The stare that told me I should stop thinking, and stop questioning, and get in bed under the covers, just where he told me I should be.

But not anymore.

Not now he'd…

Because how could he…

How could that ever be ok…

He saw it in my eyes. My pain and my hurt and my disbelief. He saw my clarity striking and my heartrate picking up even further in fight or flight, and my face take on enough disgust to send me backing out onto the landing.

"Fucking hell, Anna!" he snapped. "Going bailing on me again now, are you? You barely lasted another fucking week of the *new life* you wanted to invest in so fucking badly!"

Yes, I was bailing on him again.

I was stumbling backwards towards the staircase, wanting anywhere but there. Wanting anything but him.

I backed away faster as he appeared in the bedroom doorway, panic rising.

"You think anyone is going to listen to any more of your whining, pathetic bullshit? Everyone's already spent months of their lives trying to reason with your useless fucking brain. Do you really think they're going to pat you on the back when you tell them you've fucked up your sweet little fucking life another fucking time already?"

I didn't think that.

I didn't think anyone would pat me on the back for anything.

Let alone myself.

I'd never pat myself on the back for ever considering I could ever make this right again.

I was just scared.

Lonely.

Destroyed by the man I'd prayed would help me heal.

I backed my way down the stairs and raced to the kitchen.

I grabbed my handbag from the counter, and managed to pull my shoes on and rush towards the front door, and I didn't even grab my coat on the way back through, my heart was racing too fast to care.

I heard him before the door shut behind me, shouting down the stairs at me like I was the same sad little invalid he'd been babysitting for years.

"Fuck you then, Anna!" he called after me. "See who else puts up with your disgusting little ways, and your disgusting little bodily functions to go along with them. We're fucking done!"

Yes, we were.

Yes, we were fucking done.

And so was I.

Only this time I had nobody I could run to.

This time I was well and truly alone with nowhere to go.

Chapter Thirty-Four

LUCAS

I could barely sleep all over again – tossing and turning in the now so familiar blur of self-pity and regret, hating myself all over again for losing Anna in the first place.

In the day, I was making it through, but nights were harder. So much fucking harder.

At least I wasn't drinking my way to salvation this time around.

I think I'd been dreaming. Yet another mash up of running after Millie and running after Anna too. But getting nowhere. Always getting nowhere.

I cursed my life and rolled over to the edge of the bed. The beside clock said 4.18 a.m. and I cursed the dark as well.

My phone was there on the bedside table, and I picked it up for the distraction, emails and bullshit social media streams that didn't mean shit to me, but my thumb didn't click on them. It took its usual route to my work identity and login, and I called up her details, just like always.

Anna's phone. No doubt on standby as she slept soundly next to Sebastian bastard Maitland in her new life without me.

But tonight it wasn't on standby.

It was active.

Active at 4.20 a.m.

I propped myself up on an elbow, suddenly switched on and wide awake, because I didn't understand it.

There was no way Anna's phone would be active at 4.20 a.m. Not with Sebastian Maitland taking care of her.

And if he wasn't...

What the hell did it mean if he wasn't?

I dug further and I shouldn't have done it, but I shouldn't have done many things associated with Anna on my work identity. I clicked on the tracker and my gut twisted as the dot positioned itself over the street view.

The Neptune fountain.

Her phone was active at the Neptune fountain at approaching half four a.m.

What the fuck was she doing at the Neptune fountain at half four in the fucking morning?

I couldn't ignore the weird tension in my chest as I flicked on the bedside lamp and got myself out of bed. I tried her phone as I was getting dressed, but my number was still blocked. The line was dead to me.

It was probably nothing. I was probably still dream-drunk and half sane, and this crazy flash of panic was nothing short of ridiculous, but I couldn't stop myself.

I headed downstairs and I got my shoes on and grabbed my keys.

Even the dogs looked at me like I was crazy when I made my way through the kitchen. They tried to follow me to the front door but I sent them back to their bed, and then I stepped out into the night.

The lanes were empty, and so were the roads into Cheltenham. Parking was easy at this time of night, and I pulled up in a side street just along from the fountain, cursing myself all over again as I jumped out and headed over. It was probably nothing. I was probably being ridiculous, and it was all probably ok.

Only it wasn't ridiculous.

And it wasn't ok.

She wasn't ok.

My heart stopped dead when I saw her there, a tiny huddle on the grass in front of the fountain.

My feet pounded the tarmac as I raced to her, and I was calling her name but she didn't turn around, not until I was right on top of her and reaching out.

And then she screamed.

She screamed and shuffled away and turned towards me wide-eyed and scared. And she didn't know me. Barely registered who I was. Barely knew anything through her own fear.

"Jesus Christ, Anna. What the fuck happened?!" I called out to her, and her eyes focused on mine.

"Lucas?!"

I was down on my knees and reaching out, but she was so scared. It was only when my hand took hold of hers and pulled her closer that she broke and cried, and I was there. I was right there.

My voice was quiet, and my arms were holding her tight, and she was freezing. Freezing and trembling, with ragged breaths and tears.

I asked her what happened, calmer this time, but she wouldn't answer, just shook her head.

I took off my coat and wrapped her up, and asked her to come with me, pulling her to her feet, but her legs were weak and she collapsed right back down onto the grass.

"Please just talk to me," I begged, and I was straight back down beside her.

This time she sucked in a breath and tried to calm herself. Her hands were shaking as she held them out, and I thought she was reaching for me, but she wasn't.

She let out a gut-lurching rumble of a scream and twisted the diamond ring from her finger, then threw it into the water with more rage than I'd ever seen in her.

"What the fucking hell did he do to you?" I asked her, and I knew it was bad.

I knew it was really fucking bad.

She shook her head all over again, then pulled my coat tighter around her, and it was something in the way she tugged her knees up to her chest and squeezed them closed so tight.

"Anna," I said, and my voice was so soft and so low, "come with me, please. Let's get you back in the warm."

Her lip trembled and then she nodded. She breathed and nodded.

I took her hand and helped her to her feet a second time around, but this time I was ready. I took her weight and held her steady, and then I lifted her up from the floor.

Her arms wrapped around my neck, and she was holding so tight, and it was the most natural thing in the world as I carried her back to the truck and lowered her into the passenger seat.

"Do you need a doctor?" I asked her as I turned on the ignition, but she shook her head.

Then she managed to speak.

"No. I don't need a doctor. Please just get me away from here."

I didn't ask her where. There was only one place we were going.

She didn't respond to any questions as we drove the lanes and headed to mine, just kept her eyes on the road ahead and sucked in the breaths as her tears subsided.

My driveway was on us in what felt like seconds. I jumped out of my side and helped her out of hers, and she was steadier on her feet this time, pressing into my side as I led us to the front door.

It was warm inside. I got the lights in the kitchen and she pressed into the counter, and I could truly see her in this space. Hollow and scared and barely conscious – my beautiful little magpie with her barbed thorns torn to shreds.

Torn to shreds by him.

I had no doubt she'd been torn to shreds by him.

"What the hell did he do to you?" I asked her, but I already knew. Something deep inside me already knew.

"He…"

She paused.

"He…"

"Say it," I encouraged. "Tell me, Anna. I promise you can say it."

"I was drinking prosecco and he didn't like it… he didn't like it… and we… we argued, and he." Another pause. "And he…"

"Say it," I told her. "Come on, sweetheart. You can say it."

Her lip trembled, and I was right there all over again. I was on my knees with my hands on her thighs so steady.

"You can say it," I said again. "I promise. You're safe now, Anna."

She looked away from me, staring into the darkness through the windows. And then she said it.

She fucking said it.

A breath. Barely audible. Lip still trembling through her words.

"He raped me." Her face crumpled. "Oh my God, Lucas… he raped me… Sebastian raped me…"

Holy fuck, my gut twisted like a knife.

"I told him to stop… but he didn't… I screamed for him to stop… but he didn't… he wouldn't stop…"

I pulled her down towards me, and she gave up the fight to stay standing. She buried herself in my arms and I held her so strong. I rocked, and she rocked with me, and she cried all over again.

"They said I should go back to him… they said he was my life… and I believed them. I wanted to believe them."

I held her face to my chest, and my heart was pounding with rage, so angry and so fucking broken along with her.

I don't know how long we were sitting there, but the first cracks of dawn were showing through the window when I eased us to our feet and grabbed her a juice from the fridge. Her fingers were still shaking as she took it from me, and she looked so awkward as she slipped a hand down between her thighs.

"It's ok," she said, and then she sighed. "I just thought I might have... I had a seizure at the fountain, and I thought I might have..."

My heart broke in two.

She'd been alone, in the cold, in the middle of the night, battling a brain that was failing her after a cunt had failed every fucking thing a fucking man should ever be.

And what if I hadn't woken up? What if I hadn't clicked on her details and found her there? It didn't bear thinking about.

I lit up a cigarette and handed it over. She was grateful. She sucked in a decent drag and pressed herself back against the counter, and I lit up one for myself.

"Tell me what happened," I said, and there was a new clarity in her eyes as they landed on mine.

It took her a long time to tell me what happened.

Her words were stuttered, and her breaths were hard, but she told me. Every little detail through her pain.

I had to fight back my own rage enough to stay calm, because I wanted to drive right back into fucking town and skin that disgusting cunt alive, but I stayed calm for Anna.

"I thought he loved me," she said when she reached the end. "I always wanted to think he loved me. But he didn't. He never did. He doesn't know what love is. Not really."

I kept quiet, because I wanted her to carry on. Freely, in the flow, and however she wanted to tell me whatever she needed to say.

Her face crumpled again as she found the next words, and I crumpled inside along with her. But still I kept my calm.

"Oh my God, Lucas..." she said, and held her stomach. "Oh my God, there was so much I never wanted to see... so much I never said... not to anyone... not even to *me*..."

I said it again.

I took a breath and I said it again, with my hands on her shoulders and my eyes fixed tight on hers.

"Tell me."

She nodded, with my hands on her shoulders, and her eyes fixed tight on mine.

And then she told me it all.

Chapter Thirty-Five

ANNA

Clarity comes like a butcher's knife when you least expect it. It slices through everything. The hopes and the fears and the beliefs you take so much for granted as you live your life.

My hopes and my fears and my beliefs had been held very tightly by Sebastian Maitland for a very long time. I'd believed in him. I'd believed he believed in me.

I was wrong.

Lucas was such a support as he sat across from me and listened to my inner voice finally find faith in itself. He was close, and warm, and he listened harder to me than I'd listened to myself in years as my niggle of intuition spiked and pricked.

Sebastian was an evil prince in a beautiful mask. Too slick behind his smile.

Far too slick for anyone to ever see the true ugliness. Least of all me.

I'd been an easy rabbit to snare. A wide-eyed piece of potential roadkill waiting for the truck to hit when he'd found me lost and held out a hand to save me.

He'd started off so kind as he'd picked me up from the floor of my own fucked up dreams. His smile, his touch, his concern.

He'd been the saviour in my storm, and I'd thanked my stars every single minute of every single day that he was in my life.

He'd ask me how my day was, and how I was feeling through the nights. He supported me through the seizures, and the scans and the epilepsy diagnosis.

He'd ask if I was warm enough for the wind outside, and what I'd been eating for lunch at work.

How much I'd slept and if I'd been staring at screens too much, or drinking too little, or whether I should really be watching the things on TV I wanted to be watching so close to bedtime.

Everyone loved him for it.

I loved him for it.

Everyone saw the beautiful mask on his face and nothing more – until his true self started to slip through the veil, but only to me.

It started in the tiny details, far too small to give them note. The pinpricks. So soft at first, you barely feel them.

Asking if you're warm enough becomes an instruction to wear a warmer coat – and that instruction to wear a warmer coat becomes disapproval if you don't wear exactly what he wants you to.

Him caring if you've eaten enough becomes an instruction to eat food that's healthy for you –

and that instruction to eat food that's healthy for you becomes him deciding your meals for you and making digs if you eat anything else.

And you listen.

Over time, you begin to listen.

Your croissant at the local cafe turns from a nice snack to a niggle of doubt that you should be eating it. So you don't.

Wearing a tiny jacket in a colour you like becomes a niggle that it doesn't wrap you up enough and keep you warm. So you wear a different one.

And then, even more slowly. Softly, softly, softly, those pinpricks turn a bit more painful.

Disapproval becomes outright criticism, and always behind closed doors where nobody is watching – but it doesn't matter by then, because you're already in so deep, you believe it.

You believe it because it's disguised as caring, and you believe it because the whole world is smiling and singing their praises of the evil prince in his beautiful mask.

You believe it when they insist that you would be a broken mess without him.

You believe it because they believe it.

Because they care.

Because they love you *so much.*

Because you *don't know what you're doing.*

Because you're so ill you *can't take care of yourself.*

Ungrateful.

You're ungrateful.

You're pitiful.

You're so lucky, Anna. What would you do without me?

Good job I love you, isn't it?

I love you so much, Anna.

I love you even though you wet the bed at night. So disgusting, but I love you anyway.

You're such a beautiful person, even though your brain is so fucked you can't remember your own name.

Nobody else would love you like I do.

Nobody else would help you change the sheets like I do.

Nobody else would tell the world how amazing you are, and how much I love you like I do.

I don't know when Sebastian turned from the man who'd stare at me with love in his eyes, into the man who controlled every scrap of everything I ever did.

I don't know when I became the woman who believed everything he said and tried to live up to his instructions, and his demands, and his expectations. But I did.

Slowly, over time, I did.

I stopped working late, and stopped eating what I wanted, and stopped feeling like I could go to bed past midnight, or reading under lamplight, or watching horror movies with the lights off.

I stopped feeling like I was well enough to go places where I wasn't holding his hand.

Yet still, it was all masked in caring and people loved him for it. *Everyone* loved him for it.

His lovely smile, and his hand holding mine so tight. Him helping me spoon the vegetables onto my plate at the dining table. The way he'd be so worried about my seizures, and what I was and wasn't doing to prevent them.

Everyone told me how lucky I was to have him over and over and over and over again. A mantra that lasted a decade and was still bleating strong now.

I believed them.

I believed him.

I believed everyone but that tiny little voice inside me.

Me.

I believed everyone but *me.*

Because I wasn't me anymore.

I was the ill person he wanted me to believe he was saving.

I was the person he'd attack with savage little verbal blades whenever I didn't do what he wanted.

And *he* was the person who needed control. Always so much control.

But when I took it back…

When he couldn't control me anymore…

I stopped for a pause as my revelations caught up with me.

"And nobody saw any of this?" Lucas asked. "Nobody saw him saying that shit, or forcing you to dance to his bullshit tune every day of the week? They just all thought he was some kind of perfect hero parading around like Jesus in a suit?"

I shrugged. "He was always so caring. Most of the time I believed it too. It was just late at night, or sly little digs, or in anything he could twist to make me feel like I wasn't good enough. And I did feel like I wasn't good enough."

"You'll always be good enough," he said.

The tears came then, and my breath hitched as I struggled for the words as it all came crashing in. And those tears weren't just about the vile savagery of the rape, or the way he'd abused me so hard on that one evening. It was about all of it. So much of the decade I'd spent at his side.

It was about the tiny ways he'd gripped me so tight with his *caring* that I'd choked on my own fear. It was in the way he'd wrapped me up so deep in paranoia that I didn't know my own mind.

"But I thought he loved me," I told Lucas. "I really thought he loved me. He was always so caring and kind that I always blamed his bullshit digs on myself. Always. I mean, I never even thought about it. He'd be vile after a few drinks sometimes, but even then it was always wrapped in a pretty bow of concern. Wanting the best for me. Seeing the worst in me. Wanting to change that."

I saw Lucas's jaw clench and I knew he was struggling to keep a lid on his rage.

"And what about helping you get better? With the seizures, I mean. How the fuck did he help you get better? Did he even want you to? I bet he fucking didn't. Bastard piece of shit."

I shrugged at that, because I didn't know. Not anymore.

As the morning broke through the window and Lucas stared over at me, I didn't know much about my life with Sebastian Maitland at all. It was all still tumbling, and I was still reeling.

I stared up at the ceiling and tried to pull myself back to my senses in the room, and then I finally registered where I was.

Oh crap, I registered where I was.

My eyes were fast to land on his.

"Shit, Lucas. Where's Maya?! Surely I shouldn't be here... she must be around... I mean, I should go... I don't want to cause any–"

"What the hell are you talking about?" he said. "Why the hell would Maya be here? She never comes here."

The confusion in my stare must have rivalled his. "Well, you're back with her, right? The three of you? Hasn't she moved back in here yet?"

He shook his head like my questions were the most absurd things he'd ever heard.

"I'd never be back with Maya. I'm doing what I can with Millie, jumping through her stupid fucking hoops to see my daughter, but I'm not back with her. I hate being in the same room as her, so there's no way I could ever share a bed with her."

I shook my head like his answers were the most absurd things I'd ever heard.

"But that's why I walked away... I thought you'd go back to her and make it right again..."

He squeezed my hands in my lap, and his eyes were so raw.

"Jesus Christ, Anna. I'd never have gone back to Maya. Even if I never saw you again in this whole fucking lifetime, I'd never go back to Maya. I couldn't. We'd never be able to make it work."

"But the family pictures..." I said. "Your mother showed me the family pictures... of the three of you all together... how happy you were..."

"How happy we *wanted* to be," he said. "But it doesn't matter what anyone pretends is picture perfect, not unless it's fucking real." He sighed. "It was never real for me, I just wanted it to be."

"But what about Millie?" I pushed. "If you don't get back with Maya like she wants you to, then how are you going to see Millie?"

He shrugged. "Fuck knows. But I can't get back with her again or be anything else. I don't love her, I never did. I should've accepted that years ago and been done with this bullshit."

I let out the most insane little laugh. A bitter, sad little giggle as my brain churned over the carnage.

It was toxic. Painful. Blunt and savage.

It was poison.

But sometimes the antidote comes from the strangest places.

Maybe, just maybe, I was staring at mine.

I breathed out. "Damn, Lucas. It's one serious pit of bullshit we've both managed to drop ourselves in. Two shitty sides of one shitty coin we've been trying to make work for a decade."

"Two shitty sides of one shitty coin we've been trying to make work without each other, more like it." He leaned in to rest his forehead against mine. "And I'm done with it. I'm sorry, but I'm done. I'm not spending the next decade without you, Anna. The world can get fucked."

The pressure of his skin on mine was enough to give me butterflies under the pain.

Because I was done too.

I didn't want another day without him. Not anymore.

"Don't leave me," I whispered. "Please, Lucas, don't leave me again."

"I won't be leaving you for anything," he said. "And I swear to you, Sebastian Maitland won't be coming anywhere near you ever again, that's a certainty. He'll never fucking hurt you again."

I took a deep breath, my forehead still on his, and then I gave up the fight.

The world really could get fucked.

I loved Lucas Pierce and he loved me, and this time he was mine to stay.

Chapter Thirty-Six

LUCAS

I took her up to bed and held her tight, but we didn't sleep. We were out of words, and energy, and everything other than the need to be together.

I was never letting this go again. I was never letting go of the woman at my side.

I loved Millie so hard, of course I did. She was my world, and my love, and my zest through life. But so was Anna. And somehow, by some means, I'd have to make that balance work without making a choice. I'd never be making the choice between them for anyone. I couldn't do it. Not even if that anyone was the mother of my daughter, and the woman I'd been a prick of a partner to for our entire life together.

Guilt is guilt, and failure is failure, but love is love too, and life is life along with it, and mine was with Anna.

Mine would always be with Anna.

The sunrise turned to morning with her in my arms, and that morning got brighter and brighter as the sun rose in the sky through the window. I heard her phone ringing and buzzing from downstairs, but she ignored it and so did I. She pressed even closer to my side and let out a sigh.

"I'm not ready to talk to anyone," she said. "I will be, but not yet."

"I'll be ready whenever you are," I said back. "I'll be right there with you."

I felt her smile against my shoulder. "I think this is the first night we've ever been together where we haven't had sex, you know."

I laughed and kissed her head. "I think you're probably right."

She looked up at me. "Don't you dare turn me into a china doll now Sebastian forced himself on me. I've been a china doll for far too long, and I don't want it from you."

I squeezed her tighter and managed a grin. "I wasn't planning on it. I certainly can't imagine treating you like a china doll. I wouldn't know where to start."

She laughed at that.

I used the conversation topic to lead into something that needed saying.

"We need to call the police, Anna. He can't be allowed to get away with what he did to you."

I felt her tense up. "It would be my word against his, what could they possibly do?"

"That doesn't matter," I said. "He raped you, Anna. It needs to be reported."

She sighed. "We can try."

Yes, we could. But I'd be doing a whole load more than trying. She just didn't need to know that yet.

Her phone sounded out again from downstairs and she let out a long breath.

"I'd better do this. The world needs facing."

"*We'd* better do this," I said. "We'll be facing the world together from here on in."

She reached out a hand to stroke my chest, and then she rolled away.

"Let's get started then."

I tried to keep as calm and steady as I could for her as she got her things together. She put on my coat and fastened her heels back up and told me she wanted to head back to her place to see her friends before she faced telling her parents. I told her we'd be heading wherever she needed to and, behind the scenes, I messaged both Maya and my mother saying that I needed to rearrange our meetups due to a weekend emergency.

Then I switched my phone off to avoid the abuse. I didn't warrant any. They'd rearranged things a million times over and given me the middle finger whenever it suited them. They could bitch about me all they liked in my absence.

This weekend was all about Anna.

She said goodbye to Bill and Ted with a smile on her face before we headed on out, but her knees were trembling in the passenger seat all the way back into town.

I reached out to squeeze one and she flinched, but then relaxed with a sigh.

"Sorry, I'm just jumpy."

"Totally understandable," I said. "Don't even think of apologising."

I pulled up in her street and turned the ignition off.

"My heart is pounding," she told me. "I'm so nervous."

"Take your time," I said.

She waited a few minutes, breathing deep with her hand in mine before she gave it a final squeeze.

"Okay," she said, "let's do this."

I was as close to her as I could be as she fished her key from the bottom of her bag and pushed it into the lock with shaky fingers.

Nicola Henshaw was in the window staring out at us before we'd stepped inside, and her face was nothing short of a typhoon of rage when she stormed into the hallway to greet us.

"Sebastian's been messaging us this morning," she snapped. "We've been worried fucking sick, Anna, wondering what the hell has been happening. But now we know, don't we?" She scowled at me hard enough that she could have burnt me alive. "*He's* been happening, hasn't he? That utter fucking cock you can't stay away from."

Vicky appeared in the hallway behind her, and she was scowling too, and I was ready to interject with some words of my own, but Anna was there before me, with enough pain in her voice that they stopped dead.

"STOP FUCKING TELLING ME WHAT THE FUCK I SHOULD BE DOING WITH SEBASTIAN FUCKING MAITLAND!" she screamed, and their jaws dropped. "HE'S NOTHING LIKE YOU FUCKING THINK HE IS!"

She pushed past them with her fingers holding mine tight, leading us both into the living room without looking back. She dropped down onto the sofa, and I sat alongside her, and my arm was wrapped tight around her waist as her friends rushed on through.

"What the hell happened?" Vicky asked. "What are you talking about?"

Nicola was right there with her. "Seriously, Anna. Please just tell us what the fuck's going on."

So she did.

She told them what had happened with Sebastian the night before. Everything from him taking her out of the club because she'd been having a prosecco, through to him storming upstairs when they got back home. And then she told them the finer details through her sobs, right up until she'd run away from him and rushed out into the night, and they were right there sobbing along with her, shaking their heads as they realised just how much of a cunt they'd been singing the praises of for a decade straight.

"We didn't know!" Nicola cried. "I swear to you, Anna. We didn't know!"

Anna was nodding through the tears. "Neither did I," she said. "Not like I know it now."

"He said you'd had an argument over prosecco," Vicky told us. "He said you'd stormed out on him when he was trying to care for you. He's told your parents that too. Everyone's been so worried."

Anna's voice was so solid.

"He raped me. No argument matters. Nothing else matters."

"Of course nothing else matters," Vicky said. "He's a disgusting cunt and he needs to pay for what he's done!"

But it wasn't the full story. Not the full story of just how much of a disgusting cunt Sebastian Maitland truly was through the days and months and years.

My hand was tight in hers, but I didn't interfere, just let her express herself however she needed to the people she counted on as friends. And they were her friends. The genuine support and horror on their faces as they digested just how much of an evil controlling prick they'd been bigging up for years was so raw, it took my breath.

Anna took a break in her Sebastian Maitland revelations to light up a cigarette outside and they didn't say a word as we smoked together. She sat herself back down with me held tight at her side, and I kissed her hard on her cheek, and they didn't say a word about that either. Not anymore.

And then she told them how I'd found her by the fountain.

She told them how I'd been with her all night, supporting her through every breath.

They listened.

They listened to her tell them how the one thing she really was still confident of was that I loved her and she loved me, and that there really had been one stupid mistake that had led to me leaving her, and that didn't make me any less of an asshole for my fuck ups and my choices, but it made me an asshole she wanted to give another chance to.

An asshole she wanted them to give another chance to along with her.

I expected their eyes to be full of disbelief and disgust as they met with mine, but they weren't.

They believed her.

They believed it was one stupid mistake and not me being a total prick of a man for months on end behind her back. I could read it in their faces.

But this wasn't about me, it was about Anna, and I cleared my throat before I pulled the conversation back to the inevitable.

"We need to call the police," I told her. "It's hard, I know. But we need to call the police."

She nodded, but then took a breath. "I need to see my parents first. I want to tell them what he's done to me before I tell anyone else."

"We'll come with you," Nicola said. "Just tell us what you want us to do."

I was ready to face telling Jim and Terri along with Anna, but she turned to me and held me tight.

"I need to do this without you there," she said. "I don't want them wrongly connecting you with what's happened. I just know they'd add two plus two and get six."

"Are you sure?" I said. "I know it would be confrontational, but I'm happy to stand with you through whatever you need."

"I'm sure," she said. "Please just be here for me later."

"I'll wait here for you," I told her. "I'll be right here whenever you need."

Her friends stood up to take her over there, and I fought the urge to charge along with them and face off the whole world at her side. But no.

This part wasn't for me.

She'd made her decision, and I would respect everything she wanted, however she wanted it.

I walked to the door with her and she hugged me tight before she stepped outside.

"I love you," she said. "I'll never have enough thanks for how you were there for me last night."

"I'll never be anywhere else," I said, and it took every scrap of me to let her go.

I wasn't expecting Nicola to grab my arm on her way past me in the hallway. I expected her to be straight on out after Vicky and Anna.

I figured maybe it was for a hiss of *we still hate your fucking guts*, but it wasn't.

Her eyes were open wide when they met with mine, a strange

expression on her face I couldn't read.

"You need to speak to Yasmin Boyle," she said in a whisper. "Believe me, Lucas, you really do need to speak to Yasmin Boyle."

"What do you mean?" I asked her, because I didn't understand it. I hadn't seen Yasmin Boyle in years. She'd been friends with Maya and around at our place at regular intervals, but then as far as I knew it she'd disappeared up to Newcastle.

What the hell would I need to speak with Yasmin Boyle about?

But Nicola didn't answer me, she just looked me right back in the eyes once she was standing outside the doorway and said it again.

"Trust me," she said, "just speak with Yasmin Boyle."

And then she closed the door.

Chapter Thirty-Seven

ANNA

My parents were so scared as I stepped through their front door. They came rushing straight on through, and their fear only grew ten times stronger as I looked them in the eyes.

The gravity was too huge to hide, and they felt it. They sucked in breath as they felt it.

Nicola and Vicky stepped on in after me, and there was a terrible silence, everything hanging in the air in my parents' hallway.

Until I burst into tears.

My mum came and held me, and eased me on through to the living room, and she was crying too as she sat me down in the chair and knelt down in front.

"My God, Anna. What happened? What on earth happened last night?"

My dad was as white as a ghost when he joined us, and Vicky and Nicola hovered to the side, and they were crying too.

I wasn't expecting it. Not when Mum asked me the next question.

"What on earth did he do to you, sweetheart? What on earth did Sebastian do to you?"

I couldn't remember a time I'd been asked that question. Not since he'd been in my life. It was always *what did you do. You do. You do.*

But not this time. This time it was all about him.

Finally, it was all about him.

So I told them. I held nothing back and I told them exactly what he'd done to me.

My dad was shaking when I'd finished, pacing the room like a man who wanted to kill. He was struggling to hold in the rage, but he was trying. His face was red, and his brow was heavy, and my mum was devastated along with him, her hand trembling as it gripped mine, her voice trying to be soothing as she told me it was *all going to be ok. It was all going to be ok. It was all going to be ok.*

And it *was* all going to be ok.

Now I could see the truth in what Sebastian was truly like, it *was* all going to be ok.

It was my mum who called the police. It was my dad that directed them inside as they came to the house and sat down in front of me and asked me what happened.

The officers listened, and they took their notes, and they had sympathy in their eyes as they listened to my story.

But that's what it was. A story. That's all they could take from it. One person's opinion which would certainly clash against another's. And there were no witnesses. No evidence. Nothing but a couple who'd gone home together where one of them was accusing the other of a terrible crime with no proof. Still, I told them it all as honestly as I could do, and they left there with a sympathetic smile and the promise they'd be looking into it as thoroughly as they could.

I went into the station with them, and Mum, Dad, Vicky and Nicola waited in the reception area. I was assigned a dedicated officer who recorded my account and sent me to a medical team to check me over, but

I knew it there and then. That same little voice of intuition I should have listened to for so long about Sebastian.

They'd never be able to prosecute a monster like him. He'd be too slick for anyone to convict him of anything with no real evidence.

Mum and Dad tried to get me to stay over in my old bedroom to wrap me up tight for the night when we were done, and part of me wanted that. Part of me wanted to be looked after like a little girl safe at home. But I'd been that little girl wrapped up in cotton wool for far too long, and I'd been without things I needed in my life for far too long, too.

I didn't want another night without Lucas for as long as I lived.

"We're right here for you, Anna," Dad said, and pulled me close before I left with Nicola and Vicky. "You'll never see Sebastian again, or I swear I'll kill the vile piece of shit myself."

I didn't doubt it.

I didn't doubt it when Mum held me tight and told me that Sebastian Maitland was gone from my life, and he'd pay the price for what he'd done.

Unfortunately, I wasn't so sure the police would be able to deliver on that.

I was quiet on the way back home with the girls, all of us exhausted and heavy with the upset, but it sure felt good to be there with them. For once in months, it felt so good to have them on my side.

Lucas was in the hallway as soon as we pushed our way in through the front door. He folded me in his arms, and I breathed deep and collapsed in the release.

He asked about the police and about my parents, and I told him everything I could do through the fog of tiredness. But it was blurred. Blurred and fading.

"Let's get you to bed," Vicky said, and reached for my hand. "Don't worry, Lucas. We'll make sure she's alright."

It was such a relief when he pulled me closer. "I won't be leaving her anywhere," he said. "Not ever again."

I expected them to argue with him, but they didn't. They didn't say a word as Lucas came through to my bedroom with me and helped me pack a suitcase with my things. They watched from the hallway as he helped me gather my toiletries together and fastened the case ready for my leaving, but didn't they make a sound in protest.

They hugged me tight as I left, and watched me leave. No complaints. No arguments. No objections.

I was grateful – truly grateful – that I didn't need to justify Lucas's place in my life all over again.

I was silent for most of the way back to his place, facing him with my legs pulled up high in my seat, staring at his profile as he kept his eyes on the road ahead. The strength in his jaw, and his eyes, and the firmness of his shoulders as he drove me home. I remembered how he'd pulled up at the train station to pick me up for one crazy day, and how I'd known from that first single moment that it would be trouble, because he was him. He was Lucas. The man I'd always been in love with. The man I'd never really moved on from, not even with Sebastian the evil prince Maitland at my side.

"Penny for your thoughts?" he said, and I managed a smile.

"Penny for my thoughts is that I love you."

"Well, that's a good thing," he said. "Because a penny for my thoughts is that I love you too."

I was desperate for bed when we got in, but I took my meds, and ate a stir fry that Lucas put in front of me, and thanked him very much. I tried to help him load the dishwasher, but he shooed me away and finished up himself, and I watched him through tired eyes, realising all over again just how hard it would be to ever let him go.

I could never let him go.

Not again.

He showered with me, and wrapped me up in a towel, but he didn't give me a running commentary on every little movement I should make.

He lit up a cigarette for me, smoked alongside me, and didn't have a word to say on what I should or shouldn't be doing for my health.

He was just him.

I was just me.

And we loved each other just for what we were. No conditions. No disapproval. No illusions.

He was so warm at my side in bed, legs twisted in mine and his arm so strong around my shoulder. My face was in his, breath against breath, and it felt so right.

Everything about us felt so right.

My brain was too tired to spin and churn, and my breathing slowed as I relaxed, skin to skin and heat to heat… and slowly… slowly and surely, I drifted off to sleep with him at my side.

"I love you, Anna," he whispered, when I was right on the edge of my dreams, and I whispered back, nothing more than a ghost of a reply, but one that meant the world.

"I love you, Lucas. I always will."

Sleep ate me up and held me as tight as he did. Dreams were a blur, and I needed them. I needed every scrap of rest I could get.

When I jolted back awake, the light was streaming in through the window, and he was still asleep at my side, breathing steady.

But I wasn't breathing steady. Not when I thrust my hand down between my thighs under the covers.

I was wet.

The bed was wet.

I'd wet the bed with Lucas next to me, and I felt the panic. The disgust. The shame.

He must have felt me struggling to get out of bed and get the dirty sheets away from him when he opened his eyes and came to his senses.

I was apologising, asking him to please roll over and I'd clean up.

I promise I'll clean up. I promise, Lucas. I promise. Just please roll over and give me the sheets.

But he wouldn't.

He wouldn't move a muscle to free the sheets for me.

His arms were reaching out, pulling me in so tight and warm and wrapping my wet thighs in his, rolling further into the dirty wet sheets I'd spoiled.

"I'm sorry," I said again, and I was fighting back the tears. "I'm really, really sorry."

He shook his head, and held me even tighter, and told me never to apologise again, because I'd never need to apologise to him. Not ever again in this life.

My heart was thumping, and my tears were ready, and I was still so sorry for the wetness in the sheets, and on him, and on me.

I was still ready to jump out and fix things, and strip the bed and make it right again, but he didn't let me go when I made to pull away.

"I'll sort it out," I told him, but he shook his head again, and his eyes were full of love, and care.

And then he kissed me.

Chapter Thirty-Eight

LUCAS

S hame.
Embarrassment.
Self-consciousness.
All things I never wanted to see in Anna.

I held her close, and her squirms turned to tension. Until I kissed her.

I kissed her deep and hard, like the Anna I loved, and nothing whatsoever like the china doll she was afraid of being. I kissed her like the man who wanted her body and her heart, no matter how dirty or raw they came. I pulled away for long enough to check the tears weren't flowing, and her eyes were open wide, still shocked in the moment – but there were no tears to be seen.

So I kissed her again.

"I need to clean up," she murmured mouth to mouth, but I had no interest in that.

My fingers took on a life of their own as they slipped down between her thighs and found her warm and wet, panties soaked right through.

I didn't care in the slightest.

I knew how to circle my thumb, and she murmured louder, her mouth still pressed to mine.

"I can clean up," she insisted, but I smiled against her lips.

"You'll never need to clean up for me," I told her, and slowly, as my thumb worked its magic, I felt her body loosen. "Tell me to stop if you want me to stop," I said. "I'll always stop the second you ask me."

"I know," she said, and wrapped her arms around my shoulders. "But don't stop. Make me forget. Make me forget him, Lucas."

"Then spread your legs for me, dirty girl," I said, and I was me, and she was her, both of us consumed by the flesh and the want and the fantasy.

I'd make her damn well forget Sebastian fucking Maitland, she didn't need to worry about that.

I grabbed her damp thighs and eased them apart, and her breaths were ragged as I positioned myself down between them.

Yes, I'd make her forget that vile cunt.

"Lucas, what–" she began, staring down as I lowered my head.

But I knew what I was doing. I knew what I wanted.

I wanted those filthy panties from her horny little pussy, and her level of dirty only added to the forbidden. My cock was throbbing and my mouth was watering, and I was ready. I was ready for everything she could possibly give me. And I wanted it all.

"Fuck–" she said, and tensed as my mouth landed. "Lucas, fuck–"

My tongue was flicking her clit through soaking wet lace, and my face was buried between her damp thighs and it was bliss. Hearing her moan, and whimper, and lose herself under those self-conscious little reservations was the horniest thing in the whole fucking world.

I knew she was battling with herself. I knew there was a screaming part of her that felt she should be stripping the bed and apologising for her *accident*, but there would never be an accident with me. There was only her, and every taste of who she was.

I wanted every single fucking taste of who she was, and I made sure she knew it.

Thankfully, the dirty little minx in her won the battle.

She bucked, then cursed as she pressed herself up against my mouth. Her fingers landed in my hair and held me firm between her legs, and she wanted it. She wanted it just as much as I did.

"This is filthy," she moaned. "Fuck, Lucas… this is so fucking filthy…"

I moaned back, my mouth hungry against her pussy, and her breaths were ragged, just like they always were when she was desperate for me to keep going. Her thighs were open wide and her clit was her sweet little bud craving more, and I gave her more. I sucked on that pretty cunt like it was my world, and the tastes of her blended, and hit my nostrils, and my tongue, and I wanted it. I really fucking wanted it.

So did my cock.

My cock was crying out even louder than the rest of me.

She was panting for more when I pulled away and shunted position. I shoved a pillow behind her head nice and high, and she watched me with her eyes wide open as I pressed my cock to the slick wet lace over her cunt.

It was horny as fuck as I worked it back and forth.

"Good girl," I said, and she let out a shuddering breath. "Spread those thighs even wider for me."

She was a good girl and she did spread them even wider for me. My dick rubbed against that gorgeous little slit through the wetness, and it was bliss. Pure fucking bliss. I stared down and watched my cock in rhythm, and I was so fucking swollen it was a strain.

"That's fucking beautiful," I told her. "That horny little cunt of yours is so fucking beautiful, Anna."

I angled the head of my dick closer to her clit, until the pressure was on just the right spot and I knew it. She let out a whimper, and her hips started working with mine, and I knew she was cresting. I knew she was going to come for me like the dirty little minx I loved so much.

"Watch," I said, and twisted my fingers in her hair to hold her head in position. "Watch my cock rubbing that sweet slit. I want you to see how horny I am. I'm so fucking horny for you, Anna."

She did see it. She saw that the desperation in me was as raw as ever. The way my cock thrust, so fucking hard. The way my breaths were so deep, and my grunts were coming so fast, and I was cursing at how fucking near to shooting my load she was making me already.

"My God, Lucas…" she managed, and she was working to my groove, both of us grinding and both of us watching.

I held back until she came under me. She moaned and arched and cursed a stream of sweet fucks from that filthy mouth of hers, and I was ready and waiting, cursing myself as my dick spurted its first load of cum right across those soaking panties.

"Watch," I said, but she was already watching. Her eyes were fixed tight on that thick white juice of mine as it landed so fucking creamy on dirty lace.

Delicious.

It was fucking delicious.

"Now rub it in like a good girl," I told her, and her fingers slipped down in a heartbeat, smearing my cum right the way across the crotch of those pretty little panties, nice and wet over her slit.

"That feels so good," she said, and her fingers picked up their rhythm.

"Play with that dirty little clit for me," I told her, and she nodded, tipping her head back and panting hard all over again.

My mouth was watering fresh, heart still pounding and cock growing back hard as I stared at my cum slicking her up. Piss and cum and the beautiful juice of her cunt, a perfect cocktail.

"Work that clit nice and fast," I said again, and her nod came with a whimper this time.

I kissed my way up her thighs and they were still nice and clammy. I pressed my mouth up close to her fingers as they strummed against her clit, and she was crying out as my tongue eased in to lap alongside, wriggling like a dirty little pixie as she came all over again.

I didn't even let her catch her breath before I was up and on her, grabbing her hand and aiming her dirty wet fingers at her open mouth.

"Suck," I said, and she gave me that tiny little moan of hers that drove me so fucking wild. That tiny little moan that told me just how much of a filthy little bitch she truly was.

"Suck them clean," I said again, and I was throbbing. My dick was so hard and grew even fucking harder as her eyes met mine.

She wanted it just as much as I did.

"Suck them," I told her, and she was a tease, poking her tongue out nice and far, but pretending she was trying to be such a little angel.

I was insane for it. So fucking insane for it my balls were hurting with the need to shoot again. I couldn't take it. Couldn't take the need to see her suck her filthy fucking fingers.

"Holy fuck, Anna. Suck for me," I growled, and she smirked. She smirked and she stared up at me with that filthy glint in her eyes I loved so fucking much.

And then my dirty little slut did what she was told.

Chapter Thirty-Nine

ANNA

My whole body was tingling when I sucked my fingers into my mouth. My clit was still buzzing, warm and wet with my filthy knickers pressed tight.

I was messy. I'd messed up and messed his bed up with it. But it didn't feel bad.

For once in my life, it didn't feel bad.

There was no disgust, and no judgement, and no idea of him being some kind of carer I should be grateful for.

He was the opposite.

The complete opposite.

My fingers tasted bitter and were thick with cum, and I wanted it. Even though I knew it was filthy dirty, and my heart was pounding fast, and I still couldn't believe Lucas had tasted my clit through my soaking wet knickers, I wanted it all.

I wanted *him.*

I sucked my fingers with moans and slurps and every scrap of need I could summon up in me.

I was still squirming, legs still spread wide, clit crying out for more when he climbed up higher and aimed his cock at my face.

It was the most natural thing in the world to open my mouth even wider, and it was the most natural thing in the world to feel him stretching my lips apart and forcing his dick in my mouth along with my fingers.

"Suck me clean," he said, and I did.

I sucked and lapped and moaned as I did it, and he thrust and cursed for more. His thighs were tense, and he was straining not to dive all the way in and fuck my mouth until he came down my throat.

"Fuck, Anna. That feels so fucking good."

Yes, it felt good.

It should have been a pit of shame, but it wasn't.

It should have had me burning up like a self-conscious little cow, but it didn't.

He'd saved me from that, and now I was soaring. Glowing. Alive.

I was *me*.

"Fuck," he said again, and stopped himself thrusting. "Keep sucking those fingers like a good little dirty bitch."

His breaths were heavy as he pulled his cock away and positioned himself on top of me. I was still sucking my fingers when he tugged my knickers to the side and the head of him eased its way inside. And then he paused.

He paused and drove me fucking crazy.

Teasing.

He was teasing.

"Please..." I whispered and he knew what I was asking for.

It was one single thrust that pushed him inside me, and he was balls deep in a flash, hard and fast and rough enough to make me yelp as the mattress bounced underneath us.

He kissed me around my fingers, his tongue wet and hungry, and I kissed him right back. Need, and want, and love. I loved him so much my heart could have burst.

I pulled my fingers free from our kiss, and we were all about tongues and lips and groans.

He fucked me. Hard. He knew the angle for his hips, dick pressing just right inside, and I felt myself building all over again. Felt my muscles clenching right the way down.

Fuck.

I was lost to everything but the sensation, moaning against his mouth as he slammed in rough.

I'd been scared that Sebastian would've made me edgy, but he hadn't. Not with Lucas. Not with Lucas's mouth and body on mine.

My hands were up and at him, fingers digging into his back, nails pinning. My knickers were stretched tight to the side, and it was anything but shame that burned inside.

He wanted this.

He wanted me.

He broke the kiss long enough to press his forehead to mine, thrusts still pounding in perfect rhythm.

"I could come like this, right here and now," he told me, but there was the dirty glint in his eyes that I adored, and his smile was pure filth to match. "I could come like this, Anna, but I'm not going to."

I cried out as he pulled out of me, but his hand was straight down to take the place of his cock, strumming my pussy like a master.

"Be my dirty girl," he told me, and I knew what he meant. I was ready when he slipped two of his fingers to my ass and pushed them in.

"Yes!" I moaned. "Fuck, yes! Yes!"

I was writhing and panting as he tore my dirty wet knickers down my thighs. They were off and at me in a heartbeat. He rubbed them against my clit, but further. Deeper. Everywhere.

He rubbed them everywhere.

"Tell me to stop," he said. "You can tell me to stop."

But I shook my head.

I didn't want him stop.

I wanted him to give me everything.

We were face to face when he pulled those knickers up between us. I couldn't tear my eyes away as he opened his mouth wide and pinned that lace between his teeth. And then he sucked. He sucked on my filthy panties with filthy groans, and rubbed his cock between us all over again, but this time it was flesh to flesh, and I couldn't stop myself wanting more. I couldn't stop myself opening my mouth nice and wide to meet his, and it was crazy, and it was filth, but it was us.

Oh fuck, it was us.

He kissed me with filthy wet lace between our tongues, and my senses were burning, and my body was bucking against his, panting and moaning and grabbing him tight.

Crazy.

Hot.

Lucas.

This was the Lucas Pierce I'd fallen in love with. No restraints. No judgement. No barriers.

Unapologetic wants. Unapologetic filth. Unapologetic him.

He made me come for him all over again in dirty wet sheets, with dirty wet knickers between our open mouths, and I was lost. Lost to the explosion. Nothing else but the sensations and my heart burning bright.

I was still breathing frantic when I broke the kiss enough to meet his eyes, and he knew what I wanted. He was already moving with his cock in his grip before I said the words.

"Come in my mouth," I whispered. "Please, Lucas, come in my mouth."

He angled my head back and kneeled over me, and his cock was rising high, precum dripping as he stared down at my wide open mouth. The lace was on my tongue, and he stretched it tight across my lips, working his dick so hard I could hear the wetness.

"Take it like my dirty bitch," he groaned, and then he came. A spurt of pure fucking cream that drenched my face, splattering my open mouth and my cheeks along with it, but the fountain kept on going, another stream landing right in my eye.

Fuck, I wanted it all.

He was shuddering when he finished.

So was I.

"Holy fuck, Anna," he said, and lowered himself back down, his chest to mine. I wrapped my legs around him, and he was warm, and strong, and everything I'd ever wanted.

I didn't need to ask him to kiss me, he was already there. He licked his cum from my cheek and pushed his tongue into my mouth all over again. And there was no shame in me. No urge to rush to my feet and disguise my weakness. No hating myself for my disgusting bodily functions and how I couldn't control them.

My soul soared.

My heart burst free and made me fly.

I was happy. So damn happy I could touch the sky.

Lucas was catching his breath when he finally pulled away and took the knickers from my mouth. He rolled onto his back and dropped them onto his stomach like some kind of victory banner before reaching out for my hand.

He squeezed my fingers and he was grinning at the ceiling.

So was I.

I was grinning too.

And then I was laughing.

"I've got spunk eye," I giggled, and I did have. I could feel it getting sore already, certain it would be bloodshot in minutes.

He was laughing along with me, and it was a beautiful sound. "Well, dirty girl. I think it's safe to say I won't be treating you like a china doll anytime soon."

I caught my breath myself, and we relaxed into the buzz of the aftermath, holding each other tight – until the practicalities of Sunday morning eventually kicked in on us.

It was time to get moving.

My meds were easy to grab from my suitcase, and I took those with juice while Lucas stripped the bed.

There was no self-consciousness inside me at all as he bundled the sheets up in the laundry. I was still grinning hard as we brushed our teeth in tandem and I smoothed my ragged hair down into some semblance of order.

We were having breakfast and watching the dogs charging around in the yard when conversation inevitably made its way around to the day before – but today it landed on somewhere it hadn't stopped before.

It landed on Nicola grabbing him in the hallway before we left the apartment yesterday.

"She said I need to talk to Yasmin Boyle," Lucas said, and pulled a face of confusion. "Do you have any clue what the hell Yasmin Boyle would have to talk to me about? I haven't seen her in years."

I shrugged. "She doesn't like Maya. She was trying to tell me so at girls' night, and then again at Amy Miller's wedding, but I didn't listen. I couldn't bring myself to hear it. Didn't seem relevant."

"She doesn't like Maya?" he asked, and his confusion intensified. "They used to be great friends when we got together."

"Not anymore," I told him. "She definitely doesn't like her now. She said I owe her nothing. She said neither of us do."

He finished up his toast and grabbed his phone, and I stared over as he flicked through his contacts.

"She's in Newcastle now, I think. I don't have her number."

"I'll get it."

I grabbed my phone from my bag, and pinged Nicola since she must have had some contact details to get her to girls' night.

I also asked her what was so important about Lucas speaking to Yasmin Boyle, but all I got back was a number and a *Get Lucas to ask her himself.*

Under normal circumstances, I'd have pushed her harder, but she turned the conversation into a run down on how I was doing, and when I was through with replying Lucas had already grabbed her number from me and made the call. He was on the phone to her when I finished up answering Nicola, and I messaged my parents and Vicky to let them know I was doing ok while he was speaking.

I didn't listen, because it wasn't my place, just kept my attention on my own conversations. But it seemed it wouldn't have made all that much difference to his privacy if I had have done.

He looked puzzled as hell as he hung up the call and came back to me at the kitchen table.

"She wants to tell me in person. She says phone or text doesn't cut it."

I tipped my head. "But she's in Newcastle, isn't she? When is she down next?"

He reached for the cigarettes. "Not anytime soon," he said, and lit one up.

This time I decided not to join him, and left the pack alone.

"Maybe I can push Nicola. She was trying to chat through something with me after Amy Miller's wedding, but I didn't want to listen."

He shook his head. "I think I need to speak to Yasmin herself. I have a weird feeling about it. Dunno what. Slightly spooky."

I smirked. "Not like you to believe in psychic intuition."

He let out a laugh. "No. But I do believe in secrets and bullshit revelations."

He barely smoked any of his cigarette before he stubbed it out in the plant pot by the side.

"You could head up to see her," I said. "I mean, she'd give you her address, I'm sure."

I expected he would brush it off as a no-go, such a long drive away across country, but he didn't. He looked out of the window as he weighed it up, pulling at his beard in the way he so often did when he was thinking.

His eyes were the deepest mottled green in the sunlight, and I stared.

Stared and watched him pondering.

Hell, I loved him so much.

Hell, I wanted to know what on earth was so important that Yasmin Boyle had to say.

So did he.

"I could get back before sleep time tonight," he said. "And I could take the dogs in the car."

"So do it," I told him. "If you really think there's something weird and worth knowing, then do it today." I paused and weighed it up. "I mean, I could come with you. For the drive."

His eyes were hard on mine. "Are you sure you'd be up to it? I could drop you back with your parents and pick you up later. Or I could stay, Anna. I'm not about to leave you anytime soon."

I gave him a fake scowl at that. "No china doll, remember?"

He laughed, then got straight to his feet. "Alright then, little miss filth. Let's head up to Newcastle for the grand revelation."

So we did.

We drove up to Newcastle, stopping on the way to let Bill and Ted chase their ball.

We stopped for lunch at the services and talked about the world and life and the past decade en route.

We found Yasmin Boyle's sweet little Newcastle terrace house easily enough by using the sat nav, and pulled up on her driveway, and she welcomed us in with a nervous smile and sat us both down for a cup of tea.

And then he asked her.

He asked her what the hell he needed to drive all the way to Newcastle to hear from her, and what the hell she could possibly know that had Nicola Henshaw grabbing his arm in our hallway.

She cleared her throat, and she looked him in the eyes, and took a breath.

My belly did a weird lurch, because I could see it.

I could see that what was coming was going to be every bit as serious as the build-up promised.

"I didn't tell anyone the full story," she told him. "Not even Nicola Henshaw, I just told her bits."

"Go on," he said. "Don't hold anything back now."

She nodded. "I'll tell you everything," she said, and pulled out her phone, and called up a screenshot and handed it over.

Lucas's eyes were wide and wild before I'd seen it, and he swallowed, and paled, and it was enough to have my fingers shaking before I took the handset from him.

But his eyes were not nearly so wild as they were when she started talking.

Neither were mine.

Chapter Forty

LUCAS

I managed to keep my shit together until Monday morning.

I talked with Anna happily enough all the way back from Newcastle, even though we were both frazzled to fuck. I cuddled up to her that night until she was asleep, then slipped away from her just long enough to use my laptop at the bottom of the bed.

Sweet fucking Jesus, I was glad I did.

I was back beside her when the alarm went off. We ate breakfast together and I dropped her at work when she insisted on going in as normal. I watched my beautiful minx smile back over her shoulder and blow me a kiss before she stepped in through the door and I blew her one right back.

And then I took my action.

Hell knows, there was enough of it to take.

I pulled up in the car park behind Lewton's Consultancy and logged into my work office account from my laptop. I dropped a message to my team, saying I was too sick to make it in for the day, and then called up my

Sebastian Maitland shitstorm from my embedded system files.

The police would do nothing with Anna's word against his, and I knew it. I'd have relished the thrill of hunting him down and tearing his dick from his balls, but it wouldn't cut it. Not to a son of a bitch like him.

Pain hurts most when it slams its punch straight into the heart – and Sebastian Maitland's heart was firmly fixed in one position. So, I took it from him. I cut his fucking heart from his chest with one swift swipe and pressed send from my anonymous email server to seal his fucking fate.

And then I took my action, round two.

I drove out to Maya's village and waited until she was back after Millie's school run before I pulled up onto her driveway and stepped up to her door.

Holy fuck, I hammered that door to let her know I was out there.

To say she wasn't expecting me was an understatement. She jolted back in shock when she answered, and then her shock turned to warmth with a glowing fake smile on her face.

Confused.

She was so fucking confused.

Smiling.

Fake.

Trying to fathom what the hell I was thinking. Doing. Wanting.

Just like fucking usual.

Just like the whole last fucking decade.

Her expression changed when she saw the rigidity of my shoulders as I stepped over the threshold and headed on through to her living room. There's no way she could've missed the bristle of disgust in my jaw when I turned to face her.

"Well?" she said, as though I was the asshole, just like usual. "What's with the impromptu call? I could've done some coffee, but some notice would've been nice. Millie isn't home from school until three."

"Yasmin Boyle is the impromptu fucking call," I said. "I went to Newcastle yesterday. We had quite a chat."

I saw the flash of fear in her eyes at Yasmin's name, but she shrugged it off and pretended to busy herself picking some of Millie's toys up from the sofa. "Yasmin Boyle talks a load of shit sometimes, Lucas. I hope you didn't make that whole bloody journey just to hear her bullshit stories."

"No," I said, and pulled my phone from my pocket. "It seems I made that whole bloody journey to hear *yours*."

I called up the screenshot and handed it over, and if I'd have had any concerns whatsoever that there was anything misleading about Yasmin Boyle's version of events, Maya's expression of guilty horror in that one heartbeat of recognition would have sealed the deal forever.

"It's not quite how it looks," she said, but her cheeks were already burning bright fucking pink.

"Really?!" I spat. "Because it's looking pretty fucking bad from where I'm standing. So how about you fucking enlighten me?"

She dithered, and shrugged, and then the look on her face came up that I'd seen a million times over. Victim Maya. Poor Maya. Poor innocent Maya being judged so bad.

She sat herself down on the sofa, and acted like the whole world was on her shoulders, but this time I was done. I was done with the whole fucking lot of it and everything she stood for.

"Just remember before we start this," she whined. "Just remember that we got Millie out of it. We have Millie, and she's everything!"

"Don't fucking tell me what to remember!" I hissed. "Just fucking tell me what happened!"

She took some deep breaths and told me I should sit down to hear her out, but I didn't want to sit down. I was edgy as fuck, hands in my pockets, pacing, pacing, fucking pacing. My heart was thumping and my gut was wrenching, because no matter how much you know someone's a self-centred bitch at the core of them, it's another thing to have it slammed in your face beyond all denial.

I watched her read through the screenshot over and over, my gut twisting a little harder every time. Then, finally, when I guess she knew there was no easy way out, she shook her head and dropped my phone on the coffee table.

"It's quite a story," she said, and I cursed under my breath.

"Go on, then. Get started."

She took a deep breath, faking a trembling bottom lip that would have usually moved mountains in guilt, but not this time, and then she started.

"We went to Psychic Showdowns, that big fair over by Leominster, me, Dawn, Hannah and Yasmin. It was a weekend thing and we'd been getting ready for it for months, doing all the workshops and preparing for the classes and everything." She paused. "You must remember what I was like back then, Lucas. Psychic spirituality was my whole life. Always chasing the higher purpose and applying it to the road ahead. That was my thing. Dawn's too. And Hannah's."

"I remember plenty about what you were like back then, Maya," I told her. "Just carry the fuck on, please."

She shook her head a bit more, and I saw those victim's tears brewing, but this time I wasn't having it. Not any of her fucking bullshit. Not anymore.

"It was an intense weekend," she said. "We were all sinking really deep into the therapies and the courses, and part of that was having a session with Kade Riley. You remember Kade Riley? You must remember Kade Riley?"

I stared blankly. "Who the fuck is Kade Riley?"

"The psychic guru, Kade Riley. The guy who has the TV show and does the weekend courses across the world. He's incredible."

"I don't have a fucking clue who Kade Riley is," I told her. "What the hell does it matter?"

"BECAUSE HE WAS THERE!" she snapped. "Because I'd been aching to see him for years! And he was THERE! And we were able to have a session with him, one on one with Kade fucking Riley! You can't substitute that, Lucas! He was too good!"

I was still staring blankly, not quite believing just how much she was still buying into the fluffy New Age bullshit she'd been into for years.

"So?" I asked. "How does that apply to you being a lying fucking bitch, Maya? How the fuck does it apply to you fucking up my whole entire fucking life?!"

She breathed in deep, and there it was again, the whiny little victim part of her shining out through her eyes.

"Because he told me our destiny was together! Me and you!" Her stare was crazy intense. "I asked him to read my cards, and he did. He read them and told me about the man in my life who'd bear me a child and be my world, and how the road would be hard, and it would involve betrayal, but we'd make it. He said one night together would lead to a whole new life, and it was with someone I knew I had feelings for... someone I couldn't resist..."

"WHAT THE FUCK ARE YOU TALKING ABOUT?!" I yelled, then cursed again under my breath. I kept it steady, forced myself to keep pacing, and she was shaking her head, finding the words.

"IT WAS YOU!" she yelled back. "It was you I had feelings for and couldn't resist! I knew it as soon as I saw you that night out without Anna, and you were stumbling, and you climbed into the back of the taxi with me. I knew that you were the man in my life Kade was talking about."

I stared in shock and started shaking my head, but she was nodding right back at me.

"It's true, Lucas. You're the one Kade was talking about. He even described you perfectly. Broad shoulders, and that dirty twinkle and the hard jaw... and the beard and the hair... and the suits you like to wear. He even said you'd be in a green suit, Lucas. Just like your favourite one. Hannah and Dawn said it was you straight away as soon as I told them. They said *that's Lucas Pierce, Maya!*"

I stepped up closer, and my glare must have been pure fucking spite.

"So you lied to me about being pregnant with my fucking baby because some spiritual fucking headcase told you we were *meant to be*? That's what you're saying, is it? That you thought it was *destiny* to be a malicious, twisted, fucking bitch and wreck my fucking life?"

She shook her head. "No! I thought I might well be pregnant when I told you that. I thought it was better to get the betrayal out of the way when Anna first got home from her retreat. I thought it would be better for everyone that way around."

"So you LIED!" I spat, and my rage was boiling over, I turned away long enough to catch my breath and she was bleating on in the background, mumbling on about how she'd been so sure it would be right, and so sure it should've worked out between us, and still could.

"FUCK YOU!" I screamed, and it was hard to keep it together. So fucking hard. My eyes must have been pure fire when they crashed back into hers. "You handed me that pregnancy test with shaky fingers, like you were scared for the whole fucking future, Maya! You saw me fight back the urge to fucking vomit, knowing I was losing my whole life to that bullshit you were spewing out at me!"

"For the bigger picture!" she insisted, but my hands were up to my temples.

I couldn't hold back the roar. "THERE WAS NO BIGGER FUCKING PICTURE!"

She shook her head. "There was! The bigger picture was Millie! You can't take away that the bigger picture was Millie, Lucas. We had Millie!"

I stepped up close and leaned right into her. My voice was nothing more than a hiss, filled with rage and hurt and hate. "Don't you ever, ever fucking use Millie against me again, you vile fucking bitch. I owe you fucking nothing."

Her tears blubbed over then. "We had a good life all mapped out for us, Lucas. If you'd have just let yourself love me, we'd still be having one now."

My voice was low and cold, without a scrap of sympathy left inside me to dull the blade.

"I held you while you sobbed over a miscarriage that never fucking happened, Maya. I tried to give myself over to you because of guilt.

Because of trying to be a decent fucking man. But I didn't need to be, did I? I didn't need to be shit to you. Not then, not ever."

"I thought I'd be pregnant by then!" she countered. "Honestly, Lucas, I thought I'd be pregnant for real by the time it came to it. I wanted to be."

"So you faked the loss? And faked the pain seriously enough that I wanted to make it work between us? You're a sick bitch, you fucking know that?"

But she didn't know that. She was still victim-eyed and delusional.

"I thought it was short-term betrayal for long-term destiny. I didn't realise you'd be such a selfish prick to live with and that you'd never get over Anna fucking Blackwell, did I? I THOUGHT WE'D MAKE IT!"

Even hearing Anna's name from her mouth was enough to send me reeling. I stormed out to the front door and lit up a cigarette and puffed in deep drags while I heard Maya sobbing inside.

This time, for once in my life, I didn't go in after her.

She could sob until the end of time and I still wouldn't go in after her.

She was dead to me.

Yasmin's screenshot had been enough to shine the light on the bullshit I'd been fed by Maya and her stupid fucking circle, but it was still so much harder hearing it for real.

I'd seen the message from Maya to Yasmin asking her to forget whatever she'd heard from Hannah Ames about borrowing her positive pregnancy test to show to me in the pub that one sad little day, and how we were so very happy, and sometimes people have to do bad things for the greater good, don't they? Don't they, Yasmin, hey?

The message was from a long time ago, but the implication was still fucking timeless. She was a vile bitch, who'd played on my drunken night and stupid mistake to snare me for the rest of my life. If there had even been one stupid mistake on that one drunken night.

If I really had been able to get my dick up that night in her bed.

But I couldn't go there…

Even I couldn't bring myself to challenge that much of a cuntish pack of lies and come out the other side being civil enough to handle the logistics of our daughter together.

I smoked my cigarette and went back in, and she was still blubbing on the sofa, her usual switch from being the self-righteous bitch ruling the world to the poor little princess who was being treated so bad.

I'd bought into it for so long.

I'd believed it for so fucking long.

"You do know that Anna got epilepsy when you fucked me out of her life, don't you?" I said, managing to keep my voice calm enough to speak. "You do know that I've spent the past decade hating myself for what I did to her?"

"We made Millie!" she snapped. "My God, Lucas! We made Millie! That's all that matters here!"

But it wasn't all that mattered.

All that mattered was that she was a piece of shit who deserved nothing from me, not even the slimmest little scrap of respect.

I cleared my throat before I sat down beside her, and I was bristling so fierce she didn't even try to worm her way up close.

I was very calm, and very clear, and every scrap the man I should have been a thousand times over across the years.

The man I truly was, with the spine that I should have made sure was damned fucking solid all the way through.

I told her that she wouldn't be moving to Hampshire, she'd be staying right here, and Millie would be splitting her time just fine between us.

I told her that she'd have to accept that she was a lying bitch who'd twisted me around her warped fucking wishes for too fucking long, and now was the time she'd be letting me go.

I told her that we were getting a divorce, and if she had so much as a sliver of sense in that calculating brain of hers, she'd see it'd be in her interest to sign on the line and keep her games to herself from here on in.

I told her I loved Anna.

I told her I'd always loved Anna.

I told her she'd never be coming between me and Anna Blackwell again for as long as I lived.

And fuck, I meant it.

I'd have signed that declaration in blood.

She cried.

She wailed.

She told me it had never been like that, and she'd loved me, and the road was the road, and we had Millie and yada yada fucking yada.

I asked her if we should let people make their own call on that and bring them into the story of how much of a twisted lying bitch she'd been when it mattered, and she paled before my eyes.

If there was ever anything more important to Maya than getting what she wanted, it was that the world saw her as Mrs fucking Perfect with her perfect fucking smile.

So, I used it. I told her I'd be very happy to keep the deviant truths of her bullshit lies to myself, just so long as she didn't stand in my way of living my life with the woman I loved – and allowing my little girl to be a part of that.

Hell, she blubbed some more, but it didn't matter. I'd have eaten my own shit before I compromised for one single second with that scheming bitch.

I told her it was my way or no way, and I'd destroy her in every way I could, in every court in the land if she didn't swallow down her cuntish ways and draw a line in the sand for a new life. A separate life. A life where we were never going to be together again.

And then I left.

I didn't wait for a response, I got up from the sofa with her wailing in her seat and I left.

Fuck her.

Fuck her lies.

I lit up another cigarette on my way down the path, and my heart was thumping, and I felt sick from the confrontation, but I left with a greater feeling of freedom than I'd had in years.

I was free of Maya.

I was free of being the asshole who was never good enough.

I stubbed my cigarette out in the truck ashtray and set off back to my house. I walked the dogs and logged into work from home, and checked out what was in the freezer for dinner.

And then I did what I should've done a decade ago.

I went to pick up Anna and tell her exactly what I'd just done with Maya fucking Brooks.

Chapter Forty-One

ANNA

Work was surreal.

Stacey and Lucia had spent photocopy breaks through the morning telling me all about their weekends, and I'd listened and smiled and said nothing about mine. There was a comfort in the familiarity of my daytime routine. Meeting rooms, and coffee breaks, and people's shoes making the same familiar sounds across the carpet when they passed by my desk.

But still, my whole soul was spinning.

Spinning with Lucas, spinning with hope, and fear, and dreams.

Spinning with the possibility that Maya Brooks could have ever told those lies and torn our world apart.

Spinning with the possibility that her friends could have ever supported that. Because how could you? How could you ever watch someone lie to tear other people's dreams to the ground?

It was only when I grabbed my handbag from my desk and stepped out onto the street to find Lucas waiting there that evening that I realised none of it really mattered.

You can't ever change the past, no matter how much you want to, so why give it any more of your future than you have to?

I was damn well determined not to give either Sebastian Maitland or Maya Brooks any more of ours.

Lucas was smiling bright as I climbed up into the passenger seat of the truck with him, reaching straight over to squeeze my fingers in his just as soon as he'd pulled away.

He asked how my day had been and I told him. I gave him the small talk little catch up with a grin and gossip, but it was there, and we both knew it – a whole topic was brewing right under the surface.

"Tell me about Maya," I said to him. "I know you must've been to see her."

He looked vaguely surprised that I knew that, but of course I did. I knew him.

We were back onto the Lydney lanes when he took a breath and started the rundown of his morning. He told me how Maya was every bit the spiteful scheming bitch Yasmin had painted her as, and she was right when she said we owed her nothing.

He told me about the New Age psychic crap she'd bought into when she'd wanted to believe their *destiny* was together, and it made me feel queasy just to think about it. Queasy to think that Hannah Ames really had been pregnant with Jamie, her eldest, and handed over her positive test to Maya to use for her games.

I had to say it, so I did, even though it made Lucas visibly flinch.

"Do you think you really had sex with her that night?"

"I can't think about it," he said. "Because if I even begin to think she lied about that too, I'll never be able to be in the same room as her again. It's bad enough already."

"But she might have lied about it," I pushed. "I mean, if she can lie about being pregnant with your child for the sake of psychic destiny, then surely she can lie about anything?"

He pulled onto the driveway and turned off the ignition, but he didn't move from his seat, just stared out at the house across the garden.

"I was absolutely fucked that night," he said. "I should never have been that fucked, and I should never have been in a state bad enough to end up in some random woman's bed, regardless of what happened or not when I was in there." He turned to face me. "I should never have been in a position where I *could* believe I'd make a mistake that bad, regardless of whether or not I actually made it or not."

"But you might not have made it," I said. "You might just have got so drunk, you stumbled out of a taxi and thought you were home."

"Or I might have been so drunk, I stumbled out of a taxi into Maya Brook's bed and thought she was you enough that I fucked her. I'll never know."

He was right on that front. She was sure as hell never going to admit it, whatever the case.

I sighed and leaned back in my seat, staring out at the house along with him.

"So this is where it starts again, is it?" I asked. "Our whole new life, a decade later."

"This is where it starts again," he said, and his hand was right back in mine. "It's been one fuck of a road getting here, but we're here. Jesus Christ, Anna. I'm so glad we are."

I tried to imagine living in the house, with him and the dogs. I tried to imagine this being home now, and meeting his sweet little girl and being Daddy's girlfriend.

The whole thing would be so bizarre.

So bizarre, but so right.

"Let's get it going then," I said, and I was smiling as I dropped down from the truck.

He cooked me dinner, and we moved the conversation back to the more positive sides of life and we were laughing by the end of it, staring at the ceiling in bed, hand in hand and throwing around our ideas for the year ahead. We talked about summer trips, and whether we should get a batch of chickens for the garden, and how maybe, just maybe, we could get ponies for our new countryside life.

Because that's what this was. A countryside life. The life we'd contemplated having one day when we were living our regular lives in the city way back when.

And now we had it.

Now we really had it looming ahead.

I knew what was coming before the police turned up a few days later. I knew as soon as they sat down opposite me in Lucas's living room and began the conversation.

My word against his, unfortunately not enough evidence to prosecute, and I managed to nod my way through it without crying, because I'd tried.

I'd been honest and at least I'd tried.

After they'd gone, he held me tight, and I let out the fears I'd been pushing away for days on end.

"What if he comes after me, Lucas? Because he might. He never lets things go, and he'll be raging. Totally raging that I went to the police about him."

"He won't be thinking of coming after you for long, Anna, I promise you," he said, and put his hands on my shoulders and pushed me back enough to look me straight in the eyes. "I never let things go, either, and he isn't going to be capable of coming after you for very long. I've made sure of that."

There was a flash of panic inside, because I knew whatever he was talking about would be serious, but his eyes were so steady and so true.

"Tell me," I said. "Please, Lucas, just tell me."

So he did.

He finished making dinner and we sat down at the table together, and he told me all about how Sebastian Maitland was a corrupt little prick who'd used his career position for fraud and bribery. He told me how Sebastian was arrogant, and over the years had become careless with his bullshit, and it had been so easy to piece together behind the scenes by checking out his communications activity from three different phone accounts.

And how easy it had been to assemble and report anonymously.

"It's just time," he said. "I can assure you, his career days are reaching their end, and he'll be suffering the consequences of the life choices he's made for his own gains."

"But you shouldn't have done that, right?" I asked him. "That's abusing your position, isn't it? What if they come after you, too?"

"I hope I'm a little more careful than he is," he said. "But yes, I've abused my position. It's a rarity, but I've abused my position, there's no denying that." He shrugged. "I think it's worth it, though. I wouldn't have been able to use anything he hadn't done himself. One day someone would have found him out for it, I've just sped up that process."

I reached out across the table to take his hand. "You didn't have to do that. You didn't have to make Sebastian pay for what he did."

"I didn't have to do that," he said, and took both of mine. "I wanted to."

We stared at each other in silence for long seconds, both of us lost in that moment.

"Please don't do that again," I said. "You aren't some super moral hero behind the scenes, trying to make the world a better place. You're Lucas Pierce, here with me, having chickens and ponies and walking the dogs. I love you that way, please don't change it."

"I wasn't planning on it," he replied, and kissed my hand. "I'm very, very happy to be Lucas Pierce, here with you, having chickens and ponies and walking the dogs. I'm not intending to change that. We've got more than enough time to make up for." He paused. "I just wanted Sebastian Maitland to get what's due. I could have dug a lot deeper and done a lot worse to him, I assure you."

I let it settle at that. I took a deep breath and we cleared the plates and my heart was thumping with a nice wave of comfort that I was really here, out the other side of the battle.

Because love is a battlefield. It really is.

We'd taken our blows, and we'd hidden in the trenches, and luckily, finally, we'd won the war.

Or so we thought.

It was just a shame the enemy didn't want to surrender.

Even now, there was one final wave of attack still to come.

Chapter Forty-Two

LUCAS

Within a few days we were living in bliss, waking up in the mornings and being so happy to be there. We'd eat breakfast in dressing gowns and shower together, then take Bill and Ted out before work. I'd drop her outside her office, and we'd ping each other through the day, and I'd be there every evening to pick her up for home. Sometimes we'd grab the rackets and hit the tennis court, and some games she'd get so close to winning that she'd dance along the net, blowing me raspberries. Fuck me, I loved her for it.

Sometimes we'd be too desperate for flesh on flesh to do anything other than rip each other's clothes off the moment we were back in through the door.

We'd talk. We'd laugh. We'd hold each other tight. Just like we should have been doing the past decade through.

She'd talk to her parents, and Vicky, and Nicola, and message the girls from work. I'd be on video chat to Millie every evening, talking about her school day without so much as a peep from Maya in the background.

My mother was silent. Just like she should have always been when it was none of her pissing business.

We were happy.

Really happy.

It was that first Friday in our new life that I took Anna out into the city to celebrate. We ate pizza, and laughed as we tore into garlic bread, and toasted our happiness with a prosecco at the table.

But she wasn't smoking, not anymore, and neither was I.

She hadn't had any seizures either. Not in days.

"Maybe we could do a pizza night again when I meet Millie," she suggested, and I smiled over at her.

"Millie does like a good slice of pizza," I told her. "Maybe we could do an ice cream sundae to follow."

I had a strange tingle of excitement every time I pictured Anna meeting my little girl. I loved the thought of them laughing together in our kitchen, and eating popcorn on the sofa and watching old kid's films, and Millie's explosion of absolute joy if we really did go through with our potential plans to get her a pony in the paddock.

Yet still, I was nervous.

I was so fucking nervous for the two most important parts of my life to combine and make a new one.

"You're thinking," Anna said across the table, and I jolted back to my senses. "What are you thinking about?"

I took another sip of prosecco.

"I'm thinking of you meeting the little princess."

"I'm looking forward to meeting the little princess," she told me, with a big smile on her face. "I'm sure I'll love her loads if she's even a tiny bit like her dad."

I hoped so.

Holy fuck, I hoped so.

"Maybe we'll make another little princess one day," I said, and her eyes shot open wide. "Sorry," I added. "Thinking out loud there."

She pulled off another piece of garlic bread. "Maybe we will." She took a bite. "Maybe if the epilepsy eases, and things settle down with everyone around us, and we can be that little family we want to be."

"Maybe," I said.

"Maybe," she smiled.

"Maybe in the meantime we should hit the bars, and head on out for another prosecco or two."

"Maybe in the meantime we should indeed hit the bars, and head on out for another prosecco or two," she laughed. "I think the girls from work are out at Bar Royale tonight."

So out we went.

We met up with Stacey, Melissa and Lucia and I watched Anna join in with their work chat with a big grin on my face.

We danced to some terrible tunes that neither of us liked, laughing right the way through, and resisted the urge to head out onto the smokers' terrace like true champions.

I couldn't keep my hands off her when we left the club, my mouth on hers all the way up the street on our way to the taxi rank. Her arms were around my neck, and her tits were pressed to my chest, and clothes were a barrier I'd tear off in a flash just as soon as we were out of the realms of public indecency.

I hadn't had quite enough proseccos for that just yet.

It was Anna who suggested we take a detour a few streets over and head to the Neptune fountain.

It was me who grinned right back at her and said I'd love to go the Neptune fountain, just so long as she didn't expect me to be making any wishes with any damn coins.

Neither of us expected to be standing on the lawn at the front of the spurting water, staring up at Neptune himself, hand in hand, when the charge of stumbling feet sounded up the street behind us.

And there he was.

The cunt himself.

His tie was loose around his neck as he stumbled his way down the road, and I knew straight away where he was heading. His path was from Oscars to Casey's Casino, with two of his suited idiot mates rocking along at his side.

They were oblivious, all three of them, clearly off their fucking heads as they made their way out for more of the same.

It would have been so much better if he hadn't seen us standing there, but unfortunately Anna was looking divine enough to stop the world in her burgundy satin and heels.

He stopped in his tracks the very moment he saw her, and his jaw tightened as he looked her up and down. Angry, and bitter, and pure fucking spiteful.

His two friends tried to call him along with them, but he wasn't having any of it, just kept on heading over towards us.

I pulled Anna closer to my side, and stepped ahead of her, but the prick was oblivious. His eyes were burning right on her as he closed the distance.

"So-called *rape*?" he sneered, and jabbed a finger at her. "That wasn't fucking *rape*, Anna. You were fucking begging for it. I told the fucking police so, too. Good job they fucking believed me."

"Stop," I told him. "Seriously, Maitland, just fuck off and leave us, please."

Anna pressed up close to me, edgy with nerves, but her voice was so fucking tough when she answered him.

"That *was* fucking rape, Seb, and you know it. I wasn't begging for anything, you disgusting prick!"

His friends tried calling him over again from the street corner, but he gave them the middle finger.

"You're a slut," he sneered at Anna. "You're a slut, and you were begging for it. And this is the loser you spread your fucking legs for, isn't it? Lucas fucking Pierce, the pervert freak."

He glared at me, and he was so vile. So fucking vile.

"Shut the fuck up," I said to him. "Honestly, you need to fuck off now before this escalates. Call me whatever you like, but don't you dare think of speaking to Anna like that again. Not if you've got any sense in that cuntish head of yours."

"She's a slut," he spat. "A filthy, little, invalid slut."

My gut twisted and my fists clenched. "Shut your fucking mouth right now."

But he didn't.

The cunt didn't.

"You're an ungrateful bitch," he sneered. "You know that, Anna? You're an ungrateful fucking bitch and always were."

I was so fucking ready for him when he reached out to grab for her.

I twisted his arm behind his back, wrenched it hard and cut him off in his tracks. "Just get the fuck away from here," I snapped, and shoved him away.

Still, he fucking didn't.

He swung for me as soon as he spun around, teeth bared and eyes fucking wild as he came at me. Again, I was fucking ready for him.

I shouldn't have taken nearly so much pleasure as I did from slamming a fist into the cunt's jaw and sending him flying from his feet onto the goddamn grass.

I definitely shouldn't have taken so much pleasure as I did from grabbing him by his shoulders and dragging him through the soaking wet lawn, muddying his suit to fuck as I wrenched him over to the fucking water.

"You can sober the fuck up," I barked at him, and plunged his face in the fucking pool.

"Lucas!" Anna shouted, but I was on a fucking mission.

The piece of shit spluttered and squirmed, but I didn't let him come up for air. Not until he'd well and truly taken a gulp full.

He spat and retched when I let him up, and I gave him the option to walk away again.

"Leave," I told him. "Just fucking go, yeah?"

But still he was a cunt, glaring up with spite towards Anna.

"She's a fucking slut! Nothing but a pathetic little slut!"

I plunged his head back under.

The next time I let him up he was squirming worse, and the rage in his eyes was nothing short of primal.

"I'll take you fucking down for this, Pierce!" he choked. "The police won't do shit about Anna's bullshit claims, but they'll fucking listen to me when I tell them about your fucking assault. Believe me, they'll listen to me!"

"Lucas!" Anna called out again, but she was the only one intervening. His so-called *friends* had bailed to the street corner at the conflict and were hovering well and truly on the outskirts. Typical for his bullshit circle and its bullshit loyalty.

Sebastian was still too wrecked to swing for me when I leaned in close and pressed my mouth to his ear. I felt him tense as soon as I started speaking, and I shouldn't have taken nearly as much pleasure as I did from his panic either. But holy shit, how I did.

"Nobody is going to give a toss for what you say, Maitland," I hissed at him. "The police may not have any evidence to prosecute you for rape, but I swear to God they'll have enough evidence to prosecute you for fraud. I made sure of that when I submitted it."

"Fuck off," he spluttered. "You don't know shit about me."

"Quayside Finance," I whispered. "Sound familiar? Quayside Finance and Logan Randall? Don't suppose you siphoned off a few mill from one to the other last September by any chance, did you?"

Oh fuck, how he tensed up at that.

"I know everything about you," I told him. "If you have any fucking sense in that cuntish head of yours, you'll fuck off from here and never even breathe Anna's name again. You go anywhere near her and I'll be pulling a whole load worse up to slam you with. I'll burn you alive, I fucking swear."

I dropped him on the lawn, and he was a wreck, coughing and trying to scrabble to his feet.

I walked right on past him with Anna's hand firmly in mine.

"You have a few days tops to get your things in order. They'll be coming for you," I told him.

"I'll tell them it was you!" he snarled, using the fountain bannisters to get to his feet. "I'll tell them it was you who fucked with my affairs and take you the fuck down with me!"

"You can try." I shrugged with a smirk on my face. "We'll see who they are most interested in, shall we?"

"I'll take you the fuck down!" he yelled, but he was still stumbling around on his feet like the idiot he fucking was.

He didn't intimidate me. Nothing about that cunt intimidated me and never would.

I shoved him back to the floor on our way past, beyond giving a shit for any useless bullshit the cunt had to say.

I'd have happily torn his limbs apart, but a swollen jaw and soaking wet suit would have to do. That and taking his career and freedom away from him for all fucking time.

It was Anna that surprised me as we walked on by, hanging back just long enough to spit at him on the floor.

"You disgust me," she hissed. "Don't ever fucking come near me again, you vile piece of shit!"

The other suited pricks were still hovering on the corner, pretending to be busy on their phones when we walked on by.

"If you have any sense, you'll keep your distance from that cunt," I told them.

And then we went home.

It took a few more days before the Sebastian Maitland headlines hit the local papers.

He'd been arrested and charged with fraud and bribery, and had been detained behind bars until the court trial.

It appeared he didn't have all that many real friends after all – since not a single one of them came forward to pay his bail charges.

It was a few days on from that still when Moose, the introverted work genius, cornered me in the meeting room when Keith and Ralph had made their exit after our weekly debrief.

I was still packing up my laptop when he cleared his throat and stepped up close.

"Saw the Sebastian Maitland shit going down on Gloucestershire Live TV," he told me. "Got well and truly shafted by an anonymous email, didn't he? Weird that."

I shrugged. "Yeah, pretty damn weird, hey? Still, the guy always was a cunt."

His smirk was eccentric, and his eyes were strangely bright. "Seems there was a system glitch around your login in the last week or two," he said. "Seems the Sebastian Maitland searches were spiking all over the place from your account. Pretty big coincidence."

My blood turned to ice, but I kept a calm face on it. "Really? That's quite strange, Moose. Quite strange indeed."

"Yeah," he said. "It is. I was thinking that you were checking it out via enough proxy that hardly anyone would have ever been able to see the action, especially not from our team login. But with me putting the automation protocols in place and tracking user behaviour… I guess it puts me in prime position to pick up any glitches like that."

"I guess it does. And what are you going to do with that prime position, Moose?" I asked him.

He shrugged, and his eccentric smirk grew bigger. "Well, I fixed the glitch," he said. "Don't want our system throwing any other little balls ups like that around, do we? So, I made sure I cleaned it up. Not a single Sebastian Maitland glitch to be seen now."

I was surprised.

Surprised enough for the shock on my face to be seen, I'm sure.

Moose shuffled on the spot. "Won't be any more glitches now though, will there, Lucas?"

I shook my head. "Absolutely not, Moose. I'm sure the system is well and truly fixed now. No more glitches to be had."

"Good," he said, and then he nodded his head at me. "Sure nice to have you back, boss. Keep up the happy, will you? It's a whole load better than the sads."

He was at the meeting room door when I called his name.

He turned to face me and I realised for the first time in a long time that I really did have true friends. I'd lost sight of just what they were over the years.

"Thanks, Moose," I said. "It means a lot that you cleaned that up for me."

He shrugged at that. "No biggie," he said. "Can you just make it to quiz night next week please? Marketing team caned us last month and I want to come out with the trophy."

I laughed out loud and gave him one hell of a smile.

"I'm damn well sure I can be there."

Anna was looking incredible, head to toe in a cream dress suit when I met her outside her office that evening.

I leaned in to kiss her and she lingered for a few beautifully long seconds.

"Good day?" I asked, and she nodded.

"Very good day," she said. "Got an invite from Mum and Dad for Sunday dinner over the next few weeks."

"Nice," I said, and took her hand as we set off on our walk to the car park. "You haven't been to dinner at theirs for a few, have you? About time they started back up again."

She stopped me in my tracks, and shook her head, and she was so alive. So fucking alive that it took my breath.

"No, no, no. I've got an invite from Mum and Dad for *us* to go to

Sunday dinner," she told me. "Both of us."

Jesus Christ, it took me a second to digest it.

"You're serious? Your parents have invited me for Sunday dinner?"

She nodded. "Yep, sure have. Took me quite by surprise as well."

My smile was all genuine. "I'd be very honoured to accept the invitation."

"I know," she said. "I've already said we'd love to be there, just need to get it pencilled in. Can't wait to get you suited and booted for the big event."

My heart was already absolutely pounding at the thought. Jim and Terri must have absolutely despised me for a whole damn decade, and I didn't blame them. I never would.

The very thought of them welcoming me across their threshold was quite surreal.

Anna pulled me back in my tracks again before we rounded the corner to the car park.

"Can we just take a detour?" she asked me. "I have a wish for the fountain…"

I looked at the sky, such a lovely day in spring. The clouds were pink and the air was warm, and the city was bustling just right with evening life.

"Sure, let's go see Neptune," I said.

I don't know what her wish was that she made that evening. I just watched the usual addictive sparkle in her eyes as she pulled that coin from her purse, gripped it tight, then tossed it into the water.

She turned to me, just like always, and asked me the question, just like always.

"You going to make a wish today, Lucas?"

The words were right there, right on my tongue ready to flow, just like always.

The universe isn't responsible for my road ahead, Anna. I am.

Only today those words didn't come.

I surprised myself as I reached into my pocket and dug around for a coin.

Her eyes widened in shock as I held it up in front of her, and I loved it. I loved the gorgeous enthusiasm on her face.

I loved her so fucking much it hurt.

So, I wished.

I wished to the universe that Anna would one day be my wife, and Millie would love her almost as much as I did.

I wished that our road ahead would be long and blessed, and I'd be every scrap the man I'd intended to be for her before I fucked up the past decade.

I wished to be her world, and everything she ever deserved, and make right all the stupid wrongs I'd ever pushed on her.

"Made your wish?" she asked, and I nodded, and kissed her head.

"Made several of them actually," I told her.

Then I tossed that coin into the water and took my beautiful Anna home.

Epilogue

ANNA

A few weeks later

Amy Miller's face was a picture of mischief as she slammed a pint glass full of wine down onto Nicola's coffee table.

"Exactly what's going on between you and Lucas Pierce, Anna? Truth or dare?"

Nicola laughed, and so did Vicky, and so did Vicky's new flatmate, Claire.

And so did Yasmin Boyle. Freshly down for a weekend from Newcastle and sitting across in the armchair on the other side of the table.

I tipped my head to the side and pretended to think about it.

"Well... I dunno... that's a tough question..."

"Truth or dare, truth or dare, truth or dare!" the girls chanted, but we were all giggling like fools.

Because we all knew the answer.

Every single one of us knew the answer beyond all doubt.

"Everything," I told them, and pushed the wine away. "Everything is going on between me and Lucas Pierce."

"Including Sunday lunch at your parents' place tomorrow, right?" Vicky asked, and I nodded.

"Including Sunday lunch at my parents' place tomorrow."

And that was indeed going on.

I was crapping myself about it going on, but it was. Picturing Dad and Lucas making any kind of conversation over roast potatoes and broccoli was enough to bring me out in tremors, so hell knows what it was doing to Lucas.

He was pinging me right through the evening, sending me snapshots of him and Millie in front of the TV and saving me some popcorn, and every one of them had my tummy fluttering.

I'd met her once and she was incredible. A pretty young princess with a feisty little mind and a fiery little heart to go along with it. We'd taken Bill and Ted out on the hills for a great afternoon walk, and topped our own pizzas to eat for dinner when we got home.

I think she liked me.

I hoped she liked me.

Lucas sure seemed to think she did, and she was keen enough to come back and stay over, so at least round one was a success.

Maybe, just maybe, we'd be lucky enough to make another sweet young prince or princess to share family life with her one day. Hell knows, we were having enough sex to practice.

He'd dropped her back at Maya's, so was more than happy enough to come and grab me from Nicola's front door at 2 a.m. It was hilarious being the taxi service to Amy and Yasmin along with me, and I laughed along with their silly sing songs in the backseat like we were teenagers all over again.

"Tomorrow is the big showdown, then?" Amy quizzed as we headed to hers, leaning through to the front seats with a big grin on her face. "Do you think Daddy Blackwell is going to kick your ass tomorrow, Lucas?"

He shrugged, and flashed a grin right back at her. "I'm sure we'll find out. I'll be expecting it, that's for sure. I'll give him three straight punches on my jaw before I bail and run like a wimp."

"He isn't going to punch you," I laughed. "He might call you a prick and spit in your carrots, but I don't think he'll floor you in the hallway."

"We'll see," he said, and squeezed my knee.

We dropped Amy and Yasmin off at theirs then headed out to home. The dogs jumped up at us as we walked on through to the kitchen, and I fussed them like crazy, loving the furry bundles of fun more and more each day.

It was still so weird so see the house so fresh with all my stuff in there. My pictures up on the wall – my favourites of magpies, and a giraffe in a hat, and a photo of me, Mum and Dad at my school play when I was seven. My books on the bookshelves next to his. My clothes in the wardrobe next to his. My tennis racket permanently hung up above the shoe rack in the hallway, right next to his. My cutlery in the drawers, and my plates in the cupboards.

I was grabbing myself a juice when Lucas arrived behind me from the living room. His smile was magic as he held up a piece of paper, bright with wax crayon.

"Millie drew this for you," he said, and pointed to the sketched out people. "You, me, her."

It made my heart do a strange little flip in my chest.

He pointed across the page. "Bill and Ted."

"She drew this for me?"

He nodded. "She said she really likes you. That you're one of her bestest, bestest people."

"Aww," I said, and took the drawing from him with a tear in my eye. "She's one of my bestest, bestest people too."

He pulled me close. "And tell me, Anna, who else is one of your bestest, bestest people around here?"

I put the drawing down on the counter and wrapped my arms around his neck.

"Hmm, that is a good question, Lucas. Let me think about that for a minute…"

He kissed my cheek, and I grinned, loving the feeling of his mouth on my skin.

"My bestest people…" I started. "Well, I do really like Nicola, and I like Vicky, too…" I paused as he lowered his mouth to my neck. "And Mum and Dad, of course… oh, and Stacey… I really like Stacey…"

I sucked in a breath as he dropped his kiss to my tits, tugging my dress down just enough to free my bra.

"And who else?" I whispered. "Who else is on my bestest, bestest list?"

"How about you show me who else is on your bestest, bestest list?" he asked, and there was that growl in his throat I couldn't resist.

My belly was fluttering, and my heart was racing, and I wanted him so much it made me dizzy.

I pulled away long enough to finish my juice, and then I giggled and ran, racing past him and bounding upstairs like a horny teenager, poking my tongue out at him over my shoulder.

He caught me before the bedroom doorway, scooping me up from my feet and carrying me over to the bed while I giggled.

He dropped me backwards and lowered himself down on top, and his body was so hot and so firm, and so fierce as his hands worked their magic.

"What delicious dirty panties do you have on for me this evening?" he asked, and he was already kissing his way down and tugging my dress up to answer his own question.

White lace.

His favourite.

The slip of the thong had been pressing tight between my ass cheeks all evening at girls' night, and I knew they'd be messy. I knew he'd love them for it.

And he did.

His breath turned ragged as his face arrived down between my thighs, and I was desperate for it. Desperate for him.

He ran a thumb over the crotch, pressing tight against my slit.

"Who did you say was one of your bestest, bestest people?" he asked, and I couldn't hold back a moan.

He worked his thumb in circles, and I could feel the heat of his breath through the lace, and I needed it. I needed it so damn bad.

"You," I whispered. "You are my bestest, bestest person, Lucas. You always have been."

His mouth landed hard, and I was ready, arching myself under him to get as much as I could.

"Be my bestest person, Lucas," I told him. "Make me come really hard."

"Oh, I'll be your fucking bestest," he said, and did it.

His tongue was divine, and his hands were so strong as he held my ass cheeks, and I came for him. I came for him so hard there was white behind my eyes, and my heart was in my temples, and my clit was sparking like dynamite.

Then he came up and kissed me, with a mouth that tasted of me, and a hunger in his tongue that set me on fire all over again.

He slipped my dirty knickers down my thighs and rubbed them against his cock, and I knew what was coming. I always knew what was coming.

"Open wide," he said, and I did.

I opened my mouth nice and wide and kept my eyes on his while he worked his dick sheathed in dirty white lace and aimed it right up to my face.

I sucked him, deep and wet until he shot his load, the delicious taste of his cock, and me, and drips of precum through lace. His balls tensed, and his breaths quickened, and I was begging through slurps.

Yes, yes please. Yes, please. Please, Lucas, now.

"Good girl," he growled, and gave me what I wanted. A mouthful of his cum through the crotch of my knickers, and he was right down and at me, his fingers pushing it deeper and deeper, right the way to the back of my throat. "Don't you dare swallow," he said, and I murmured my agreement.

He was already hard again when he repositioned himself. His thrust inside me came so naturally that I was already grinding back up and at him to meet his hips.

It was hard. Fast. A rhythm that spoke to my soul.

So was his tongue in my mouth along with wet lace and cum.

That was a rhythm that spoke to my soul too.

My arms were holding him so tight, and his body was so hot against mine, I could've stayed there forever, entangled with him in perfect bliss.

I came before he did, mouth still full of knickers, and cum, and tongue. A bucking, moaning mess of joy as he picked up pace and reached his own thrusting high.

I was grinning as soon as I swallowed, pulling the lace from my mouth and tossing it up at his chest as he grinned back down at me.

"Another one for the never to be washed pile," I laughed at him. "I need to get a subscription order from Panties R Us at this rate."

"You'd get an order from Cum on Demand at the same time," he laughed back, and dropped down at my side.

He took my hand and kissed my knuckles, and I grinned up at the ceiling, catching my breath.

"Have I ever told you that you're amazing?" I said to him, and he laughed fresh.

"Have I ever told you that you're amazing too?" he said to me, and I couldn't hold back the post orgasm giggles.

"Hopefully my dad will be telling you you're amazing over dinner tomorrow, hey? We can dream."

We laughed together into the night, me rolling into his side and him holding me tight.

It was so easy to fall asleep like that, happy. So happy my heart could fly.

This was me.

This was him.

This was us.

And finally, it was forever.

***

LUCAS

I was as edgy as a naughty schoolboy as we made our way up Jim and Terri Blackwell's front path.

I was suited and booted, and my shoes were polished, and I felt like this was prom night and I was waiting for parental approval.

Anna had a bunch of flowers for her mum. Lovely yellow roses with a box of chocolates for the dining table after lunch.

I had me. Just me.

Me and a whole bundle of nerves.

She knocked on the door and I held my breath.

It was Terri who answered, hair tied back in a messy bun and a bright pink apron around her waist.

She was just like I remembered, and my belly lurched at the memories.

I wasn't expecting her to pull me in for a hug after squeezing Anna tight. I wasn't expecting a *Lucas, nice to see you* as she let me go and gestured us inside.

Anna was grinning as we headed on through to the living room, and there he was. Jim. Every bit the strong shouldered gentleman I remembered, just a little more grey.

My mouth was dry, and my heart was pounding, and I'm sure my forehead must have been clammy with sweat as he stepped on over to meet us.

I was ready with a whole rush of apologies, and assurances that I'd be different this time, and how I was a monster for ever hurting Anna the way I did, and I'd never be doing it for anyone, ever again.

I didn't need them.

He grabbed my hand and shook it hard, and his eyes were firm in their stare as they met mine.

But they weren't angry.

I was truly shocked when he let my hand go and slapped me on the back on the way through to the dining room. Anna was already up ahead and handing over the roses to her mum, and Jim held me back in the doorway, leaning on in with his voice down low.

"I heard Sebastian Maitland had a pounding on the jaw," he said. "Know anything about that?"

I shrugged. "He sure had one due to him."

"Yeah, Lucas. He sure did."

We watched the women laughing at the side of the dining table and arranging the roses in a vase.

Jim spoke again, and his voice was so much nicer than I ever expected to hear it.

"Sebastian was cursing your name, so I heard. Seemed pretty certain you were the one who landed him behind bars."

"Sebastian is a paranoid asshole," I said, but I was smirking.

Jim slapped my back again, and his eyes were smiling. "Glad you floored the vile prick," he said. "I'm grateful you gave the piece of shit what he deserved."

"So am I," I said, and my heart did a flutter to see the woman I loved giggling with her mum.

"Ten years can make a lot of difference," Jim told me. "I think sometimes people deserve another chance to right their wrongs."

"I won't be making any more wrongs," I told him. "Not where Anna is concerned, I swear."

"Good," he said, and walked us through to the dining room. "Because believe me, Lucas, if there's another wrong to be righted, I'll be righting it my fucking self."

"You'd be very welcome to," I told him, and thanked my lucky fucking stars when he got me a beer.

***

ANNA

You know, it's a strange thing.

There's so much in life you think is toxic. You think you know so much about what you are allergic to, and what is bad for you, and evil and poisonous.

So many people tell you what to avoid, and what will do you harm, and what is setting out to destroy you.

But poison is often in the places we least expect it.

Sometimes the antidote looks like the curse, and sometimes the curse looks like the cure.

And after all that – a decade of twists and turns – there was one thing definitely for sure…

Lucas Pierce wasn't the poison.

Lucas Pierce was the cure, the antidote for a better life, and a future full of nothing but love.

The End

POISON

Acknowledgements

This has been quite an intense few years.

That's an understatement.

Losing Jon, and trying to find my feet again, through to my epilepsy diagnosis and starting on treatment, and finding my whole personality coming back to me.

Thank fuck, it did come back to me.

And with it came Poison.

It's eaten me up in the most delicious way I know. Through the words.

But that wouldn't have been able to happen without a whole ocean of support from so many people close to me.

The biggest support for this novel came from the man who all out inspired it.

Timmy, you are an incredible human being, and I love you in ways I never expected to feel again. I can only thank you for so many things about this creation – not least for putting your mouth on the cover. That's quite a thank you due in your direction.

John, for editing, as always. You are such a support to me, and your feedback is insanely valuable. Thank you. That's John Hudspith, to anyone looking for editing services. You won't regret it.

Letitia, your cover work always blows me away. This one is another that had me open mouthed and so happy I could burst. Thank you! That's RBA Designs, everyone. She's fantastic.

Gel, for teasers, you rock, thank you.

LJ Designs – thank you for the beautiful paperback pages!

Samantha, for helping with my street team, and for dipping into some glorious graphics for me, too. You are awesome, thank you.

For my beta readers on this one – Sharon Standke and Mary M Maberge. Your feedback has been so valuable. Thank you!

Isabella – for helping me with formatting as per and being the amazing friend and author you are. You are just epic. Thank you.

Bloggers and reviewers, and Give Me Books – thank you so much for your time and support! Social Butterfly – thank you for being there and helping so much!

To my street team members, you are tireless and fantastic. Thank you.

To other incredible author friends of mine, there are too many to list. I'm blessed to have support from so many amazing friends. Leigh, Lauren, Willow, Siobhan, Jordan, Penny, Jo, just to name a few. Love you all, and thank you.

And my other friends. I love you all. Boo, Maria, Lisa, Tom, Hanni, Sue, Nick, Luba, Lynne, to name a few.

Jackie – it's been an absolute blessing to have you so close these past few months. You are such a powerful and positive woman. I'm beyond lucky to spend so much time with you.

My family. I'm so grateful to have such a great one.

Mum and Dad, Brad, Stevie, Nan, Misha and Rodion. Andrew, Julie, Deb. My cousins Kim and Jen, and your beautiful kids. Couldn't do this without you.

And of course, to my readers. You make this possible. I'll always be grateful to every single one of you. Thank you all.

About Jade

Jade has increasingly little to say about herself as time goes on, other than the fact she is an author, but she's plenty happy about it. Spending her time in imaginary realities and having a legitimate excuse for it is really all she's ever wanted.

Jade is as dirty as you'd expect from her novels, and talking smut makes her smile.

She lives back home with her parents now, at thirty-seven years old. Yeah, she smokes around the side of the house to hide from her dad like a fifteen-year-old.

Yes, it's been a rough couple of years since losing Jon, the love of her life, to an aortic dissection, and being diagnosed with epilepsy. BUT, it's getting better.

Thank fuck, it's getting better.

Not least due to all the support she's been getting from everywhere in the universe. Thank you for that everyone!

Plus, everything in this world is inspiration for more stories. That's a win at least! :D

Find Jade (or stalk her – she loves it) at:
www.facebook.com/jadewestauthor
www.twitter.com/jadewestauthor
www.jadewestauthor.com

POISON

Printed in Great Britain
by Amazon